# THE *Other* PARKER

# SARAH ZANE

To all the queers and misfits still navigating the halls of ~~hell~~ high school – it's cliche, but know that things get better

Sincerely,

An elder queer who was too scared to come out in high school and now writes and publishes queer books with happy endings

And to everyone who watched John Tucker Must Die and wondered, why didn't the girls just date each other – I fixed it, you're welcome

# CONTENT WARNING

This book is suitable for high school ages and up. If it were a movie, it would be rated PG13. Please be advised the book contains the following:

Mentions of parental substance abuse

Underage drinking (not by main character)

Mentions of bullying

# Playlist

God Sent Me As Karma – Emlyn

Vigilante Shit - Taylor Swift

Boyfriend – Dove Cameron

Thank God You Introduced Me To Your Sister – Sarah Barrios

Dirty Little Secret – The All-American Rejects

Accidentally in Love – Counting Crows

Girl's Girl – Emlyn

I Could Have Been Worse – King Mala

Buzzkill – Mothica

Oscar – Melina KB

I Can See You (Taylor's Version) – Taylor Swift

Force of Nature – Melina KB

Beggin' On Your Knees – Victorious Cast

# Chapter One

My younger cousin was supposed to be with her friends all day today. I wasn't sure why she was texting me, but knew it couldn't be good. As the bubbles appeared that she was typing, I started mentally doing the calculations for how long it would take me to get from the cafe I was at back to our house. I was thinking I could be out of here and at the house in ten, fifteen if I needed to stop for ice cream or anything else Lyndsey might need.

I was just about to call her when her response came through, but it wasn't an answer, just a link.

Confused, I clicked on it. It brought up a Facegram page for a profile called The Tiger Shark Tea. It wasn't until I saw the bio mentioned her school, soon to be my new school, that I remembered that Harris High's mascot was the Tiger Sharks. I clicked on the most recent post. It took me a long minute to realize what I was reading and why it mattered.

## Tiger Shark Tea

*It's no secret that Shawn Parker, Harris High royalty, the Tiger Sharks football team's fearsome leader, has no problem with the ladies, but I can't help but wonder if his luck is about to run out. He was spotted out to dinner with his suspected girlfriend, Ava, but later that same night, he was seen making out with the raven-haired rebel, Roxy, during a party at the Parker Palace. Double timing would be bad enough, but it seems our quarterback wasn't going to end his night without a touchdown, since later that same night, he was seen escorting a curvy redheaded freshman, Lyndsey, to his car with his jacket wrapped around her shoulders. Turns out Shawn might have a thing for freshmen. To the incoming freshman class of Harris High, you've been warned. Shawn Parker's on the prowl.*

*I know what you're thinking, gossip isn't fact, and you're right, but I certainly do my research and you know I've got receipts. Swipe to see.*

I swallowed, knowing I needed to swipe, but not wanting to. Lyndsey had been telling me how happy she was lately and how excited she was about a new relationship that had just started. She wouldn't tell me too much about him, though, saying they were keeping things low-key. I'm guessing this was why.

For a split second, I wondered if she knew, before dismissing the thought almost as quickly as it had come. Lyndsey was a hopeless romantic. Anything less than pure devotion from a partner wouldn't be tolerated. There was no way she knew he had been seeing other people. I just wasn't sure if the cheating was on or with her. It didn't really matter, though. What mattered was that she was hurting and I couldn't believe that anyone would hurt her like that.

I sucked in a deep breath and swiped. First there was a photo taken over the top of a menu of a boy with a gleaming smile and messy blonde hair that had to be Shawn and a beautiful black girl with long, thick braids. I tried to go to her Facegram for a closer look, but she wasn't tagged.

The next photo was of the same blond boy, Shawn, locking lips with a raven-haired girl in a short black skirt, fishnet tights, and combat boots, up against a tree. They must have thought they were hidden because the straps of her top were down and it looked like her top was halfway to coming off. You could see a party in full swing behind their tree. Clearly, they weren't as alone as they probably thought.

I wanted to look at her page, but I knew I needed to keep going and get the worst over with.

Next was a photo of Lynds smiling up at Shawn adoringly as he led them to his car. She was wearing her favorite green sundress that brought out the green in her eyes, and his jacket was wrapped around her.

*That's not even bad,* I thought with relief, until I realized there was another photo.

I swiped to the end and saw the next photo was of his tongue down her throat.

Yikes.

I was right; this was an ice cream level emergency.

I'll be there in 15

I quickly shoved my phone into my pocket, put away my laptop, grabbed my keys, and got in the car.

# Chapter Two

She was inconsolable. There was no amount of ice cream or bad movies that could fix it. I didn't expect them to, but seeing her sobbing, afraid to go to school and face her friends, was heartbreaking.

I didn't know what to do except be there for her. I tried to convince her everything would be fine, but even to me it felt like a lie, and a weak one at that.

Since the photos had dropped, none of her friends had been in touch with her. Even her best friend Grace was silent. Worse than silent, actually, since Grace seemed to be leading the charge to isolate Lynds. Lynds had sent me some screenshots of Facegram posts of her friend group hanging out without her. I hated them for that. The broken heart and betrayal were hard enough without her so-called friends piling onto her misery.

I wasn't used to dealing with emotions like this. Sure, when my mother would sober up from one of her benders, she'd cry it out for a while, but I learned early on that there wasn't anything I could do that would help more than her next fix. I didn't know how to deal with something like this. I was only a year older than Lynds. I should've had a good deal of experience to help me, stories to tell her about how things looked bad now but would get better, but I had never been in any one place long enough to have many stories.

I was in over my head, but that was the upside of my new situation. Unlike my mom's breakdowns, this wasn't something I had to hide. I didn't have to hesitate about calling for backup.

I scrolled through my contacts quickly, pulled up 'Oxen Free' and hit video call. Sure, it was rude as hell to attempt a video call without a warning text, but I was desperate. I needed advice.

I was about to give up when a head of shaggy purple hair and a dorky grin showed up on the screen.

"Heyya cuz!" he said, grinning wider. "What's going on?"

"Ollie Ollie," I said, grinning.

He rolled his eyes, attempting to look annoyed, but it didn't meet his eyes. "Oxen free," he finished. "You and Lynds are never gonna get sick of that, are you?" he asked.

My smile slipped a little at the reminder of why I was calling. Whenever I couldn't get through to Lynds when we were younger, I would turn to Ollie, my cousin and her older brother. He was always quick with a joke and a goofy grin that forced smiles out of most people.

It was a shame he wasn't here. Ollie was ten years older than me and had moved out to Portland a while ago with his best friend, Gwen. At first, the family thought he would come back, but from the way he talked about it since he got there, we knew they both loved it there and had grown to accept it. With his best friend Gwen, and now also his boyfriend Eli, living up there, even with as great as San Fran was, NorCal couldn't compete with the hold Portland and the PNW had on his heart.

Lynds and I had given up on him coming back. It was a shame, though. From everything Lynds said about Gwen and the video calls I'd had with her and Ollie, I was sure I would've loved Gwen as much as I loved Ollie.

"I need some advice," I told him.

His smile slipped a little when he saw I had grown serious. "That bad?"

I nodded before shaking my head, not sure how to answer. "Yes and no. Everyone's fine physically."

He looked around, saying, "Gwen's here, but everyone else is out. Is this a headphones or speaker talk?"

"Speaker, definitely. Gwen actually might be more helpful for this."

He furrowed his brow in a playful way, asking, "Are you implying I'm not helpful?"

I laughed despite myself. "Of course not. You're just not as big into socials as Gwen is."

"Hi Bri!" I heard a cheery call from the background.

There was some shuffling as Gwen plopped down on the couch with Ollie and they adjusted blankets, settling in. I couldn't help envying their closeness. I had had friends throughout my life, but my constant moving meant I had never really been close with anyone like that. As Ollie slung an arm over her shoulder and she cuddled into him, I found myself craving that closeness, that connection with another person. Maybe things would be different here, though. Maybe I would finally be somewhere long enough to make lasting friends.

Lynds and I were close, of course, as close as two cousins who hadn't spent much time together, until a month ago when I moved in, could be. She, my aunt, and uncle all welcomed me with open arms and I was incredibly grateful for it. Even if I did miss my mother sometimes, things felt calm and safe here in a way life with her never did. Lynds made me feel right at home, but still, she was family. I'd never been close with anyone not related to me, never had anyone choose me like that.

"So, what's up, cuz?" Ollie asked when they were settled.

"Everything okay?" Gwen asked, her big blue eyes widening with concern.

Looking at the two of them, anyone would think Gwen was the one Lynds and I were related to. We had similar big blue eyes and red hair. Lynds and I both had a lot more freckles than she did, but Gwen looked a lot more related to us than Ollie did with his dyed purple hair and warm brown eyes.

"Not really. Lynds is having guy trouble."

They exchanged a knowing look before Ollie said, "Well, that can't be too bad, is it?"

"He's an ass. He cheated on her, or with her. I'm honestly not really sure on that point."

They both winced.

"I didn't want to ask too much, but it seems like he had her and two other girls on the hook."

"Guys are the worst," Gwen groaned.

Wisely, Ollie nodded. "Don't I know it."

I raised an eyebrow at him.

He smiled a little. "I don't make excuses for my gender, only apologies. What happened, though? How'd she find out? And what can we do?"

"Do we need to put someone on blast?" Gwen asked with some interest.

This was why I loved Gwen. Even though we weren't family, she loved and cared about me and Lynds because Ollie did, and her threat wasn't an idle one. Gwen was a social media influencer with over half a million followers and somehow managed to make enough of a living off that to not have to hold down a job. It was inspiring, but also helpful. I knew all we needed to do was say the word and she could spread whatever news we wanted or needed. It was good to know, but probably not the ideal way to handle the situation.

"Someone sent pictures into the school's gossip page. Lynds-"

Before I could keep going, Ollie asked, "Your school has a gossip page?"

"Most do now on Facegram," Gwen told him, elbowing him saying, "Geez Ollie, get with the times."

We both laughed when he just groaned. "Fine, fine, making me feel like an old man over here," he said before turning back to me. "So someone posted about him cheating?"

"Yeah, the school has its own page for gossip, apparently. Whoever's behind it posted about the guy Lynds liked being with her and two other girls."

Ollie paled, and I quickly corrected, "Not with with, just with."

"Take pity on him," Gwen said to me before turning to Ollie and saying, "She didn't mean what that sounded like."

Ollie sighed. "I knew you and her weren't gonna stay babies forever, but to me you're both still little and need looking after."

"We still need you, Olls," I said quickly. "Always have, always will."

"How can I help?" he asked.

"I was hoping you would have some good big brother advice or that Gwen would have some advice on how to deal with negative press?"

She laughed at that. "The world knows I've had enough of that. It feels fake to say it, but the best way to deal with things like that is to be yourself and embrace what's being said."

I grimaced.

"I know, I know," she continued. "It sounds like mom advice. Trust me, I feel old saying it. Everyone knows it took me forever to take the advice myself, but being yourself, or Lynds being herself rather, would be the easiest way to get this to die down. If she shows she doesn't care, people will get bored."

"But she can't be herself and act like she doesn't care."

They both considered for a moment before Gwen said, "What about her friends? There's safety in numbers."

"No help there. They've been radio silent since the news dropped."

"Seriously?" Ollie asked.

"Girls can be the worst, too," Gwen said with a sigh.

Ollie perked up at that and said quickly, "Wait, girls. That might be the answer."

I looked at Gwen, who looked just as confused as I felt, so we both turned our attention to Ollie. He waited but neither of us said anything, so he said, "Girls," and again watched us expectantly, and when neither of us said anything, he said, "Girls, as in more than one, as in not just Lynds."

"Yes," I said slowly, "you're grasping the problem."

He shook his head empathetically. "No, you're not grasping the solution. Lynds's friends are being awful and none of us really know how she's feeling right now, but I can guarantee there are two other girls out there right now that know exactly how she's feeling."

It took longer than it should have for understanding to dawn. "You mean...?"

He nodded enthusiastically, seeing I was finally caught up. "I mean, they're the only ones that will get it. It's worth a shot."

It didn't sound like a half bad idea, but then again girls could be cruel. I looked at Gwen. "What do you think?"

She considered it for a moment. "It really depends on the others, but I think if they're the right type of girls, it could be good for them all." She considered before nodding and adding, "Yeah, actually, I agree with Ollie. Go for it, worst-case scenario, you don't hear back from them; best case, Lynds might end up with a new friend or two."

I thanked them and promised to update them. Ollie said he could come visit if things didn't get any better, but I told him things weren't that bad yet. I didn't want to drag him away from his life. He had taken care of Lynds for years. I could handle this.

At least I hoped I could.

The advice rotated through my mind over the next few days, eating away at me. I wasn't sure if it was the right move, especially if the initial contact came from me. I didn't feel comfortable bringing the idea up to Lynds, though, until I knew if it was worth it. I didn't want to get her hopes up if neither of the girls were receptive.

I had tried every trick up my sleeve to help her and to distract her, but what she needed wasn't something I could give her by myself. I was doing my best, but I could only do so much. I didn't really know how she was feeling. Ollie was right; there were only a couple other girls who really got how she was feeling... but being screwed over by the same guy didn't automatically make them friends.

For the millionth time since he suggested it, I considered it. The experience didn't make them friends, but it bonded them in a way that I couldn't relate to. Maybe with the right push, they might become friends.

I was out of other ideas, and it was worth a shot.

I clicked over to Facegram and went to the Tiger Shark Tea page and found the post. I clicked through the text pages and stopped at the photo of the girl with the braids. I clicked on the photo hoping she might've been tagged since the first time I checked. Unfortunately, she wasn't. It wasn't surprising, but it was disappointing. Keeping my fingers crossed, I scrolled to the next picture and clicked on it. I was elated to find that the raven-haired girl was tagged.

I clicked on her username KickRox, and it brought me to her profile. Roxy had a punk rock meets witchy aesthetic going on that I couldn't help envying. I could never pull it off, but she killed it.

I clicked on her most recent post, not really sure what I was looking for, but wanting to get to know her a bit better before deciding whether to actually reach out.

The post was a middle finger over purple painted lips with the caption "Kiss my ass Shawn Parker. For anyone wondering, no, he's not even good."

I barked out a laugh and hit follow, loving her a little already. I scrolled through some of her other photos, debating whether this was really a good idea. I knew Lynds didn't blame the other girls. She blamed Shawn, and unfortunately blamed herself a lot more than I would like, but she didn't blame the other girls. I wasn't sure if the other girls would feel the same, though, but from the anti-patriarchy and girl power radiating from Roxy's profile, it seemed like a worthwhile risk to take.

I opened a message to her and started and deleted a couple of tries before settling on:

"Hi Roxy, I know you don't know me, but I'm Lyndsey(the redhead from the photos)'s older cousin. I've been trying to help her, but I don't know how. I'm sure you have a lot on your plate, but I'm so impressed with how you're handling things and thought that maybe you could use someone to talk to, too. I'm sure you have plenty of friends and support, and Lyndsey would kill me for saying this, but she doesn't. I don't know anyone in town, so I don't have anyone to reach out to. It's probably too much to ask, but if you want to come over and talk, I'm sure it'd help her. Maybe we can even help each other. What Shawn did was unforgivable and karma's going to be looking for him... maybe we can help it along. ~ the New Girl in Town."

I couldn't decide if I was kidding about getting revenge. I knew it wouldn't help anything, not really, and Lynds had been insisting for days for me to leave it, and him, alone, saying revenge wouldn't help her, wouldn't change anything, but I couldn't help thinking she was wrong.

After all, two wrongs don't make a right, but three wronged girls could.

# CHAPTER THREE

To my surprise, Roxy was quick to message back.





I thought for a minute about whether or not to lie. I wanted to protect Lynds as much as I could, but this seemed like a risk worth taking. Roxy seemed nice enough and had messaged me back, and more importantly, she and the other girl were the only ones who really understood what Lynds was going through. It was worth a shot. If this backfired, at least I would be there with Lynds when school started in another week. At least she wouldn't be alone.

Of course, since she was a sophomore now, and I was a junior, I wouldn't be in her classes, but at least I could be there to watch her back since her friends had turned on her, too.

I decided to go with the truth.

I hoped she might have a suggestion. I didn't have much experience with heartbreak. I hadn't exactly been popular at any of my old schools. I'd been on a few dates but never seriously dated anyone. I used to tell people I was bisexual, but I had secretly worried if there was something wrong with me. I hadn't met anyone yet that I felt more than a momentary attraction to, no one I actually wanted to be with.

As I got to know a little bit more about queerness, I learned I might be somewhere on the asexual spectrum or demisexual. There wasn't anything wrong with that, but it felt weird to me. Everyone was always talking about crushes and dating and hooking up and none of it had appealed to me yet. I claimed the label demi because it felt more romantic to me, like if the right person came along, I could feel the attraction that others experienced so easily, but I'd yet to have that proven true. So I didn't know the first thing about romantic heartbreak.

I was glad I was here for Lynds, though. I couldn't imagine how she'd be dealing with things if she had been truly on her own. I hated that she was experiencing this, but I didn't hate feeling needed. Lynds needing me reaffirmed I was welcome and wanted here and that my new home wasn't temporary. I wanted so badly to thank her for that, to help her, but I didn't know the first thing about how to.

> I don't even know. Her friends aren't talking to her, and I don't know anyone around here.

KickRox

> I might be the last person she wants to see - but me and Gavin can come over. He's been my rock; he's better at the emotion shit than I am. I'll bring some spiritual cleansers, though.

I was so far in over my head that I didn't know where to start. I wanted to ask what spiritual cleansers were and why they would help and who Gavin was, but I didn't want her to change her mind, so I didn't

KickRox

> I'll try Ava, too. I'd be surprised if she answered, but it's worth a shot. You're right, guys are ass-hats and she shouldn't be suffering alone.

I started to type and then stopped, not sure what to say to that. Before I could come up with anything, my phone buzzed again.

KickRox

> Can I plan to crash there tonight?

> You want to sleepover?

KickRox

> If it's cool, sure.

My aunt and uncle weren't particularly strict. I would have to double check with them, of course, but I couldn't imagine they'd say no. They kept telling me to make myself at home, and with how sad and down Lynds had been lately, I couldn't imagine they would begrudge anything that would cheer her up.

Yeah, definitely cool

KickRox

Sweet - I'll try Ava but no promises

# Chapter Four

My aunt and uncle were cooler about it than Lyndsey was. "You invited Roxy?! Here?! Why?!" she asked loudly as she sprung up from the blanket cocoon she had been swaddled in on her bed. Her wide eyes had me worrying I made a mistake. "Are you crazy?" she asked. "Roxy can't come here!"

"Why not She seemed really nice. She said her and Gavin were going to come over and that she was bringing the spiritual cleansers, whatever that means."

Lyndsey groaned. "They can't come here. After what happened, I'm sure she hates me, too, just like the rest of the school."

"No one hates you-" I started, but she cut me off.

"Of course they do! I was the stupid band geek freshman who thought I was good enough for the quarterback."

"Stop-"

"It's true, though!" she groaned, collapsing back onto her bed.

"The only stupid one is Shawn. He's an idiot for letting you go, for hurting you the way he did, and for messing with Roxy. I've been scrolling through her feed and I wouldn't be surprised if she'd already hexed him."

I heard her giggling as she moved the pillow from over her face. "I hope she did."

"You can ask her yourself, but I promise you she wouldn't be coming if she hated you."

Lynds looked a little calmer now, which I was incredibly grateful for, especially when she said, "Thank you. I hate that you feel like you have to look out for me, but I don't know what I would do without you here."

I grinned at that. "Well, without me here, you'd have a much harder time getting our room in shape for company."

Her eyes widened as she surveyed the room. There were clothes all over the floor and makeup and jewelry strewn on the dresser and desk from last night. I had thought makeovers would cheer her up, but I'd been wrong. The room wasn't as bad as it could have been, but it certainly wasn't ready for company. Her momentary smile had dropped from her face and her eyes widened in alarm.

"Hey, don't worry about it. We have plenty of time to get it back into shape before they get here."

# CHAPTER FIVE

"Girls, your friends are here!" Auntie Jen shouted from downstairs, just in time, too, since our room was a lot less messy now.

Lynds looked nervous, so I shot her a reassuring smile and squeezed her shoulder. "It's gonna be fine. If she's rude, I'll just have to fight her."

Lynds laughed at that. I was glad to hear her laughing, and the idea of me fighting the incredibly tough-looking, witchy, combat boot wearing Roxy was laughable.

I had been mostly kidding, but I would kick her out of the house if necessary. Yes, Lynds and I were basically the same age, but still, no one messed with my little cousin.

Lynds took a deep breath, and we both exited our room, trotting down the stairs to meet Roxy and Gavin. I wasn't sure if Ava would be with them, but since I was surprised enough that Roxy had agreed to show up, I didn't really expect to see Ava, too.

When we rounded the corner toward the front door, I was surprised to see Roxy was already inside with a tall skinny boy with warm brown eyes and curly brown hair who must be Gavin. Auntie Jen was laughing at something Roxy had said, which put me a little more at ease. I'd been a little worried since Roxy, with her dark eyeliner, purple lipstick, fishnets and combat boots wasn't what most parents would call a good influence. I was glad that my aunt didn't seem phased, and I was surprised to see Roxy smiling. Her Facegram page made me feel like I knew her and, as much as I had scrolled, I hadn't seen a single picture of her smiling.

She saw us and her smile broadened into a grin. She waved, holding up a brown paper bag. "I brought supplies!"

Auntie Jen laughed, saying, "I'm so glad you guys are having a girls' night, but there better not be drugs in there."

I froze, feeling instant relief when Roxy waved her off. "Of course not, just some sage, moon water, and chocolate."

"Chocolate?" Gavin asked.

"Not everything has to be magic to be good," she said, shrugging.

"Well, it's great to meet you both," Auntie Jen said. "Please make yourselves at home. I've been telling the kids for a while now they're more than welcome to have their friends over, but it's been awfully quiet here lately." I saw Lynds wince, and I went to say something, but my aunt kept going. "But we're happy to have you both. Of course, Gavin can't spend the night."

Gavin jumped in, saying, "Of course Mrs. Matthews. Roxy drove me over but I'm a five-minute walk from here. Just let me know when you want me out and I'll hit the road."

Auntie Jen smiled at that and I was relieved that Roxy and Gavin were much better with parents than I had expected.

"Well, I'll leave you guys alone. Dinner's at 6. We're having pork chops if that's okay with everyone? No allergies? Vegetarians? I can make tofu or pasta instead."

"Pork chops sound great!" Gavin said.

"Sounds great!" Roxy echoed. "Thank you so much for having us."

"You're both perfectly lovely and welcome here anytime," Auntie Jen said, smiling. She turned, heading for the kitchen before turning back and adding, "Since it's a summer weekend, does ten sound fair for Gavin?" Lynds nodded quickly. I glanced at Roxy and Gavin and was happy to see they didn't look phased or upset by it, so I nodded, too.

"Sounds great. Thanks Mom!" Lynds said.

"Why don't we go upstairs?" I said, leading the way to our room.

We trooped upstairs and Lynds tensed when we entered the room. It was clean now, but I knew she was worried about and wondering how it would look to Roxy. It was a pretty spacious room, even with my twin bed on one wall and hers on the other. We had a big closet that was overflowing with clothes, mostly

Lynds's. I was lucky, though, that while I was a little less curvy than her, I could fit in most of her clothes and she was happy to share.

We had vines on the walls and glow-in-the-dark stars on the ceiling. I thought they were cute, but Roxy might not.

She looked around and turned back to us saying, "Love the vines."

Lynds grinned, sending relief coursing through me. Lynds and I took a seat on her bed and Roxy and Gavin sat on mine.

"Thanks so much for coming," I said. "It's so good to meet you guys."

"Of course. Any enemy of my enemy is a friend of mine," Roxy said. "Besides, I don't like what we're walking into next week, if I'm being honest. I'd been thinking about reaching out, but thought I'd be the last person you'd want to talk to, Lyndsey." She grimaced, saying, "I should've said it before, but I'm so sorry. I didn't know he was seeing anyone. Boys are trash."

I waited to see if Gavin would take offense, but he chimed in, "Amen to that. Boys are the worst."

"You're the exception," Roxy said, grinning, bumping his shoulder.

"Obviously. I'm the best of the bunch, but even my magnificence can't make up for the trash that is Shawn Parker."

"If anyone could, it'd be you," she said before turning back to Lynds, "but we're getting off topic. I'm really sorry. I hope you know I wouldn't have intentionally hurt you."

I held my breath, waiting to see how this would play out. I didn't think Lynds blamed Roxy for Shawn's actions, but sitting face to face with the other woman would be tough for anyone.

I was incredibly proud of her when she said, "You don't have to apologize. I know you didn't mean to hurt me, and I don't blame you."

She stayed quiet for a few moments and I couldn't help saying, "Exactly. There's only one person to blame for it-"

Lynds cut me off, saying, "I feel like there's two."

My brow furrowed, and I was sure the confusion was painted across my face. I looked at Roxy, whose face mirrored my own. She spoke before I could think of what to say. "If you forgive me, it's not really fair to be mad at Ava."

Lynds huffed. "I'm not mad at Ava either. I'm saying I was stupid. I blame myself. Besides, Ava at least makes sense for him."

Roxy and Gavin nodded, showing I was missing something. "What do you mean?"

"She's cheer captain," Roxy said with a shrug.

"And I'm just on the bleachers," Lynds said. "I'm no one. I was a band geek freshman, and it never made sense he wanted me."

"Fuck him," Roxy said quickly. I shot her a grateful smile. Hearing Lynds put herself down hurt me.

I was shocked when Lynds laughed and said, "I'm so glad I didn't."

Roxy grinned back. "I thank the universe for that daily."

Lynds's eyes widened. "You didn't?"

"Nah," she said, shrugging.

"Not that he didn't try, though," Gavin piped in. "I still can't believe those pics you showed me."

Lynds and I looked at each other, her eyes as wide as my own.

"You mean..." I trailed off.

Roxy grinned. "Do I mean that I was the single worst person for him to decide to fuck over? Yes, yes, I do. You guys wanna see it?"

I shuddered. "Not even a little."

"It certainly is," Gavin chimed in.

Lynds's mouth dropped open and I couldn't help laughing with Roxy, especially when she mouthed, "tiny" holding her fingers just barely apart.

"Think Crayola marker," Gavin added.

I couldn't breathe when Lynds asked, "Length or girth?"

I still struggled sometimes to remember that she was only a year younger than me. To me, she would always be my little cousin.

"Both," Roxy answered, and then we both started laughing at the horrified look on Lynds's face.

"So why doesn't the school know about that yet?" I asked Roxy.

Her face turned serious, and the mirth left the room. "Would you believe I didn't want to sink that low?"

Lynds nodded, but I found my eyes meeting Gavin's, who shrugged and mouthed, "I tried."

"It's not the same as what he did to us," Roxy insisted. "Besides, I don't know how, but it would backfire on me. He gets out of everything, just like I'm sure he's going to find a way to wiggle out of this one."

"There's no way," I said quickly, expecting someone to back me up, but Lynds and Gavin stayed quiet. "He can't actually talk his way out of this, though, can he? He got caught cheating."

Roxy huffed out a sigh. "Wouldn't be the first time he's done something heinous and gotten away with it."

"Why though?" I pressed when no one else said anything.

"Because he's a cis-het white man," Roxy said.

"With the audacity of one," Gavin added.

I looked at Lynds, who shrugged. "He has a lot of audacity, but the whole school is wrapped around his finger."

"He could get any girl, boy, or in-between he wanted," Gavin added.

"And he does." Roxy said. "We're obviously all done with him, but even knowing what he did to us, I bet there's still a line around the block."

"I bet he's never been told no," Lynds added.

Hearing that Shawn had not only hurt Lynds but was probably still going to end up hurting a lot of other girls had my blood boiling. I wanted to hurt him for hurting her. I wanted to knock him down a peg or two. Then it came to me.

"What if we could change that?"

"Change what?" Lynds asked.

Roxy turned to me, a smile forming on her lips that gave me chills. "Are you thinking what I'm thinking?"

I honestly wasn't sure.

"Depends what you're thinking," I said hesitantly.

"What are both of you thinking?" Gavin asked impatiently. "Come on and share with the class."

"I'm thinking he could stand to be knocked down a peg or two."

"And?" Roxy prompted.

"And you'd dump him?" Lynds said. "I know, I know, but he hasn't been answering my texts. He left all my texts on read, and I can't really dump him if we were never actually together."

"That's not what I was going to say. I didn't say break-up. I say we get even."

"There is it," Roxy said, smiling. "I knew I liked you."

"Get even how?" Lynds asked.

"Whatever it is, I'm in," Gavin said quickly.

"I hadn't thought further than the vibes of a plan," I admitted.

"What if we give him someone who will finally say no to him?"

"You mean play the player?" I asked.

"Exactly!" Roxy cried out.

"It wouldn't work," Gavin argued. "Anyone who you shove in his direction will take one look at those gorgeous hazel eyes and fall harder than a cheerleader dropped from the top of a pyramid."

Roxy had lost some of her grin, but Lynds said slowly, "I might know someone."

We all quickly turned to her, but she wasn't meeting our eyes.

"Who?" Roxy asked.

We all waited as she bit her lip and nervously twisted a strand of her hair. When she looked up a moment later, she was looking at me.

"Who?" I asked.

She just continued to look at me. I looked toward the others, but now they were looking at me, too.

"Who?" I asked again, turning my attention back to Lynds.

She still didn't say anything, just nodded at me. She couldn't be saying what I thought she was. I waited for her to crack a smile, anything to show she was joking, but she didn't.

"You can't be serious?" I asked. "Me?"

"Yes, you. You'd be perfect."

"I'm probably the least qualified person in the room," I said.

"Really?" Gavin asked with a raised eyebrow. I considered it for a moment.

My gaydar wasn't the best, but he was giving rainbow energy. Even if I was wrong and he was straight, I was sure he was still more qualified, so I nodded and said, "Yup, you're more qualified."

He laughed. "Clocked me just like that, huh?" He looked at Roxy and asked, "Am I that bad at cosplaying straight?"

Roxy ignored him, finished assessing me, and turned back to Lynds. "You're right, this could work."

"It really really won't," I said.

"You'll do just fine," Roxy said. "You're stunning. Besides we'll make you into something Shawny-boy won't be able to resist."

"I'm sure I'm not anymore his type than he is mine," I said, trying to slow them down.

"Shawn's only type is a challenge. The moment you turn him down, he'll have to make you love him. He loves the chase."

I looked at Lynds for support, but she was smiling, and the smile killed the rest of the protest on my lips. This was the longest I'd seen her looking happy since the photos came out. He had done that to her, and yes, I wasn't the best person for the job, but someone had to make the boy pay. Besides, if it would make her happy, I could try for her.

"You're perfect for it," Lynds said.

She knew me better than anyone, and if she thought that maybe she was right, but Roxy didn't know what she was working with, and they deserved to not go into this challenge blind.

"You guys don't get it, though. I'm demi."

"Which is why you're perfect for it," Lynds said.

Roxy grinned. "You're just what we needed!"

Now I was the one feeling lost. "How is that an asset? I don't know the first thing about flirting with anyone."

"Don't worry about that," Roxy said, waving her hand through the air dismissively. "Boys are easy. Plus, the less interested you act, the more interested he'll be. The hard part was gonna be finding someone who wouldn't fall for his crap."

"Exactly," Lynds chimed in. "You're perfect. You can be our secret weapon, because no matter what he throws at you, you won't fall for him."

The more I thought about it, the more sense it made. They were right. I'd never fallen for anyone before. I'd never been in the same place long enough to get close enough to fall for anyone. My mother had moved us around too much continually changing jobs to try to hide and support her habit. This was going to be the first year I got to spend completely at the same school. From what Auntie Jen had told me, I was here for good if I wanted to be.

My uncle and her had held an intervention for her sister, telling her that either she had to get clean or

I was going to move in with them before she lost custody of me.

She didn't make the choice I thought she would, but I was settling in nicely here.

Sharing a room was weird, but a good weird. This was the most time that I had spent with Lynds our entire lives. We texted all the time, but actually being here with her was so much better. I didn't want to imagine how she would be coping if she were dealing with it alone. She wasn't, though. I was here with her, and she needed me. For once, it sounded like my inability to fall for anyone easily was going to come in handy. I wasn't used to thinking of it as an asset.

"Okay, fine. I'm in."

Gavin laughed. "Roxy wouldn't have let you rest until you agreed."

"I'm not that bad. Unlike Shawn, I understand consent."

Gavin immediately clarified, "I didn't mean it like that."

Roxy waved him off. "I know, I know." She turned back to me and said, "But really, if you don't want to, we won't make you."

"Speak for yourself," Lynds said, grinning. "They might not make you, but I'd be annoying and persuasive."

I laughed. "You don't have to be. I'll do it. He hurt you. He deserves more than whatever we're going to do to him." I paused a moment before asking, "What exactly are we going to do, anyway?"

We spent the next few hours floating plans out there, waiting for something to stick, but nothing seemed right. We wanted to humiliate him, but we were only willing to go so far. The only thing that Roxy and Gavin agreed on was that I needed a new name to go with the character I was going to be playing.

"Why though?"

"It'll help you get into the mindset better," Gavin said. "Think of it like a stage name."

"Any ideas?" Roxy asked.

I shrugged and Lynds suggested, "Bridgette?" She gave it a French accented lilt that my actual name Bridget didn't have. I was almost positive she was joking, but apparently the others didn't agree.

"It's perfect!" Roxy said.

"Really?"

"Definitely." She nodded. "Simple but sultry."

"And French," Gavin said nodded.

"Really?" I asked again.

"It's erotic and exotic," Gavin said, grinning.

I was already in over my head.

Dinner passed uneventfully, with my aunt mentioning a few times that she was glad we had found some nice friends and that she never liked Lynds's old friend Grace. I couldn't agree more. Grace had been nice enough when I used to visit when we were younger, but the older we got, the meaner she got. She acted nice, but was constantly using her religiousness as a reason to put other people down. She thought she was better than almost everyone, and she acted like it. It wasn't at all surprising that she dropped Lynds the second something happened. What was surprising was that she had stuck around this long.

After dinner we talked through another couple of plans, before Gavin had to leave, not that that stopped him from video calling us the moment he got home lamenting how being a guy left him out of sleepovers.

We stayed up concocting plans that grew wilder as it grew later. When Lynds suggested hoisting him up the flagpole by his boxers, I figured it was time to call it a night.

We got Roxy set up on the air mattress and snuggled in for the night with Gavin set up on Roxy's phone on my nightstand and tucked into his own bed at home.

My last thought before I was lulled to sleep by their rhythmic breathing was how nice it was to get to spend the night laughing and gossiping with friends. I had never been in one place long enough to have formed bonds like this. Nothing brought people closer together than a common enemy and even as new as it was, I knew me and Lynds had stumbled onto something special with Roxy and Gavin.

# CHAPTER SIX

The first day of school was less eventful than I expected. I floated through most of my morning classes until fourth period English. English class had always been my favorite. I found an empty desk near the front and plopped my books down on it. It was next to a friendly-looking blond girl who I smiled at, but she was looking down at her book. I caught myself wondering what she was reading; if it was something she was reading for fun, or if she was getting a head start on the class.

I looked to the front of the class and saw our syllabus was written out on the board and grew even more excited when I saw we'd be covering a lot of my favorite classics. I couldn't wait to reread Pride and Prejudice. The Great Gatsby was on the list, too, and I wondered if this teacher would be any more receptive than my last one had to my ranting about how incredibly gay the book was and how it was most likely mostly stolen from F. Scott Fitzgerald's wife, Zelda.

I was still thinking about that when our teacher cleared his throat and started doing roll call. I startled when he said, "Parker". I turned my head, not sure how

I could have possibly missed Shawn Parker after how much time I'd spent talking about him. Scanning the classroom, I didn't see anyone that matched what I remembered of him.

"Parker," the teacher repeated.

Someone whispered, "Shannon," and I turned around, surprised to see the blond girl's head whip up. She quickly pulled out a bookmark and marked her spot, closing her book with a wince. She was too quick for me to make out the title, though, and it wasn't a cover I recognized.

"Here!" she said quickly.

I must have misheard. I continued staring at her, waiting for things to make sense. Before I could force myself to look away, she took in my confusion and said, "Shannon Parker, also known as the Other Parker, since I'm guessing you've heard of my brother."

"B-brother?" I choked out over my surprise.

I don't know why I was so surprised. The more I looked at her, the more sense it made. They had the same honey blonde hair, the same hazel eyes if his pictures did him justice, and even the same dimples when they smiled. It wasn't surprising anymore that they were related. It was more surprising that I hadn't noticed until now.

None of the girls had mentioned it or warned me, though, which was weird. I wondered if Shannon had any idea how awful her brother was.

"I can see you've met him already, and I'd say I'm sorry, but I refuse to take any sort of responsibility for him or his pigheaded actions. He might be my brother, but he's not my problem," she said with a shrug.

"I wasn't going to-" I started, but she cut me off with a snort.

"Yes, you were. It's okay, everyone does. I haven't seen you around, though. You must be new?"

"Yeah, I am. I'm Bri-" I started before stopping and correcting myself, "Bridgette"

"Well, Bridgette, consider this your warning. Shawn may be pretty," she grinned, saying, "it runs in the family." I laughed at that. The same dimples that looked sinister on his lying face looked softer and somewhat mischievous on hers. Her honey blonde hair fell in loose waves that looked incredibly soft. In short, she was beautiful in a way that felt more authentic than Shawn's cultivated beauty. "But seriously, though, in case no one else in the school warned you, he's not a good guy."

I wasn't sure what to say. She was nice enough and was trying to help. It was sweet of her, but I knew I wasn't going to listen. The others were counting on me, so I knew whatever I said next had to be convincing. The last thing I wanted was for her to suspect I was trying to hurt her brother. I was glad she wasn't defending him, but he was still her brother. I clearly couldn't trust her. I hesitated before going with the worry that had been plaguing me all day.

"What makes you so sure I'm his type?"

I held my breath, waiting for her answer. I wasn't insecure really, but I didn't feel like I was objectively anything special looking. My face was a bit sharply angled and had a lot more freckles than most people liked. I wasn't cool and tough like Roxy, or preppy and popular like the others said Ava was. I was a little similar to Lynds since we're related, but I didn't have the curves that she did. I couldn't see a world where he would pick me over Roxy, Ava, or Lynds. They seemed sure that he'd be interested in me, but I couldn't be less sure about that. The whole plan hinged on me being his type, on him finding me alluring, so I was worried.

She examined me for a minute before chuckling to herself. "You're his type alright. You're a girl."

I grinned at her. "He's that bad?"

Her smile dropped a little, and she nodded. "I've seen him break too many hearts and you seem nice, so I hope you'll take my advice."

"Quite the poet there, Parker," a voice interjected.

We both jumped, and when Shannon turned to the front of the class, I realized we'd caught the teacher's attention.

Her cheeks flushed, and she brushed a stray blonde hair out of her face. "I try. You should hear my written poetry."

I was relieved when the teacher chuckled and said, "Save it for the poetry unit, Shannon."

She grinned at that. "Will do."

He turned to me saying, "That must make you Tanner comma Bridget."

"It's actually pronounced Bridgette." I was proud of myself for remembering to correct him.

"Well, Bridgette, I'm Mr. Hayes. You don't know me yet, but I'm tough but fair. I run a tight ship around here, but as long as you have a passion for literature, you'll get along here just fine."

The class chuckled at that. He turned his back to us, moving back to his desk.

"He's a hard-ass," came a call from the back of the room.

"Language," he said without turning around.

"A stubborn mule," the voice corrected to a chorus of laughter.

If I hadn't been sure already, I knew now. This was by and far going to be my favorite class.

# CHAPTER SEVEN

The moment the last bell rang, I pulled out my phone.

**Shawn Parker Must Die**

Lynds

> Bri, can we do a diner meet-up?

Roxy

> FUCKING BULLSHIT.

Lynds

> We need to talk

Gavin

> Spill it!

> Definitely. Meet you at my car. What happened?!

Gavin

> You guys were in there a while. You guys okay?

Roxy

> PATRIARCHAL BULLSHIT. Notice a certain golden boy was absent.

> I'll head right there.

Lynds refused to debrief until we were all together, but she looked more annoyed than sad, so I took that as a good sign. She blasted an angrier sounding pop punk playlist than she would normally choose, though, which had me a little worried.

When we got there, Roxy and Gavin were waiting outside. We took them to our regular booth, Roxy sliding in next to Lynds and Gavin next to me. Our regular waitress came over right away and I ordered my normal Oreo milkshake and fries.

When everyone ordered and the waitress left, Roxy started in. "The absolute patriarchal bullshit, Bri. You won't even believe what happened."

"What happened?" I asked.

"That's what I've been asking," Gavin said quickly. "But did she tell me anything? Noooo. Said it had to wait until we were all together or something. Revenge club rules yada yada."

"Hey," Roxy stage whispered, "first rule of revenge club?"

He groaned. "Don't talk about revenge club. I know."

"And what happens if someone can't keep his mouth shut?" Roxy asked.

"Exile."

Roxy laughed at that. I shot her a questioning look, and she explained, "I told him that if he can't keep his mouth shut, he'll get excluded from the group chat."

He rolled his eyes. "Yeah, that's what I said, exile."

I grinned at that and was happy to see Lynds was smiling, too. I took the chance to ask her, "Are you okay?"

I shouldn't have, since the smile immediately disappeared.

"I'm fine," she said. "It wasn't anything worse than I expected."

"We shouldn't have to expect it, though. Why were we given a warning when he got off scot-free? Shawny-boy wasn't even dragged out of class for the joke of a disciplinary meeting," Roxy complained.

"What happened?" I asked, still confused. Luckily, Lynds took over the conversation.

"I was pulled out of class to go to the principal's office and was told it was to discuss a very serious matter. I checked my phone on the way there thinking something was wrong or that it was an actual emergency," Lynds said, rolling her eyes. "They couldn't have been anymore cryptic about it if they tried."

"Probably some sort of 'let's make them really think about what they've done' bullshit," Roxy added.

"Well, whatever it was, it worked," Lynds picked back up. "I thought something was seriously wrong, but nope. I walked in and saw the man I'm assuming is our principal-"

"He is. We're well acquainted," Roxy interjected.

"Well, I'd only ever seen him in passing at assemblies and he's not really unique looking. Anyway, he's just sitting there with his arms crossed. Roxy and Ava were sitting there, too. He told me it was about time and to take a seat."

"Which is such bullshit. We had barely been waiting a minute," Roxy added.

"So I took a seat, and he asks us if we knew why we were there, and then Roxy almost got us suspended," Lynds said, shooting a look her way.

Roxy chuckled and shrugged. "Hey it was funny, and he was being a dick."

"What'd you say?" Gavin beat me to asking her.

"I told him if he was trying for a Charlie's Angels situation that I wasn't down and that if he was going to suggest we start a band, we were short a drummer."

Gavin and I made eye contact before bursting into laughter.

"You didn't!" I said.

"She for sure did," Gavin said.

"She did," Lynds continued. "You should've seen how angry he got."

"And then he launched into his lecture about how 'Harris High' girls are expected to act more ladylike and have more decorum and respect for themselves than that."

"And I told him it was bullshit and that it was a 'Harris High' boy's actions that were the reason we were all being scrutinized in the first."

"What'd he say to that?" Gavin asked, looking impressed with her audacity but not surprised.

"That Shawn had already been spoken to," Lynds answered for her.

Roxy rolled her eyes. "Fucking bullshit. There's no way he got more than a slap on the wrist and maybe a clap on the back."

I raised an eyebrow before Gavin explained, "He couldn't have gotten into any actual trouble since, if he was, he wouldn't be able to play in the first game of the season."

"Guarantee Mr. Perfect has scouts coming out to see him, too. Certainly wouldn't want our school to look like a joke," Roxy said with disdain.

"The principal said he talked to Shawn, and the boy had learned his lesson."

"There's no way I buy that bullshit," Roxy said quickly. "If he apologized at all, it's because he got caught."

"I mean, maybe he felt bad?" Lynds asked.

"Hard to feel bad without a heart," Roxy quipped.

I raised an eyebrow at her. "Weren't you with him?"

"For like a millisecond for a few nights. I never said I make good decisions, clearly. No offense," she said, looking at Lynds.

Lynds just shrugged. "You're not wrong."

The waitress came and handed out our drinks and food. I was glad since a moral boosting milkshake was just what I needed.

Roxy looked back at me and said, "You should've seen how he was acting, like kissing a boy was me basically selling myself. He's acting like I wanted those photos out there," she said, rolling her eyes. "If I wanted risqué photos of myself out there, I would've posted them. Actually, matter of fact," she said, looking at Gavin, "that's not a bad idea. You think I should?"

I had been taking a sip of my milkshake and almost choked on it at that. Gavin just raised an eyebrow at her and asked, "Why?"

"To reclaim my power, obviously. If we're on a destroy Shawn Parker mission anyway, I might as well go full tilt."

"Destroying Shawn Parker?" a voice said.

We all startled and looked over. Roxy was the only one that relaxed at the sight of the cheerleader watching us. She had dark, impossibly smooth-looking skin and her dark hair in thick braids. Her glossed lips were plump, but not smiling.

She looked familiar and I couldn't figure out why, until her face broke into a mischievous smile and said, "Sign me up."

She was the cheerleader from the photos. Ava.

"Glad you made it," Roxy said with a grin.

"I wasn't sure if I was going to come, to be honest, but after that ridiculous meeting, I'm not feeling as generous and forgiving as I was."

"Bullshit, right?" Roxy said, rolling her eyes. "Scoot over?" she asked Lynds, who had been too distracted staring at Ava. She immediately did, making room for Ava next to Roxy.

"Seriously! I couldn't believe the principal was implying we had done anything wrong. I mean geez, I was just holding his hand," she said before blushing and quickly saying, "not that there's anything wrong with your photos either. The only one that should be embarrassed is Shawn, not us."

I looked at Lynds and was glad to see the comment hadn't phased her. When I turned my attention back to the others, Ava was looking at me. She extended her hand across the table to me, offering a handshake that I hesitantly returned.

"I'm Ava. You must be the new girl-" She paused, thinking a moment before saying, "Bridgette, right?"

I nodded, hesitated, and then shook my head. "Yes and no. I'm Bridgette, but you can call me Bri."

She nodded. "Nice to meet you, Bri. Wish it were for better reasons."

I nodded quickly. "I'm so sorry about that, but um-"

I started and then stopped, not sure how to ask how much she knew. I looked at Roxy, who just said "She knows."

Relief washed over me at that. I had been worried how it would look to Ava if I started dating her ex. I knew the rest of the school was going to have their opinions on it, but I didn't want her to be hurt by it, especially when I was only doing it to help Lynds and Roxy get back at him. I didn't want to hurt Ava more in the process.

"So, you're okay with the plan?"

She grinned. "Are you kidding? Am I okay with him publicly getting his just desserts? Definitely. I want a front-row seat. I'll be right there shaking my pom-poms, cheering."

No wonder Roxy had been trying to get her to come. I looked around at them, taking in our little ragtag group of avengers and couldn't help saying, "You know, this might actually be a little fun."

"A little?" Roxy said, quirking an eyebrow.

"Try a lot. This is going to be the best year yet," Ava said confidently.

I looked at Lynds, who was looking hopeful. I felt a burst of joy at seeing her hopeful and it stiffened my resolve. Together, we were going to destroy him.

# CHAPTER EIGHT

Cafeterias at new schools were a personal hell of mine that I was well acquainted with. At least this one had outside seating, though. The school's massive court-yard was open for lunch anytime the weather allowed. I thought about ditching the food and camping out in my car again like I had yesterday. It was incredibly tempting. This was the first time I had somewhere I could go hide, but I shook off the thought. New school, new me. Besides, hiding in my car wouldn't be very mysterious new girl of me. Shawn had to be intrigued by me. That wouldn't happen if he couldn't even see me.

I looked around, hoping for a friendly face, or even just a familiar one. I was still scanning the tables when I felt my phone vibrate in my bag.

I balanced my lunch tray with one hand as I rum-maged in my bag with the other for my phone.

When I pulled it out, I saw with relief that it was the group chat. None of them had the same lunch period as me, but the moral support was much needed.

## Shawn Parker Must Die

Roxy

How's it going?

Gavin

Have you seen the target?

Lynds

How's your second day going?

Roxy

Yeah, yeah, that too, but have you seen him yet?

Ava

I have lunch now, too. You can sit with me if you want.

I couldn't believe my luck. I didn't think any of them had lunch with me. Maybe things really would be different this year. I wouldn't have to find strangers to sit with since I knew Ava now.

Thanks guys. Ava, where are you?

Roxy

You sure you guys being seen together's a good idea?

Ava

Better than her sitting alone. Wouldn't want her looking like a loner anyway.

Roxy

Fair enough

I looked up and saw Ava waving at me from a mostly full table of cheerleaders. Well, I was diving right into the deep end, I guess.

In my past lives, I had tried on different high school personas for size. I'd been one of the academics, an artist, a loner, a band kid, and even tried being an athlete once. It was track, and I hated it. I hadn't been a popular kid or a cheerleader in any of my past lives, but now, I guess I was trying it on for size.

Hopefully, Shawn liked cheerleaders.

Looking at Ava and the rest of the table, I knew he must. These were some of the prettiest high schoolers I had ever seen - unfairly pretty.

I whispered, "Thank you," to Ava, who smiled back and said to the table, "Guys, this is my new friend, Bridgette."

"Ohh fancy name, new girl," a friendly-looking brunette said.

"Bridgette, that's cute," another girl said, looking me up and down for a second before saying, "Suits you."

That was about the last thing I expected anyone to say.

"Th-thank you," I stuttered. She just grinned before turning her attention back to another one of the cheerleaders.

Ava introduced me to everyone before turning back to me and asking about my classes and how my day was going.

I had just been happy to have a familiar face to sit with, but I couldn't believe how nice she was being. A small part of me wondered if it was just because of our plan, but the larger part of me didn't think that was true. She actually seemed like she cared and was spending way more time talking to me than she had to. When her friends pulled her into conversation, she made sure to find a way to include me, too.

I didn't know how to tell her how much that meant to me, but I knew I was going to have to find a way to thank her. Lunch flew by thanks to her company. Thanks to her, Harris High's cafeteria wasn't looking like the hell the others had been.

# Chapter Nine

At the end of the day, I was headed to my car when I saw a group of football players by the front entrance. In the middle of their cluster was a tall muscly blonde with the same dimpled grin as Shannon's. I knew it was him, but just in case there was any doubt left, he turned around to talk to one of his friends and I saw his name in gold letters on the back of his jersey.

Parker.

Shawn Parker was in front of me, and I didn't know what to do.

*Should I go say hi? How do cool girls handle things?* I wondered, starting to panic. I didn't know why or how the others thought I could handle this.

I took a breath and pulled out my phone.

**Shawn Parker Must Die**

Target acquired. Do I engage?

As I hit send, I was already worrying about what I was going to say to him.

Roxy

NO!

Gavin

Girl! What? Absolutely not!

Ava

Where are you?

Lynds

I'm at the car. Do you need backup?

Okay fine fine. I won't say anything. I just have to walk by him. I can do that.

Roxy

Don't let him see you notice him

Ava

Maybe look back at him

Roxy

If you can look unimpressed while you do it.

Roxy

I'm calling

The phone started ringing seconds later. I wasn't sure why she bothered typing out the message.

"Hi?" I said, knowing it sounded too much like a question, but not sure why she was calling.

"What's going on? Where are you, and where is he?"

I looked around quickly to see if anyone could overhear and figured I was probably safe, but kept on the quiet side anyway.

"I was going to leave the school, but he's outside."

"Which doors?"

"Um," I hesitated, "the main ones, I think?"

She sighed. "I'm too far off. It's gonna have to be a solo mission, but you've got this."

*I did?*

"I do?" I didn't mean to say it, but she laughed.

"Definitely, just keep me on the phone."

"Won't that be rude?"

"It might be if you were going to talk to him, but you're not."

I nodded, before remembering she couldn't see me, and said, "Okay, so you just want me to walk past him?"

"Sort of. I want you to repeat after me when you do."

"What do you want me to say?"

She laughed. "Trust me?"

I was surprised to find I did. "I do, but trust that my acting skills are better when I know what's coming."

There was silence for a moment while she considered before she said, "Fair enough. I want you to walk past them saying, 'Girl you're so lucky you don't have to go to school here, the boys are so,' then you're going to pause, look back over your shoulder, and make eye contact with Shawn like you're just noticing him. Give him the once over, arch an eyebrow, and say 'unimpressive.'"

I laughed. "You can't be serious."

"Dead serious. It'll have him panting after you."

"Insulting him will help?"

I could hear the grin in her voice when she said, "Absolutely."

I couldn't believe I was doing this, even as I made my way to the door.

"Exiting now," I said as I pushed the door open.

"You're going to be watched," she told me. "Walk like it."

I had no idea what that meant, but I added a little extra sway to my hips.

The short walk to the group of guys seemed to take forever, and I still wasn't sure this was going to work. I wasn't sure why they would even pay attention to me in the first place.

"Laugh."

I thought of the expression I knew Lynds would be wearing if she could see me now and laughed.

I could feel their eyes on me and was hoping it was intrigue and not because they thought I had a horrible laugh.

"Good, now say, 'Seriously, you're so lucky you don't have to go to school here'"

She waited, and I repeated her phrase somewhat louder than I needed to.

"The boys are so," she said, and I repeated.

"Now, look at him over your shoulder."

I turned my head and was a little surprised to see that all of them were looking at me, but my eyes were instantly drawn to Shawn with his eyes that looked more amber than his sister's hazel. From his honey hair to his amber eyes, the whole boy felt like a warning, like a trap that once you sank into wouldn't let go of you.

I let my eyes drag over him down and then back up. He shot me a cocky grin with the Parker dimples. I quirked an eyebrow at him and said, "Unimpressive."

The cocky grin instantly disappeared and a chorus of "ooooohs" and "oh shits" came from his friends, none of whom were pretending anymore they hadn't been listening. I turned my head back and kept walking, knowing they were watching.

"Damn, you killed that!"

"How would you know?" I asked, looking around. "Are you out here?"

"Don't have to be. I could hear Jeremiah and the rest of the guys through the phone. Shawny boy's ego will have taken a hit. Guaranteed, you've piqued his interest now."

I let myself smile at that. Maybe I could handle this after all.

"We'll have to have a meeting before the party, though."

"Party? What party?"

"His beginning of the year party. It's this weekend, and you'll have just scored an invite."

"If you so say," I said incredulously. It was hard to believe that one small interaction like that would be enough for me to get an invite to his party.

"Trust me."

"I do, but what if it doesn't work?"

"If it didn't work, you can go as Ava's plus one, but it'll work."

"Are you going?"

"I didn't get invited."

I scoffed. "That wasn't what I asked."

She laughed. "Fair enough. Maybe. Depends on if I think you'll need backup."

"I might not even get invited."

"You will, trust me."

# Chapter Ten

She was right, and it didn't take long. After the last bell the next day, I was waiting outside for Lynds when I caught his attention.

I had stationed myself a little ways from where him and his friends were hanging out yesterday, acting like I was scrolling through my phone. The girls said it would be a good idea to be in his line of sight, just in case he wanted to make a move.

I didn't believe he would, but sure enough, Roxy was right. I looked up from my phone and locked eyes with him as he came out of the school.

I had seen him briefly yesterday, but now I was able to fully take him in. It was almost cinematic the way the sun was hitting his golden hair like a spotlight, making Harris High's golden boy shine even brighter. Apparently, even the sun wasn't immune to his charms since it bowed to his whims.

His reputation proceeded him, but I still hadn't really been prepared for how heavily Harris High worshipped him. I had been asking around about him today and hadn't heard a single bad word about him from anyone. It seemed like everyone besides my friends and his sister loved him. Even with his being exposed as a cheater, people were only saying positive things about him. It was infuriating. If I didn't have it out for him already, I would now. The girls were right; he needed to be taken down a peg or two.

After how much everyone worshipped him, I was surprised to find he was just a normal boy. He was good looking, of course, with his shaggy blonde hair that fell just so and his boyish smile with the Parker dimples, but he was just a boy with hazel eyes that sometimes veered amber and a good throwing arm. I couldn't for the life of me understand the hype.

I didn't bother hiding that I was watching him as he made his way over to me. The bulky football jersey did nothing to hide the muscle he had packed on under it. Lucky for us, if I could be said to have a type, muscled jock wasn't it, especially a muscled jock with the swagger and ego he had.

His smile was the only thing that gave me pause. It didn't seem to fit with the rest of his image. The boyish grin lighting up his face seemed to promise there was more to him, a deeper, softer side hiding under his tough exterior.

It had to be purposeful, but still, with his thousand-watt smile turned on me, it was hard to reconcile the idea I had of him with the boy in front of me.

He was halfway to me now. Before he got any closer, I quickly schooled my features into disinterest, turning my attention back to my phone.

This was the true test, whether he would bother approaching me without any encouragement.

I wasn't sure if he would. I didn't know if I had intrigued him enough for him to brave this level of disinterest, but Roxy said it would work and no one had argued. We all agreed if it didn't, we would come up with a new strategy before his party Friday night.

Whatever happened now didn't really matter. If he didn't take the bait now, we'd find another way. Karma was coming for Shawn Parker; I wouldn't let him escape it this time. Before he even knew what was happening, I was going to have him at my mercy, and spoiler alert, there's nothing about a woman scorned that leaves room for mercy.

I looked back up and was surprised to see he was still making his way over. His smile hadn't faltered. I smirked at him and watched his advance. He paused where his friends were, slapping hands and backs with some of them. He nodded at me, which I took to be a cue to come join them. I looked back down at my phone, not dignifying that with a response. I wasn't going to make this easy on him. He didn't even know me. I certainly wouldn't be summoned with a head nod and come fawning all over him. If he wanted to talk, he would have to come to me.

I was still looking at my phone when I noticed movement in front of me and looked up. Shawn and his easy smile were standing in front of me. His amber-ish hazel eyes were glinting like he was letting me in on a secret, like that smile was just for me.

It was a compelling act, and if it weren't for the others, I might've believed it. But if it wasn't for the others, I wouldn't be standing here as Bridgette trying to attract his attention. If it weren't for them, for how he hurt Lyndsey, I would be Bri, off in a corner worrying about making friends at my new school instead of plotting with my new friends and trying to get him to notice me.

He waited for me to smile back. A smirk played across my lips as I pocketed my phone that was just starting to buzz. It had to be the group chat, but it could wait. I knew the girls were somewhere with their eyes on me, and I was nervous to see how they thought I was doing, but it wasn't the time, not yet.

I waited, willing to wait however long it took to make him speak first. Whoever broke the silence gave up some of their power, and I was prepared to stand here in silence all day if I had to.

His grin faltered again before he plastered it back on.

"Come here often?" he asked.

I blinked, and he laughed, running his fingers through his hair with a self-depreciating smile.

"Okay, okay, that didn't land. Dumb joke. I don't recognize you, though. You must be new."

After a long pause to see if I could draw anything else out of him, I asked, "Because you know everyone here?"

He laughed at that. "I wouldn't say that, but you don't look like you recognize me, and I know if I had seen you before, there's no way I would have been able to forget you."

That line might have meant something if I hadn't been warned verbatim about it. It had been the exact same routine he'd used as a junior on Lynds as a freshman. The anger bubbled up in me, but I pressed it down.

"Touching, but unfortunately, I can't say the same. You have the cookie cutter jock look going on; a dime a dozen around here," I said, gesturing to his friends.

"Ouch," he said, throwing his hand over his heart and bending back a little as if I had struck him, but beneath the jokes I saw the glint in his eyes dim, saw the confusion there. I suppressed a smile that my blow had landed. "You don't know me yet, but that sounds like a challenge, and you'll come to learn I don't back down from challenges. Tiger Sharks don't lose, and as the quarterback I'm no loser."

I almost rolled my eyes, but instead arched my eyebrow. "Am I supposed to be impressed, because you'll have to try harder than that-" I paused, pretending to not know his name.

He eagerly supplied it.

"Parker, Shawn Parker, but you can call me yours."

I required a long pause for my internal gagging. The James Bond style introduction, the false promises about a future, it was all too much. He sure was laying it on thick. My smirk played across my lips. "Parker, I'd say it's nice to meet you, but I'm not a liar. The pleasure's all yours."

His startled confusion multiplied, but he quickly hid it. "You'll be changing your tune soon, you'll see. Why don't you give me your number so I can let you know what we're doing this weekend?" He made it sound like a question, but I knew he didn't expect to be denied.

"Woah there, slow down, Parker. Where are your manners? You don't even know my name."

He brushed his hand through his hair again with an apologetic, guilty looking smile. "I'm so sorry. I'm really not all that good at this, and you're quite disarming-"

He paused, and I answered the implied question, "Bridgette."

"Bridgette," he said slowly, tasting the word. "I like it. Bridgette and Shawn sound good together."

"Presumptuous, since you don't even have my number."

"Easily fixable," he said, quickly whipping out his phone from his back pocket and trying to hand it to me.

I pushed it away and reached into my bag, pulling out my favorite purple pen. "Tell you what," I said, uncapping it and reaching for his phone-free hand. "Since I feel bad for you, I'll throw you a bone." He perked up a little at that as I took his hand and scrawled down 628. "The first three digits. You'll have to earn the other seven," I said, releasing his hand.

His eyes widened at that, and an amused smile crossed his face. I pulled my hand back, recapping my pen, buying time, unsure of what to say next.

"Yo Park," I heard from the table.

I glanced over and saw most of his crew staring in our direction. I couldn't tell if they were throwing him a lifeline, or thought he was succeeding, but it didn't matter. I used his momentary distraction to pull out my phone. Our group chat, newly dubbed The "Shawn Parker Must Die" group chat, was blowing up as text notifications popped up quicker than I could scan them, my phone buzzing nonstop in my hand.

I looked up and caught him watching me. It was his turn to quirk an eyebrow at me. "Someone's popular."

"I have to go. Impress me and maybe you'll be lucky enough to be the one blowing up my phone."

I started to walk away, but he reached out quickly saying, "Wait."

I stopped, turned back, and waited. I had gotten a little carried away with my acting and had forgotten to give him the opportunity to invite me to his party, but I hadn't been ready to give him my number. I was going to make him work much harder than he had to earn that.

"I'm having a party this weekend. It's a back-to-school thing at my place. Everyone cool'll be there. You should come."

"I'll think about it."

I went to step away, only taking a half step before he said, "Wait," again just like I anticipated. "I don't have your number. How'll you have my address?"

"You said everyone cool'll be there, right?"

He nodded quickly. "Yeah! You have to come! It'll be fun, I promise."

"If everyone cool will be there, I'm sure someone with my number can let me know the address. See you around, Park, or not." With that, I turned on my heel, relishing in the glimpse I'd gotten of him gaping after me as I turned. I had to force myself not to look back as I walked away, no matter how badly I wanted to.

I put a little bit more sway in my step, knowing he was watching me and feeling incredibly powerful. The real me, Bri, would never have talked to anyone like that, but Bridgette did. Bridgette knew eyes were on her and liked it that way. Bridgette was unbothered and damn, it felt good.

When I was far enough away, I pulled out my phone in time to see a picture come in. I clicked on it and stifled a giggle. I wasn't sure where they were, but Roxy had somehow captured Parker's mouth hanging open as I walked away, him watching me leave.

Knowing them and what they told me of Harris High, it would be a meme before long.

# CHAPTER ELEVEN

Tiger Shark Tea

*What do you know, Tiger Sharks? It seems like our golden boy, Shawn Parker, is wasting no time cozying up to a new girl. Rumor has it, she's a junior who's new in town. Maybe that explains why she's looking less than impressed with our golden boy.*

*From the photo sent in, it looks like Shawn Parker'll have his work cut out for him with this feisty redhead.*

I swiped to the photo, already knowing what I was going to see, but busting out laughing anyway. The perfectly captured look of shock on Shawn's face was too comical not to laugh at.

I couldn't believe it took less than an hour for the photo to hit Tiger Shark Tea.

When I looked up, the others were grinning over our fries and milkshakes. Lynds high fived me and the others looked impressed.

"I'll be honest," Roxy said. "I wasn't sure you had that in you."

"But you told me I did!" I protested immediately.

She laughed. "I know, I know, it's all about confidence, but confidence and that," she said, pointing at the photo, "are two different things. You're going to destroy him."

I looked at Ava a little sheepishly. I was still a bit nervous about what she thought about the revenge plan, but she was grinning, too.

Gavin took a big sip of his milkshake before saying, "I sure wouldn't want to be him when you guys are done with him."

We all laughed at that.

# Chapter Twelve

"So I heard you made quite an impression on my brother," Shannon said to me in English the next day. "I'm supposed to try to convince you to come to his party," she said, rolling her eyes.

"Should I?"

She thought it over for a moment before saying, "For my sake? Yes, but for your own sanity probably not." I wasn't sure what she was getting at, which must have been clear because she continued, "Shawn's friends are a whole lot. It would be nice to have a friendly face there. My friends all usually steer clear, and honestly you probably should, too, but selfishly I can't not tell you it would be cool to have you there."

"Does that mean we're friends?" I asked hesitantly.

She laughed. "Wasn't it obvious?"

"No?" I shouldn't have said it out loud, but I couldn't stop myself.

Luckily, she laughed. "Well, we are now." She paused before asking, "So are you coming?"

"I'm not sure. I told him I'd think about it."

She grinned. "He said that, brilliant line by the way, really had him spinning his wheels all night on that one. He asked me to run recon for him." She rolled her eyes at that. "I can't believe him."

I laughed. "Really? You're supposed to spy on me?"

She laughed, too. "Ridiculous, right?"

"What'd you tell him?"

"To stop being lazy and put some effort in if he wanted to win someone over, and to leave you alone if you're not interested." She paused and looked at me hesitantly. "You're not interested, are you?"

I wasn't sure how to respond to that. The look of worry on her face had me wanting to be honest, but I knew I couldn't be too honest. I went with as much as I could give her. "What's there to be interested in?"

She laughed at that, saying, "I knew I liked you," before turning back to her notebook. She scrawled something down before ripping it out and turning back to me. "If you're around, you should come this weekend. I know you didn't want my douche of a brother to have your number, but just in case, here's the address and my number."

She had signed the note 'your new bestie' with a cute little smiley face that made me grin.

When Lynds met me at the car after school ended, I was folding and refolding the note, wondering what to do.

"What've you got?" she asked, nodding down at the note in my hands.

"A bit of a complication," I said with a half-smile, half grimace.

"Already? You haven't even been here a full week yet."

I chuckled at that. "It's Shawn's sister."

Lynds thought for a second before asking, "Shannon? What's wrong with her?"

"Nothing's wrong with her. She's just trying to be my friend. She warned me away from Shawn but also said Shawn's been asking her about me."

Lynds hesitated. "That's a good thing, though, isn't it?"

"I mean yes? Maybe? When everything comes out, I don't want her to feel like I was ever using her. She's being really nice to me. Invited me to the party and everything, warned me not to come but said it would be nice if I did."

"Sounds like you made friends with the one other person at this school that knows what a jerk Shawn can be. Sounds like a good thing to me."

Well, when she put it that way, it was easier to feel better about things. Shannon might not like what we were planning, but maybe she would understand. She actually might be one of the easier people to win over

after this was all over with. The rest of the school
wasn't going to be as easy to convince.

# CHAPTER THIRTEEN

"Are you sure about this?" I asked, looking down at the low v neck crop top and black skirt that Roxy had just shoved into my hands. Roxy, Gavin, and Lynds were all in our bedroom helping me and Ava get ready for Shawn's party tonight.

I hated that the others weren't going. Ava was really nice but had so many friends that it was going to be hard to stick by her all night. I was already nervous enough, but the outfit Roxy wanted me to wear wasn't helping.

"Just try it," Roxy said, so I did, and I shouldn't have been surprised that she was right.

It didn't feel like me, like Bri, but it looked good.

"It's perfect," Ava said with admiration, handing me some necklaces to try.

"You look great." Lynds nodded.

"Are you sure we can't go?" Gavin asked Roxy.

She nodded. "It would ruin the plan."

"But it's the party of the year," he whined.

Roxy laughed. "You say that about every party."

Ava responded before Gavin could. "There's going to be plenty of people there; he probably wouldn't even notice you guys."

"And doesn't he owe you a good party after the bullshit from the last one?" Gavin asked.

Roxy's eyes darkened at that and I knew that if she had been considering it before, Gavin had just ruined any chance he had. "You can do what you want, but I'm not going back there tonight. It's bad enough I have to see him at school. I'm not voluntarily going to his house."

Ava turned to Lynds. "What about you? You can come if you want."

Lynds considered a moment before shaking her head. "Thanks, but no thanks. I'm not ready."

I paled at that. Of course she wasn't. It had hardly been more than a couple of weeks since the photos had been shared, though it felt like a lifetime.

"I'm sorry," I said quickly.

"I shouldn't have asked," Ava added.

She waved off our concern. "It's fine, really. Maybe I'll catch the next one," she said in a tone that implied she would rather be anywhere else.

She met my eye after a moment and said, "Seriously it's not my scene."

Roxy cleared her throat, saying, "You've got the right idea. Besides, if you go, who's gonna keep me company?"

Gavin raised an eyebrow, saying, "Me?"

Roxy rolled her eyes. "We both know you're going to the party."

He hesitated for just a second, but that second was long enough to show his guilt. "I don't have to."

"You actually do." She grinned conspiratorially. "You're running recon."

# CHAPTER FOURTEEN

"This is ridiculous," Gavin grumbled to me and Ava as we walked away from Roxy's car toward the Parkers' house.

Roxy had gone a bit far. Gavin was outfitted with a small camera designed to look like a pin on his jacket. It fit right into his denim jacket that was covered in pins and patches. He was a rainbow of punk rock and color, and the camera pin blended right in. He also had a small wireless mic in his ear that Roxy and Lynds could talk to him through.

Her and Lynds had dropped us off around the block from what most of the school called the Parker Palace. We didn't want to be seen getting dropped off by Roxy. I looked back at the car once more before they drove off. Lynds smiled and waved to me. I knew this was part of the plan, but I still felt guilty about leaving Lynds to deal with her feelings while I went to a party. It was reassuring that at least she wasn't alone, though, and Roxy seemed to understand the assignment, turning their recon into something fun to do for the night.

Judging from Gavin's expression, Roxy was already delighting in annoying him.

As we walked, I was shocked to see there were cars lined up all the way back here. The others had warned me the party was big, but I was starting to think they had downplayed the number of people that were going to be here.

I'd been to parties before, but judging from the fact that we could already hear the music from a block away, this was going to be big.

"Won't there be noise complaints?" I asked.

Gavin scoffed, but Ava was the one to answer, "If his father weren't the mayor, maybe, but they pay off the neighbors and he's best friends with the chief of police so the rest of the cops know enough to look the other way."

"And everyone's just okay with it?"

Ava shrugged. "The other parents say it feels safer to know their kids are partying at the mayor's home and the cops say it's safer to have everyone in a central location."

"Such a cop-out," Gavin said, pausing and raising his eyebrows at me, "See what I did there?"

I laughed. I couldn't help it. I loved a good pun.

Gavin grinned. "I knew I liked you, but seriously, they're all just too worried about his father retaliating to really complain, but it works out pretty well for us."

We turned the corner, and I laid eyes on the Parkers' home for the first time, and I didn't need to wonder why they called it the Parker Palace. Not only was it huge, but it had to have cost a fortune.

I whistled softly. "That's a whole lot of privilege."

Gavin nodded. "The worst people always seem to be dealt the best cards."

I noticed Ava looked a little uncomfortable at that and changed the subject. "So, what's the plan of attack?"

"Just be yourself. You already have his attention. Make sure to keep him interested, but keep your distance enough so he feels like he has to work for it," Ava told me.

"Oh, is that it? Simple," I said, sarcasm dripping in my tone.

Ava grinned. "Okay maybe that wasn't super clear, but really you'll do great. Your instincts haven't steered you wrong with him yet."

I would feel comforted by that, but for the two interactions I'd had so far with him, Roxy had coached me through one and for the other I knew the others were watching. I supposed it wouldn't be much different this time, though, since I knew Gavin would be watching. He was still grumbling about it. This clearly hadn't been what he had in mind when he pictured coming. I was glad he'd be here, though.

Ava had introduced me to her friends, and they were nice enough, but they didn't really understand why she was trying to pull me into their group. They were all jocks and cheerleaders and I... wasn't. From what I heard, Ava and the rest of her friends were all athletic forces of nature. They were nice enough, but we had little in common.

I was glad Gavin would be there for company when Ava inevitably got swept up and distracted by her friends. I didn't begrudge her that, though. I wanted her to have fun. After what Shawn put her and the others through, I was glad at least one of them was going to his party, and I was determined that she would have a good time.

# Chapter Fifteen

I quickly lost both Ava and Gavin. Ava got swept up into dancing with her friends. They had invited me, but I waved them off. I saw Shawn was in the middle of the throng of people and didn't want his attention yet. I had turned to Gavin to ask where to go now but he had gotten swept up with Ava's friends, too. He tried to mouth something to me, or yell it, I wasn't sure. With the blaring music, it was hard to tell the difference, but either way, I didn't hear him. It seemed like an apology, so I waved him off, too. I'd be fine. This wasn't the first party I had braved solo. Being the perpetual new girl, I was used to being on the outside looking in.

I surveyed the party, more out of curiosity than anything, looking for familiar faces. I recognized a few people from my classes, but most were strangers. It wasn't surprising. It was probably almost all seniors. It still felt weird being one of the "lucky" juniors to have been invited.

I made my way to the kitchen, pushing through the door, hoping it would dull the music. The door opened onto a group of football players playing beer pong. I couldn't hear them over the music, but they tried to wave me over. I shook my head, and, spying a glass sliding door that led outside, skirted around them and made my escape.

I breathed a sigh of relief as the cool air hit my face. I could still hear the music, but at least it was quieter. There were people milling about and others splashing around in the pool, but overall, the energy was a lot more subdued than the mob inside. I made my way carefully around the pool, spotting a pool shed that looked like it had been converted into a bar. The shed had a large open window looking out onto the pool, complete with a counter and barstools. It even had fairy lights strung around the roof and a wooden sign that said, "Parker's Pub".

I couldn't help being a little impressed at how adorable it was. I made my way over, curious to look at it. I wasn't much of a drinker; I was stalling. Sooner or later, I was going to have to head back into the house to find Shawn. I wasn't looking forward to it. It was loud and cramped in the house, and while it wasn't quite peaceful out here, it wasn't terrible either.

I headed for the door to the bar shed, but before I could reach it, a blonde head popped up from behind the bar.

I gasped in surprise, instinctually taking a step back.

She looked at me, and it took me a moment to recognize her as Shannon from English class. It took me another second to realize it wasn't weird she was here. Of course she was here. It was her house, too.

"Bridgette? You came!"

I was surprised at the little burst of joy that rushed through me at the sight of her.

"I'm sorry," I said quickly, pointing at the door. "I didn't know anyone was in there."

"Don't worry about it," she said with an easy grin. "With how these parties usually go, you're not the first or last person to try to breach the fortress tonight."

"The fortress?" I asked, raising an eyebrow.

She laughed. "It's a bar now, but it used to be a killer fort back when we were kids."

"Oh, I believe it," I said, and then surprised myself by asking, "Is it just you and Shawn?"

She nodded toward the bar stool, and I took a seat.

"Yeah, believe it or not, he used to suck way less back then than he does now."

I laughed at that. "He doesn't seem all that bad," I hedged, not quite sure what to say.

She raised an eyebrow at that. "I'd think you of all people would know that's not true."

I paled at that. Why would she say that? She couldn't possibly know anything, right? There was no way I tried to reason with myself. "What's that supposed to mean?"

She watched me appraisingly and asked, "Wasn't your cousin one of his latest victims?"

I knew this was going to come up sooner or later and I'd talked a little with Lynds about how to play it, but I still didn't feel right about it. She told me to say I thought she was being dramatic about it, but there was no way I could do that to her, especially when I knew that was what she actually believed. She was mad at Shawn, too, of course, but she was more mad at herself. She kept telling me she should've known better.

I hated that he made her feel so low about herself. Whether or not he was the catalyst for her self-esteem issues, he definitely made things worse.

"Lynds told me he's a bit misunderstood."

Shannon laughed harshly at that. "If you're about to tell me you believe that, I'm gonna need you to pause so I can get you and me both drinks cause I don't think I can handle that sober. What's your poison?"

I didn't drink much and certainly didn't have a go-to drink. I wasn't sure it would help with the cool girl persona I was trying for, but if I wasn't going to be honest with Shannon about much, I could at least be honest with her about this. "I don't actually drink much," I told her.

"By choice or by chance?" she asked.

"Huh?" I blinked, not really understanding the question.

"Are you sober by choice or do you just not get the chance to drink?"

I considered that for a moment. "A little of both, to be honest. I don't love the feel of being drunk or the taste of it, but I'm pretty sure the last one is a chance issue, though, since I doubt I've had the good stuff."

What I didn't tell her because I didn't like to think about it myself, was that I worried about drinking since addiction ran in my family. I didn't want to chance losing myself like my mother had.

"Fair enough. Want to try something new?"

I thought for a moment before shaking my head. Even if I did want to drink, I didn't want to lose my inhibitions here. I couldn't afford to mess up the mission by saying or doing something I shouldn't.

"Gotcha. No worries," she said. "What about I make you something sweet?"

"No alcohol?"

She laughed. "None, but those assholes in there probably won't shut up if they see you without a cup."

I figured she was probably right. "Alright, do your worst."

"For you? Never."

I couldn't believe myself. Of course it was rude of me to have just assumed she was going to make me a drink, but before I could say anything else she said, "A girl like you deserves my best, never my worst."

I laughed at that. "Good drinks and bad pick-up lines, got it."

She laughed hard at that. "If you think that was bad, you should count yourself lucky. That was one of the better ones."

She grabbed some glasses from under the bar and filled them with ice. As I watched her practiced hands go through the motions, I couldn't help wondering why she was talking to me in the first place. She wasn't anything like me. She was rich, for one, but more than that, she was effortlessly cool in a way most people struggled to achieve but never could. I wasn't sure if I wanted to be friends with her or be her, but it was clear she was a level of cool that I would never achieve. Even as Bridgette, Shannon was far too cool for me.

She turned her back to me and I watched in surprise as she opened a full-sized fridge I hadn't noticed before. It was fully stocked with sodas, juices, and other drinks.

She turned back with orange juice and pineapple juice before turning back to the fridge. I wondered if they stocked the fridge weekly or if it was more of a special occasion thing. I couldn't wrap my head around anyone being rich enough to waste money on stocking an extra fridge. They probably had an extra shopping list for their pool house pub drinks.

I wanted to ask how often they restocked, but I stopped myself, realizing it was a Bri question. Bridgette wouldn't ask, so I shouldn't.

Shannon turned back with a red bottle, grinning. "Our special ingredient."

My face fell.

"No, no," she said quickly. "It's just grenadine, no alcohol."

She poured first the orange juice, then the pineapple juice, and then got a spoon with a long skinny handle and asked, "Wanna see a trick?"

She was full of surprises, and I was coming to look forward to it. "Definitely."

She twirled the spoon around her fingers fast enough that it started to blur.

"Impressive."

She laughed. "Oh, come on, that's not the trick."

She flipped the spoon face down over the glass, deftly spun the cap off the grenadine and slowly poured it over the spoon. The red liquid slowly oozed over the spoon, settling on the top of the drink.

"I call it the Shannon Special, aka the liquid sunset."

She pushed it towards me. I picked it up, but she put out her hand to stop me. I gently put the glass back down. "Wait a second," she said.

She didn't pour the grenadine over hers with the spoon, instead she just poured it straight in and mixed it with the long-handled spoon.

Then she ducked under the counter saying, "Where did they go?" I heard some rustling before she said, "Aha! Here we go!" She jumped up, now holding two little umbrellas. She plopped one in my drink and the other in hers. Again I went to pick it up, but she stopped me again. "You're not supposed to drink it like that. That's just for the selfie"

"Selfie?" I asked, but she was already pulling out her phone. "You want a pic of my drink?"

She smirked. "You're funny, I like you. I want a picture of us. I want proof we're best friends for the next time brother dearest gets on my last nerve." She looked at me quickly and said, "As your self-appointed newest best friend, believe me, you're way too good for him."

She leaned across the counter to get closer to me, pressing her chest against the counter, which showed off her cleavage. I politely kept my eyes trained on her face. "Grab your drink," she directed. I picked it up, and she pressed into me. She was close enough I could smell her. She smelled like coconut and strawberry, summer and sunshine. She extended her hand to take the picture and kissed my cheek. It was unexpected, but nice. I was surprised to feel myself blushing at her closeness, but I didn't feel uncomfortable.

She snapped a few pictures before pulling away and examining them. "We look adorable." She held out her phone to me for approval. I glanced at the picture and was surprised to find she was right. I knew she would look good, but I looked good too. I was surprised at how happy I looked.

"I'm gonna post it if that's cool?" she asked.

"Yeah, sure." I heard my phone ding and saw she had followed me and tagged me in the photo. "That was quick." I pulled it up and grinned at the caption 'New girl with her favorite Parker, aka her new bestie'.

This was new. I wasn't used to having many friends. I had Lynds, of course, and Roxy, Gavin, and Ava, and now it seemed I also had Shannon.

"Can I ask you something?"

She didn't look away from her phone but said, "Yeah shoot."

"Are you just being nice to me to annoy Shawn?"

She immediately looked up from her phone. "Trust me, as much as he annoys me, I wouldn't go out of my way for him like that. I like you."

I hated the insecurity I was feeling and decided it couldn't hurt to ask, "Why though?"

"I had a good feeling about you, and I haven't been proven wrong yet, but if you want, I'll give you the speed round friendship test."

"Um, the what?" She had a friendship test? What kind of person had a ready to go friendship test? What if I failed? I hadn't known her long and I'm sure I would be okay without her friendship, but I wanted it anyway. I wanted to impress her. I wanted her to like me.

"Friendship test, the classic lit edition."

"Are there multiple editions?" I asked, partly out of curiosity, but mostly to stall.

"Yes, but this is yours. I can feel it."

"Okay fine, hit me."

"Rank the following: Pride and Prejudice, Wuthering Heights, Little Women, and Jane Eyre."

"Easy. Pride and Prejudice, then Little Women, then Jane Eyre, then Wuthering Heights."

She grinned. "I knew I liked you. Follow up; is Wuthering Heights a romance?"

"Absolutely not," I shuddered, hoping it was the right answer, but not willing to lie about it. It wasn't an exaggeration to say I worried about the girls who thought Wuthering Heights was romantic.

"And feelings on Mr. Rochester?"

"Jane was too good for him, clearly."

"See, I knew we were destined to be besties," she said.

"That's it?" I was surprised. That had been far easier than I expected.

"I have another if you want, but I was already convinced before asking you the first question. I was just hoping this would help prove it to you."

"You have more?"

"Just one more. Who's the best character in the Great Gatsby?"

I didn't pause before answering, "Jordan." She might not have been everyone's favorite, but she was hands down mine.

"I knew it. We're the same person."

She grabbed my drink and stirred it up with her spoon.

"Looks beautiful this way, but it'll taste better mixed." She handed it back to me and raised her own cup to mine. "To new friendships."

I echoed her and took a sip. It tasted like summer in a glass, like sunshine. I took a longer drink.

"Delicious right?" she said with a sigh.

"Incredible," I said when I was able to pull the glass from my lips.

"I knew you'd love it."

The music got louder, and I turned toward the house, seeing Gavin coming outside from the house. "That'll be me," I said, pointing at him. "Lost him a while ago in the crowd. Better go see what he wants."

She nodded, holding her drink up to me in a toast. "Good luck you're braver than I am to be heading back in there."

There was no part of me that wanted to. I had been enjoying talking with her and I didn't want to get thrown into the crowd, but there was no avoiding it now that Gavin was looking for me.

I headed over to him, and when his eyes fell on me, he rushed to meet me. "Where have you been?" he asked. "Roxy's been reaming me out for losing you. Had to take out the earpiece; it was getting too loud." He popped it back into his ear and grimaced. "Happy now? Yeah, yeah, I know, I know." He looked back at me. "You have half an hour left before your Cinderella act. You really should get some face time in with Parker. What were you doing, anyway?" he asked, looking back at where I came from. I followed his gaze and mine landed on Shannon, who waved from the secluded safety of her little pool house pub.

"Ah, getting in good with the other Parker? Smart. We don't have more time to waste, though."

He ushered me inside and my regret skyrocketed when the door slid open and the force of the music hit me like a brick wall. I had forgotten how loud it was. Gavin entered, and I followed with a sigh, reminding myself who I was and why I was here. I was Bridgette, the cool mysterious new girl, and I was here to make Shawn Parker my bitch. Okay, maybe that was a little harsh and a bit much, but I did need to pique his interest more. If I played too hard to get, he might stop chasing.

"Where is he?" I asked Gavin, who, of course, didn't hear me.

I leaned over and yelled into his ear, "Where is he?"

Gavin pointed to the throng of people and I saw Shawn was still in the middle of the crowd. Gavin gently shoved me toward him and into the throng. I stumbled into a girl who mouthed 'sorry' to me and then turned back to her friends. Shawn was only a few people in front of me now. He was dancing with someone I thought I recognized as one of Ava's friends. I watched as Shawn kept trying to spin her around to get her back to him, but she wasn't letting him.

I wasn't sure how I was supposed to get Shawn's attention. I wished Roxy was here to ask, but even if she was, she wouldn't have been able to hear me through the noise, anyway. I turned to look for Gavin for help, but he was still on the fringe of the dancers and I had been jostled in too far to reach him. I was considering moving that way anyway, but he was making shooing motions towards Shawn. I wasn't sure if the message was coming from him or Roxy, but it was loud and clear.

I had to focus.

I turned back to Shawn and found he was still dancing with the same girl. I still wasn't sure what to do about that, though. I considered cutting in. I felt almost positive that Shawn would welcome that, but because of that, it didn't seem like the right move. I could already picture the smug smirk I would get from him if I did that, and I wasn't looking forward to it. I didn't want to go to him. The plan would work better if I made him come to me.

I was tempted to drag Gavin out here and make him dance with me to get Shawn's attention, but I wasn't sure Gavin would go for it. I kept looking around and my eyes fell on a boy I recognized. He sat with us at Ava's lunch table. He was a tall, dark-skinned, handsome football player with kind eyes, and if I remembered right, him and Shawn were friends. He was perfect for the mission, and he was dancing solo.

I moved through the crowd, focused on him. If Shawn saw me now, he would see only what I wanted him to, that I was too focused on his friend, whose name I couldn't even remember, to notice Shawn.

When I got in front of the boy, I made my move, putting my hand on his shoulder and moving my hips to the music. He looked surprised at first before grinning down at me. He spun me away from him and I let him. Dancing on him like that would give me a better view of the dance floor.

I saw we had caught Shawn's attention. He wasn't paying attention to the girl he was with anymore, which worked for me. I closed my eyes and pressed myself against my dancing partner, letting myself get lost in the music. I felt my partner's hands on my hips and he pressed me into him. I would give him until the count of twenty. Twenty seconds until I moved away from him. I didn't even get to ten before I felt someone stroking my face. The thumb trailed down my cheek to my lips. When it stroked my lower lip, my eyes popped open.

I knew it was Shawn, and I knew he was cocky, but the audacity surprised me. I looked at his hand and then at him, waiting. He didn't move it, so I moved it for him, moving his hand to my waist. He grinned and moved his other hand to hold me and pulled me close to him. I let him, expecting the other boy to let go of me. To my surprise, he followed, boxing me in, between him and Shawn.

I started to panic, feeling trapped. My back was to the other boy, so I looked up at Shawn. He didn't look happy with the development either, which calmed me a little. If it bothered Shawn, it was probably a good thing. I looked off to the side, trying to see through the crowd, and managed to find Gavin. He gave me a thumbs up and held up five fingers. Five more minutes until my escape. I could manage that. I gave Shawn a smirk, pulling his attention back to me. The last thing I wanted was two boys I didn't even want fighting over me.

I leaned into the music, letting myself move in between the boys, both of whom surprisingly had a better grasp of moving to the beat than I would have expected. Shawn's attention kept fluctuating between me and his friend and I was shocked the other boy didn't find somewhere else to be. I was glad for the distraction, though. I was sure Shawn would've tried to kiss me by now if I wasn't also dancing with his friend.

I didn't love the attention we were getting, though. I was struggling to remind myself that this was the goal, that Bridgette wanted to be looked at and talked about, but old habits died hard and I knew that whatever was being said about me right now certainly wasn't good.

Shawn pulled my attention back to him when he leaned into me. I was pretty sure he was aiming for my lips, so I turned the other way. It was loud enough in here that it was believable I thought he was trying to talk to me. I waited to see if he'd say anything in my ear, but instead, I gasped when I felt his lips on my neck. I wanted to pull away, but with his friend behind me and a crowd around me, there wasn't really anywhere to go. Besides, this was good. Shawn was staking a claim, and I didn't even have to talk to him. He moved up to my ear, and he said something that I couldn't hear.

"What?" I yelled loudly in his direction.

"You wanna go somewhere quiet?" he yelled into my ear. I pretended not to hear him. Then I felt a hand on my shoulder and was relieved to see it was Gavin.

He pointed at his watch, mouthing "time". Relieved, I turned back to Shawn and moved to his ear, yelling, "I'm sorry I can't stay, other plans," and before he could protest, I ducked out from in between him and the other boy and grabbed Gavin's hand, pressing my way with him through the crowd and to the door. Instant relief washed over me with the fresh air. I turned to Gavin and saw Shawn was trying to make his way through the crowd behind us.

There was no way I was letting him catch up to us now. I pulled Gavin in front of me and said, "He's coming. Hurry up."

Gavin didn't hesitate to break into a run, and I followed behind. We were halfway to the street when Roxy's car came screeching up and the backdoor whipped open. At the same moment, my foot slipped out of one of my flats. I hesitated for a moment before deciding it wasn't worth stopping for and kept going.

Gavin dove into the back, making room for me. I quickly followed, closing the door behind me just in time to see Shawn open the front door.

"Go!" I told Roxy. She chuckled and said, "Show's not over yet," and I watched in horror as my window rolled down.

I moved closer, mashing the up button, but the window ignored me and continued its downward descent.

I heard Shawn call out, "Bridgette, wait!"

I glared daggers at Roxy before calling out, "Sorry, pretty boy. Places to be. See you around."

I started to roll up the window, glad Roxy gave me back control. Before it was all the way closed, Shawn found my shoe.

"Wait," he called out again, but I didn't. The window rolled up, blocking out the noise with a finality and we drove off.

We made it three blocks before Roxy pulled over and we all started talking at the same time.

"I can't believe it!" I said.

"We did it!" Lynds said.

"You did it!" Gavin said.

"Pretty boy?" Roxy asked, grinning.

We all started laughing. Roxy regained her composure first and asked, "What was he holding, anyway?"

I looked down at my single bare foot and burst into laughter before I could explain. They all looked down and then started laughing as realization dawned on them.

Through bursts of laughter, Roxy said, "You didn't have to take the Cinderella exit strategy literally."

Lynds and Gavin laughed harder at that.

"Come on, it wasn't on purpose!"

"Twenty bucks says he brings it to school Monday," Gavin said.

"There's no way!" I said quickly. "Right?" I asked, turning to Lynds.

She shrugged. "Tough call. He might."

I groaned.

"I hope he does," Roxy said.

I glared at her, but she didn't lose her grin. "What? It would be hilarious if he shows up with the shoe of the runaway girl he couldn't make stay. I wish I had thought of it."

"It wasn't on purpose!" I insisted.

"Accidental or not, it was still brilliant."

"Speaking of brilliant, dancing with Jeremiah instead of Shawn? Genius!" Lynds said, grinning.

"Really?" I asked.

"Definitely," Lynds said.

"Bad ass," Gavin agreed.

"Inspired," Roxy said. "I couldn't have done it better myself."

"You don't think it'll get too many people talking?"

"I *know* it'll get the right amount of people talking," Roxy said, putting the car back into drive and making her way out of Shawn's neighborhood toward Lynds's house. I was happy to be headed back. Her house already felt more like home to me than anywhere else I could remember living.

# CHAPTER SIXTEEN

Tiger Shark Tea

*Parker parties never disappoint, and this weekend was no exception. The usual suspects were there, but it seems like the new girl is stirring things up both in and out of school.*

*She caused quite a stir this weekend, dancing with both Shawn and Jeremiah. Seems like Shawn is getting a taste of what it's like to have to share.*

*Her quick exit makes it seem like the new girl is angling for a new nickname.*

*I'm nothing if not obliging...*

*Spotted: Brigderella dashing from the Parker Palace party with only a single shoe.*

*Wonder where she was going in such a hurry. Has Prince Parker already lost his charm?*

*Does Shawn have that little game off the field that girls are running from him now?*

I groaned at the picture of me escaping into Roxy's car. The other photo was a little more amusing. Shawn was holding my shoe, looking after the car dejectedly.

I swiped over to the group chat and typed,

**Shawn Parker Must Die**

Bridgerella?

Gavin

GENIUS!

Lynds's laughter from her side of the room told me she was awake. I threw a pillow in her direction, but the laughter kept coming.

"His stupid little face," she wheezed, showing the picture of Shawn holding my shoe.

I had to smile a little. Even if the whole thing was ridiculous, Lynds happy and smiling. This is just what I wanted, here she was giddy on a Sunday morning in a group chat with new friends who I knew would have her and my back in a heartbeat.

"Come on, it's hilarious," she said. I looked at the photo again and had to laugh. He did look ridiculous, and it could've been worse. They could've posted pics of me dancing with Shawn and Jeremiah. That actually would've been less surprising since a lot of people had their phones at the party. I didn't think anyone else was out front with us when I left.

"How do they even have it?" I asked.

She sat up, pulling her blanket around her tighter, and I watched as she looked more closely at the photo.

After a minute, she shrugged. "Who knows. I don't remember seeing anyone, but anyone could've been out there."

"And sent the photo in? Why do people do that?"

"Why do people do anything? People like gossip and they like to feel important."

"Yeah, but there were so many people at the party. Why me? Why's the Tiger Shark Tea page paying attention to me?"

"Same reason everyone else is, everyone loves a new girl."

"Really?"

"You having Shawn's attention doesn't hurt either. Tiger Shark Tea always pays attention to him, just like everyone else at Harris High," she said, rolling her eyes.

The group chat dinged, and I looked down to see Roxy had responded.

Roxy

> That was funny enough I'll forgive the rude awakening.

I looked at the clock and then laughed out loud. It was already 10am. I couldn't remember the last time I had slept past 8am.

Ava

> Def worth it. He looks ridiculous.

Lynds

> I couldn't stop laughing.

Roxy

Seriously, though, this is a great step - we can only hope he'll try to return your shoe tomorrow.

Lynds started laughing hysterically across the room.

He can keep it.

Gavin

Maybe we could get a rumor going he has a weird foot fetish.

Roxy

I'm sure Bri's feet aren't weird.

I snorted at that, and Lynds was doubled over trying to breathe through her laughter.

Very normal feet

Ava

You know, now that you say that... he did have a little bit of a thing about my feet...

Gavin

NO!

Roxy

WHAT?!

And you guys let me give him my shoe??

Roxy

You have to be screwing with us.

Gavin

For real - no way that's true.

Ava

...

Roxy

Give it up, Aves.

Ava

Fineeeeee but how funny would it be if it were true.

Lynds

You think Tiger Shark Tea would post it?

Roxy

Without proof? Not a chance.

Damn

Gavin

Can we add that in as a goal?

You're not getting feet pics.

Gavin

I don't want them - Shawn might, though.

Ewwwwww

So not happening

Roxy

Wear flip-flops tomorrow, though.

Do I want to know...?

Ava

He's not actually into feet, Rox.

Roxy

I'm rolling my eyes so hard I'm shocked you can't hear it - of course he's not, but he's a hoe for a grand gesture - my money's on him trying to Cinderella you.

No

Ava

Ohmygosh you're right!

I will literally die on the spot.

Roxy

We'll ready a casket.

# CHAPTER SEVENTEEN

Saying I didn't sleep well was an understatement. I had been up half the night worrying about the spectacle Shawn was probably going to make of him and myself today.

By the time I got through a couple of my classes Monday morning, the adrenaline was fading a little and I was struggling to stay awake.

I was half asleep in English when I felt a piece of paper poke me in the arm. I turned and saw Shannon, who was holding the paper out to me while watching Mr. Hayes. I quickly took it and slid it into my notebook. Watching Mr. Hayes's back, I unfolded the note.

*Dude, what did you do to my brother? Whatever you did at the party, he wouldn't shut up about you all weekend; keeps begging me for info. It'd be funny if I hadn't already decided you're my friend.*

I felt a little pang of guilt at the last part, but it was mostly drowned out by the excitement that the plan was working. I'd faked confidence with the gang, but I hadn't really known if making him jealous had been the right play. It had seemed to work, but I left so quickly after that I hadn't been positive.

*What do you mean? I didn't do anything, just danced with some guy (apparently his friend?) and he pulled me in to dance with him, too.*

I quickly passed the note back to her, feeling bad about lying, but I couldn't exactly tell her the truth.

She stiffed a giggle and quickly scrawled a reply before sending the note back my way.

*Oh my god! You didn't?! No wonder he's been bitching about it. He loves the chase and can't figure out why you aren't into him. He spent the weekend bitching about how much better he is than Jeremiah, no wonder. Disinterest is like foreplay to my brother.*

I grimaced at that, looking up at her, and she mimed a gagging motion that had me suppressing a laugh.

*Gross! You're the Shawn expert. How do I get him to leave me alone?*

Even though it wasn't the goal, it would be good info to have.

She looked thoughtful for a moment before writing back.

*Act obsessed with him.*

I shot her an incredulous look.

*Your douche of a brother needs a girl to act interested before he'll leave her alone?*

She shrugged and jotted down, *You asked. I didn't say you'd like the answer. He's grimy for sure, but most of the girls he doesn't bother with are card-carrying members of his fan club - like Grace Elms. You wouldn't catch him giving her the time of day even though she fawns all over him*

Grace Elms was Lynds's ex-best friend. I hadn't noticed that she'd been hanging around Shawn. Interesting.

*Which one is she?* I asked, thinking it was better to feign ignorance than to start talking about her since talking about her would lead to talking about Lynds.

Shannon giggled at that.

*Exactly. She's not memorable or notable to him either. She's one of the righteous mean girls. She was probably in your cousin's comments after the photos. She's always slut shaming - not that your cousin's a slut - but yeah, she puts girls down and says vile homophobic shit like this isn't the 21st century. She's the worst, but she's pretty, so none of that would matter to Shawn if she hadn't committed the carnal sin of showing she's interested in him.*

I knew Shawn was bad news, but I couldn't believe his sister was really telling me that I had to act interested to get him to leave me alone. I couldn't be the only girl at the school that couldn't care less about him, right? Did he harass the others, too, or was I just getting this special treatment because I was the new girl?

*There really isn't another way?*

She wrote out a couple different things, crossing each out before she settled on something and passed it back to me, not making eye contact.

*He'd probably leave you alone if you came onto his sister at the next party.*

I looked over at her curiously, wondering what the other versions of her note had said, but they were too blacked out to read. She was blushing and didn't look back at me. It was super kind of her to offer to help me, but I didn't want to make her uncomfortable.

*I don't want to drag you into anything.*

She rolled her eyes at me, but I was glad she wasn't blushing anymore. The last thing I wanted was to have made her uncomfortable.

*It's not dragging if I offer - but yeah, just a plan B if you can't get rid of him and are too nauseated to act like you're into him.*

I smiled at her and scrawled back:

*Thank you. It'll be quite an Oscar award-winning performance if I can manage it.*

She grinned and started to write back, but the bell rang. I hadn't even noticed class was close to over. I gathered my stuff, shoving it into my bag.

"Seriously, though," she said, "if you can't handle him, I can try to step in."

"By having me hit on you?"

"I mean, I'd offer to talk to him, but me telling him to leave my friend alone wouldn't help. Making you forbidden would make things so much worse."

"But being seen making a move on you wouldn't? Besides, I don't think he noticed me spending time with you this time. What makes you think next time would be different? Do you really think it would get him to leave me alone?"

She shrugged. "Maybe. I'm honestly not sure. I haven't seen him this hung up on someone in a while."

I groaned. "Lucky me, I guess."

She laughed. "If you ever need a safe haven, my lunch table's always open to you."

"Thanks, that means a lot. I've been sitting with Ava and her friends, and they're nice enough, but I think I might have to find a new table if Jeremiah keeps sitting there."

Her eyes widened. "Good call. You don't want to get in the middle of that."

I couldn't help wondering if that was exactly what I should be doing, even if all I actually wanted to do was ignore Shawn and sit with Shannon.

# Chapter Eighteen

**Shawn Parker Must Die**

> Can I please sit somewhere else today?

Roxy

Not a chance - you have to sit with them.

Ava

You don't want to sit with me?

> Of course I do! Just don't want to talk to Jeremi-
> ah.

Ava

I can make him move if you want.

Roxy

If you're actually uncomfy you don't have to, but you've got Parker right where you want him.

I sighed. Roxy was right, of course. I put my phone away and made my way over to Ava's table. The rest of the crew waved to me when I sat down next to her. Right now, it was just the cheerleaders, but pretty soon some guys from the team would show up like usual. So far that hadn't included Shawn, and I hoped my luck held out, but Jeremiah was one of the usuals and I doubt he would ignore me after the weekend.

I slid into the spot Ava had saved for me. She playfully bumped into my shoulder with hers, saying, "Good to see you."

I smiled back at her. I was grateful to have her and the others. I hoped they all knew that.

I had been sitting there for maybe two minutes when Ava nudged me and said, "Incoming, 9 o'clock. If you look, make it subtle."

I followed her direction and looked over her shoulder as discretely as I could and had to fight to keep my face neutral. Jeremiah was coming over. I had expected it, but seeing him headed this way was making me anxious. It had been too loud at the party for me to talk to him much, and now I wasn't sure what to say.

He slid into a seat a few people over from me. I breathed a sigh of relief that he didn't sit next to me. He nodded to the table and then he saw me and I watched the recognition flash in his eyes.

He got up and moved around the table, sliding into the empty seat next to mine.

*Damn.*

"New girl," he said, nodding at me. "Good seeing you again."

"Hey." I wasn't sure what else to say.

"Jer-bear!" Ava interjected. "How's the team shaping up this year?"

I was grateful to her for stealing some of his attention.

"Pretty good so far. I think we might actually have a chance against the Orcas this year."

"Really?" Ava asked incredulously.

"What's the big deal about the Orcas?" I asked.

I shouldn't have, cause Jeremiah's attention turned right back to me. "No one's told you about the Orcas yet?" He looked past me at Ava and the rest of the table and said louder, "No one told the new girl about our sworn enemy?"

Ava rolled her eyes, and the others shook their heads.

"Sworn enemy?" I asked Ava.

"It's not that serious," she said.

"It is definitely that serious," Jeremiah said. Some others at the table were nodding. "Their school and team is full of arrogant pricks who think they're better than us."

"Because they are," Ava said, causing the table to groan. "They kick our asses every year."

"Except this year!" Jeremiah crowed to some echoes from the table. "This year's gonna be the best yet." At this, he turned his attention back to me. "In more ways than one, if the weekend was anything to go by." He slung his arm around me. It was there for maybe thirty seconds before suddenly it wasn't.

I heard Ava gasp, looking behind me. I spun around in my seat and saw Shawn was standing over Jeremiah, who was on the ground. Jeremiah stood up saying, "Hey man, what the hell?"

Shawn stared him down. "I thought we talked about this."

Jeremiah shrugged. "You certainly talked."

Shawn took a step closer. They were almost chest to chest now. "And apparently you didn't listen."

Some of their teammates stepped in now, grabbing Shawn by the shoulders. "Hey Park, come on, you guys can work it out on the field, not here," one of them tried to reason with him. I hoped he'd listen. Shawn getting suspended wouldn't help the plan. Although who knows, maybe football players could get away with fighting in school without getting disciplined.

"Consider this the last warning, Jer. Know your place."

"You don't own her," Jeremiah said, and I froze. This couldn't actually be about me. Yes, I wanted to make Shawn jealous, but they couldn't actually be fighting over me, right? I looked over at Ava for reassurance, but her eyes were glued to Shawn.

"You're right, I don't, but I'm sure as hell not letting her get bothered by you."

"I wasn't-" he started, but Shawn cut him off.

"I didn't ask you." He turned to me, and the anger turned into his easy smile in a second flat. It was chilling how quickly he could turn on the charm. "Was Jeremiah bothering you?"

"I-" I started and stopped. Everyone was staring at me and I didn't know what to say. I looked at Ava, who was still staring wide eyed at the guys. I went with my gut instinct and said, "Not at all. Besides, I'm sure you can handle a little competition, Parker. I thought you had more game than that."

With that, I spun back around, took a swig of water, and asked Ava loudly, "Are they always like this?"

She answered just as loudly. "Usually they're a bit better, but on their best day they're still animals."

Shawn had to almost be dragged away. It was refreshing to see him at a loss for words for once.

Tiger Shark Tea

> *Apparently, new girl Bridgerella is turning out to be quite the heartbreaker. It was hard to miss how she already has half the football team fighting over her.*

There was a picture of Shawn looming over Jeremiah with me looking concerned, watching them.

I scowled over at Lynds, who was still laughing.

"At least he didn't bring the shoe," she offered, trying and failing to hold back her laughter.

"Yeah, yeah, let's get home before he decides to try to find my car."

I wasn't sure if he would, but he was probably the last person I wanted to see right now. I had thought being the center of attention would be easier than it had been, but we were only a week into school, and I was already starting to think I was in over my head. No one ever paid this much attention to me at any of my old schools, and when people did, it didn't matter all that much because I was never in one place for long enough to make lasting friendships. This time was different, this time mattered, and I couldn't help wondering if I was too quick to agree to become someone new.

Then Lynds turned up the new Savannah Hollywood song and started singing along at top volume. With the windows rolled down, the wind in our hair, the sun at our backs, and a huge grin on Lynds's face, my doubts eased. Regardless of what ended up happening with Shawn, I knew this school year was going to be the best, because for once, I wasn't alone.

# Chapter Nineteen

Jeremiah had saved me from having to deal with Shawn yesterday, but I knew I wasn't going to get that lucky twice in a row.

I was dragging my feet on the walk to lunch from chem class, trying to think of what to say to him. I really didn't want the Bridgerella nickname to stick, which it definitely would if he pulled a Prince Charming with my shoe. I was still hoping he was too self-absorbed to have thought to bring it, but the others were betting he remembered.

I was halfway through the lunch line before I pulled out my phone. I was about to text the group chat when I remembered another number I had saved. I hesitated. Staying away from her would've been smart, but she would probably be the perfect shield from Shawn.

I pulled up the contact name "The Better Parker" and texted her.



I would give it until I had my lunch. If I didn't hear back from her, I would go sit with Ava and the others and deal with whatever happened.

I didn't have to wait more than twenty seconds for the answer.

The Better Parker

> Assuming this is the famous Bridgerella, then definitely still good.

I didn't know whether to be relieved at the save or embarrassed the nickname was catching on.

> Do you invite all the new girls to your lunch table?

The Better Parker

> Nah, just the pretty ones.

I laughed at that, grabbed my lunch, and was thrilled to see Shannon waiting for me.

"So I'm pretty?" I asked, grinning.

She waved me off. "You're already Harris High's resident princess. Quit fishing for compliments. You know you're gorgeous."

I was surprised enough to not know what to say. I let her pull me to her table, distracted by the thought that both of the Parkers found me pretty, not that it mattered. I knew I didn't care about Shawn's opinion, and I barely knew Shannon. She was nice and if she was anyone else's sister, I could see myself being close friends with her, but she was Shawn's sister, which made things complicated. There were always going to be things I couldn't tell her, and because of who I had to be for her brother, I couldn't be my real self with her, either.

It was cool someone as objectively and effortlessly pretty as her thought I was pretty, too, though.

Even if I knew we couldn't have a real friendship, I was still thrilled she was taking me out of the hot seat today.

"Guys, this is Bridgette from my English class. Bridgette, this is two-thirds of the drama club aka my friends."

"And yet we're some of the least dramatic people around," an Indian girl with large glasses and long dark eyelashes said with a laugh. "I'm Priya."

I slid into the seat between Priya and Shannon as the others introduced themselves. There were too many names to remember, but they all seemed nice enough. I was instantly drawn into their discussion about what the fall play was going to be. Apparently, auditions were next week and they wouldn't find out until tomorrow what the play was.

"Wait, so how do you guys know you want to audition if you don't know what the play is?"

That got blank stares from the table, but Shannon laughed, saying, "Come on, give her a break. I don't think she was a theatre kid in any of her past lives, were you?"

"Past lives?" I couldn't remember mentioning much about my past to Shannon, but maybe I had. She was startling easy to talk to.

She blushed a little and said, "I may have deep dived your Facegram. Looks like you've been just about everywhere and everyone. Didn't look like you were a theatre kid, though."

I knew she had my socials, but I hadn't thought she'd find me interesting enough to really look at my profile. "You looked me up?" I asked.

She blushed even more at that. "I like a good mystery. Don't worry though, I didn't tell brother dearest anything new about you."

"Good," I said quickly with a chuckle. "He's quite persistent."

"Yeah, what's the deal with that?" Priya asked.

"No clue," I said. "Trust me, I've been trying to keep my distance."

That much was true, at least.

"He unfortunately has good taste," Shannon said. "He's been all over her."

"And the little scene he put on yesterday? Talk about a drama king," one of the girls said, rolling their eyes.

"You should tell him if he keeps it up, he should try out, Shan," Priya joked.

Shan laughed. "Yeah, right. He gets to be good at everything else. Drama's my thing."

"The football star wouldn't be caught dead on the stage," one of the boys chimed in.

"Thank goodness for that," Shannon said, grinning.

The others devolved back into talking about their hopes for the play naming some I recognized but a lot more that I didn't.

I leaned over to Shannon and said quietly, "If it's Shawn repellant, maybe I should consider joining."

The way her face lit up at that made me feel guilty that it was a joke. "You should! It'd be so much fun!"

"I don't know," I said quickly. "I'm not much of an actress." But that wasn't necessarily true. After all, Bridgette was more of an act than the real me.

"I bet you'd be better than you think," she said. "Besides, it's not just acting roles, there's the stage crew and costume design. Behind the scenes can be just as fun."

She started using theatre jargon I didn't understand, but I tried to follow along. I was getting distracted by how much she talked with her hands when she was excited about something. She clearly loved theatre, and I was kicking myself for not knowing more about it, for not having given it a go at any of my old schools. I hadn't been at their table long, but I felt like I fit in here a lot better than I had at Ava's table.

Everyone at Ava's table had been nice enough to me, but they were Ava's friends. They were polite, but not overly friendly. Shannon's friends hopped in and out of conversation with each other, pulling me in with them and stopping to explain things if I looked confused. They were making an effort to include me, and the effort wasn't lost on me. This was the closest I had come to feeling like myself, like Bri, at school. Lunch was over way too quickly.

I felt a little guilty when I checked my phone on my way back to class and saw Ava had texted me privately.

Ava

> Missed you at lunch! Saw you having fun, though. I was glad to see it.

> Wanna get a bite after class?

Ava

> I can't. Cheer practice, but my weekend's mostly free if you're around. Group hang?

> Definitely! No Parker party this weekend?

Ava

> Don't think so - if there is, my invite got lost in the mail.

I couldn't tell from the text how she meant that, which worried me a little. I knew it couldn't be easy on her, or on Roxy or Lynds, seeing Shawn move on so quickly. A group hang would be just the thing we needed, though. I could check in with them all and see how they were feeling about things. If anyone was uncomfortable, I could call off the plan. I wasn't sure how I would get Shawn away from me since, according to Shannon, I was screwed now, but I would do whatever it took if any one of them wanted me to call it off.

If they didn't, I would keep giving it my all. He deserved to be humiliated, but I couldn't help but secretly hope a little that they would want to call it off. Being Bridgette was exhausting.

# CHAPTER TWENTY

Wednesday passed without a Shawn sighting. I was starting to think Shannon was a better Shawn repellant than anything else I had tried before. I had sat with her at lunch again and it seemed to be enough to keep him away.

I was struggling to fall asleep, wondering if I should sit go back to sitting with Ava tomorrow. After all, none of us had heard about anything going on over the weekend, and as much as that suited me to have a weekend to myself and spend time with the gang, I was starting to worry that Shawn was more fickle than we thought and had already lost interest. After all, no one throwing a party over Labor Day weekend was unheard of, at least at my other schools.

I was scrolling on my phone when a text popped up from Shannon.

The Better Parker

It involves a shoe.

....no.

The Better Parker

I tried already, trust me - I got bitched at for
hiding you for the past couple of days.

So, it doesn't matter where I sit tomorrow?

The Better Parker

Doesn't seem like it. He'll find you. You should
probably weather the storm with me, though. At
least the crew won't encourage him.

Fair enough. Ava's table would be fawning all over
him for the grand gesture. At least at Shannon's table,
people would be real about it.

You're the best. See ya in the morning.

# Chapter Twenty One

I walked to lunch like I was headed for a firing squad. I was already cringing at whatever the Tiger Shark Tea was going to post about what was going to happen.

The gang had been encouraging me, reminding me this was what we wanted. Lynds even told me that if I didn't want to keep going with this, I didn't have to, but that only served to make me more determined to keep going. Sure, she was healing now, but he had hurt her, and I wanted to make him hurt for that.

With every step, I had to remind myself I was playing the long game.

Shannon was waiting for me the second I got there.

"Not too late to make a run for it," she said instead of greeting me.

I laughed at that. "And delay things another day? You said he was persistent."

She sighed. "He is, unfortunately."

"So I might as well get it over with."

She gave me a soft smile, saying, "I'll kick his ass if he does anything too embarrassing."

I looked at her a moment before laughing. "You're so sweet, but something tells me he'd have the upper hand in that fight."

She gave me an exaggerated pout before her face cracked into a grin. "Fair enough, but it's the thought that counts."

She whisked me off to our table. The others were excitedly talking when we showed up, but they all turned to us expectantly when we sat down.

"No sighting yet, but stay vigilant. I'm sure he's coming for her," Shannon told them.

I laughed at that, and a couple of the others did, too.

"He's seriously giving us a run for our money with the dramatics," Priya said.

"Speaking of, what's the play?" I asked, half out of curiosity and half to change the subject.

"Guess," Shannon insisted.

"Something by the bard?" It was a pretty safe bet.

They nodded. From the tight-lipped faces looking back at me, I was guessing the comedies were out. They looked a bit disappointed, too, which drove me to guess, "Romeo and Juliet?"

They nodded. "It'll be cool of course," one of the girls said quickly.

"We'll make it cool," Priya agreed.

"It wasn't our top choice," Shannon admitted to me.

"We were hoping for Midsummer Night's Dream or Twelfth Night this year, but there's always next year."

"Don't you guys have another one in the spring?" I asked.

They all stared at me. "Shakespeare is a fall play," one of the girls explained slowly. "We can't do the bard in the spring."

"Why not?"

Midsummer being a fall play didn't make much sense. It was a summer play. Since they were already doing it out of season, it could have just as easily been a spring play as it was a fall play.

"Plays are in the fall, spring is for musicals," Shannon explained. "We'll find a way to make it stand out, though."

The others started spit balling ideas, but I turned to Shannon, asking, "Does that mean you're still trying out?"

She grinned. "Of course I am. It didn't really matter what the play was, I'm definitely trying out."

"You're looking at our Juliet," Priya said, causing Shannon to blush.

"I doubt I'll get it. Steph's a senior and a shoo-in."

"Oh, come on!" one of the girls said. "She's great, but she's not you."

"Shannon's so freaking talented," Priya told me.

"The best by far," one of the boys agreed.

"You guys, I'm not that good," Shannon said, waving them off.

"I'd bet anything we're looking at our Juliet," one of the girls insisted.

"I'm sure you'd kill it," I told her, and grinned when her blush deepened.

"Speaking of Juliet, here comes lover boy," Priya said, pointing behind us.

Everyone at the table turned to watch his approach. Acknowledging subtlety wasn't an option, I turned around, too. Shannon squeezed my shoulder and whispered, "You've got this. I've heard he doesn't last long."

It was a fight for my life to not burst into laughter, and before Shawn got to us, I lost. Shannon fell into a fit of giggles with me. I took a deep breath when Shawn cleared his throat. "Bridgette, my runaway princess."

Shannon elbowed me, saying, "Aren't you fancy? Does that make me your lady-in-waiting?"

I couldn't help ignoring him to answer her. "I'd say if you live in a Palace with a brother who claims to be a Prince that makes you a Princess, too. The fairest of them all, if you ask me."

Her cheeks started to heat, but Shawn interrupted, saying to Shannon, "I thought we talked about this. You're ruining it."

"He's not wrong," she said to me. "He did talk. Does it quite a lot, actually. Unfortunately, I don't listen nearly as often."

Shawn scoffed at her before turning back to me. "You've been running through my mind ever since you ran from my party."

"Couldn't get away fast enough from the looks of the pics," Shannon interjected. "Pity you let him catch up to you now."

"Shan, come on, you're killing me here," he said, raking his hands through his hair. She seemed to soften a little at that, leaning back against the table and saying, "You really think I'm holding you back? Fine. I'll just watch. Go for it."

"Bridgette," he started again, turning to me, "I can't get you out of my mind. You left a piece of yourself with me at that party."

"My dignity?" It just slipped out. I blamed Shannon. It was probably too harsh.

"If we're going metaphorical, I was thinking part of your heart, but more literally, I have something for you."

He turned around, and I noticed for the first time that a couple of his friends had come with him. He took my missing shoe from one of them and turned back to me.

"I brought it back to you. I got the message loud and clear. You wanted a Cinderella moment, well here we are."

He sunk down onto one knee in front of me and I was sure all the blood had drained from my face. My hand flew to my mouth of its own accord. He took off my flip-flop, stroking the bottom of my foot. I barely resisted the urge to kick him. I should've and said I was ticklish, that it was a reflex, but I didn't. I let him hold my foot, waiting for him to put the flat back on.

He looked up at me and paused, "Your shoe for a kiss?"

I felt Shannon stiffen next to me. I felt the same, but fought to keep my feelings hidden. It was just a stupid kiss. I could do this. I knew it was going to happen sooner or later, but that didn't mean I was excited about it. If I were being myself, I would tell him to keep the stupid shoe and would wrestle my foot out of his grip, but Bridgette should probably be softening to him a little by now.

"You think you've earned it?" I asked him.

Shannon's short inhale next to me had me worried I might be about to ruin the budding friendship between us. I felt a pang of sadness at that, but I was doing this for Lynds, and, to a lesser extent, for Roxy and Ava. I didn't want to let them down.

"I think you've made me work for it," he said, sliding my flat onto my foot before jumping up and pulling me to my feet with him. He pulled me to him and dipped me, pressing his lips to mine. He held me there, his lips on mine, while everyone at the surrounding tables broke into cheers. I was pleasantly surprised to find he kept the kiss quite chaste. I had only counted to five before he pulled away, righting me back on my feet before spinning me around.

He pulled away and sunk into a bow. "Princess."

I giggled at that. I couldn't not; the whole scene was so ridiculous. I curtsied to him. "Prince Parker."

"Enjoy the rest of your lunch," he said with a self-satisfied grin and him and his friends left.

I turned back to the table, who were all watching me. To my dismay, Shannon didn't meet my eye.

Priya was the first to break the silence, asking, "So how was it?"

"Not worth all the fanfare," I said simply.

Shannon looked up at me surprised, and I shrugged. "With all that practice I thought he'd be better."

It wasn't strictly true. It wasn't a bad kiss. He was much more respectful than I expected, but I wasn't itching to do it again. To be fair to Shawn, though, there wasn't anyone I could think of that I would be excited about kissing. I hadn't known anyone at the school long enough to be in danger of developing a crush.

When I sat back down, Shannon slung her arm over my shoulder. "I knew I liked you," she said, grinning.

I was glad it was that easy to be forgiven, even if I knew it couldn't last. I didn't think the friendship that was growing between us would last me cozying up to Shawn and then crushing him.

*Why couldn't she have been literally anyone else? Why did she have to be his sister?*

The others pulled us back into conversation about Romeo and Juliet and what they might be able to get the director agree to to make it unique. Shannon was quietly extolling the virtues of the theatre program to me and how good it would look on college applications. She had a good point. To be honest, I hadn't given college applications much thought. My classes had all been easy enough so far, so I was sure my grades would be fine, but colleges loved extracurriculars.

"I'll think about it," I promised.

It was an easy promise to keep since I couldn't stop thinking about it for the rest of the day. I felt like it would be a lot of fun, but I was worried about it being too much to balance with our plans for Shawn and my classes already. Walking to my car, I considered talking to the girls about it. If Shawn weren't in the picture, I would've already agreed to join, but I didn't want to let the others down. Not doing it, though, felt like letting myself down, especially since I could hardly put my acting experience in my role as Shawn Parker's seductress on a college application.

I was lost in thought about how my college essay about ruining a boy's reputation would go over with an acceptance board when I literally ran into the boy himself. He was waiting in front of my car and I was surprised to see he was alone.

"Woah there. Happy to see me?" he quipped as he put his arms around me. I let him pull me into a hug for a moment before pulling away.

He gave me a soft smile I hadn't seen before and said, "I know I can be a lot sometimes." He looked around for a moment before adding, "I wanted to talk to you without an audience. It's hard sometimes. Everyone here expects so much from me. They don't really give me the space to just be me."

It felt like he was echoing my own racing thoughts. Of course, I was making the decision to not be myself, so it wasn't quite the same, but I felt a pang of empathy, anyway.

"So I wanted to talk to you alone, so I could be myself."

I wondered how many times he'd used that line before and felt myself stiffened a little. I felt like I was one of the few people at the school that actually saw him clearly. When you stripped away the smooth talking and the bullshit, he was just a boy who liked attention and praise and didn't care who he hurt while chasing the next best thing.

"What can I do for you?" I asked, hoping he'd cut to the chase. I was suddenly tired and just wanted the conversation to be over.

"What are you doing this weekend?"

I fought to make my face look sad when I said, "Sorry, girls' weekend locked in."

"You can't get away?"

The nerve of him to ask me to cancel my plans for him a day before the weekend was insane. I didn't deign that with more of a response than, "Nope."

He should've asked sooner.

He sighed. "Fair enough. I knew I should've asked sooner." He looked down at the ground before offering a small smile. "I didn't want to seem too forward, but sounds like I messed up. I won't make that mistake again." Before I could say anything in response, he added, "What about next weekend?"

"What about it? What's going on next weekend?" I asked. I wasn't going to be pressed into plans without knowing more.

"First game of the season is Friday night. I'm having a party after. I'd love to see you there."

"I'll think about it," I said.

"The whole school'll be there," he said quickly.

"At the game or your party?"

He laughed. "Probably both. Everyone comes back to my house after the game to celebrate."

"What if you don't win?" I asked.

He laughed. "It's the first game of the year, we've got this. Besides, it's against the Stingrays. They don't stand a chance."

"So you're not just confident when it comes to girls?"

He laughed at that, holding up his hands. "Alright, alright, point taken. I wouldn't say confident, though, more like I know what I want and I'm willing to fight for it."

"I'll think about it," I said, granting him a small smile before moving to my driver's side door and opening it. He grinned back, gave a little wave, and trotted back toward the school.

# CHAPTER TWENTY TWO

Friday was going great until Shannon's normal seat in English was empty. I was surprised by the worry I felt. I wanted to text her and see where she was, if she was okay, but I knew better than to touch my phone in Mr. Hayes's class. He was seldom serious, but he was about phones. Phones were the enemy of thought, apparently. It's why Shannon and I normally passed notes.

The moment the bell rang, and I was in the hallway, I pulled out my phone.

Hey are you okay??

Her response came near instantly.

The Better Parker

Yeah, are you? What's wrong?

You aren't in class.

The Better Parker

I just whacked Shawn in the back of the head for you. He was supposed to tell you. He told me he told you.

> Told me what?

The Better Parker

That we were taking an early weekend - we're up at the lake. He told me he invited you. Did he not invite you?

> Lake? What lake?

The Better Parker

Tahoe. We have a place up here. Shawn said he invited you, did he not?

> I guess he did. He never told me what he was inviting me to.

The Better Parker

Ahhh - that makes a lot more sense - I was confused you turned down a free lake house trip with me, even if my brother was involved.

> Well, tell him to get better at inviting me places in the future.

I'm not sure if I would've gone, but I would've had a much harder time turning it down than I had if I had known I was turning down a lake house vacation with Shannon.

The Better Parker

I think he got the message. He sends his apologies as well as several complaints that you didn't make me work for your number like he has to.

Next time, I'll make it easier on you and invite you myself.

I'd like that.



Gotta go - he's mad cause I told him I'd give him another digit.



He didn't like that it was my middle finger instead of part of your number. Do a lot of learning for me!

I sent her some laughing emojis and hearts and put my phone away.

If Ava was surprised to see me at lunch, she didn't let on, just welcomed me back as everyone talked about their plans for the weekend. She told them we were going to the beach. A few of her friends asked to tag along, which made me anxious, but I was surprised and touched that she told them definitely next time but that she wanted to spend time with just me this time.

No one batted an eye at that or was at all upset. I was really surprised. I wasn't sure how Ava would've explained me and her hanging out with Roxy and Gavin.

When I asked her about it when we were walking to class, she just shrugged and said, "They're used to me doing my own thing. Besides, I want to hang with you guys."

It was hard not to be a little grateful to Shawn for bringing us all together. I wasn't sure the friendships would have happened without his heartlessness.

# Chapter Twenty Three

"So what's on the agenda?" Roxy asked when me and Lynds hopped into the car, squeezing into the back with Ava. Ava gave me a half shoulder squeeze, half hug.

"Aren't we going to the beach?" I asked.

"Course we are. I meant what's been going on? You haven't spilled anything in a while. Did Shawny boy say anything to you before the Parkers left for Tahoe?"

"Sort of? He asked me what I was doing this weekend, but I figured he was trying to ask me out, so I told him I was busy."

"Wonder what his plan was," Gavin said from the passenger seat.

"Well, Shannon said that was his feeble attempt at inviting me to Tahoe."

"No way!" Ava basically screamed in my ear.

I turned to her, saying, "That's what she said, anyway. Why?"

"I've only been trying to get invited there since I've known him, but I've never gotten an invite. He always brings a couple of the guys when he goes," Ava explained.

"Damnnnn this is working better than even I could've planned," Roxy said.

"Boy's down bad," Gavin agreed.

"About that, should I maybe cool things off a bit?" I asked tentatively.

Gavin's head whipped to me, Roxy met my eye through the mirror, Ava shifted toward me in her seat, and Lynds gave my thigh a quick reassuring squeeze.

"Why? What did he do?" Roxy asked quickly. "If he messed with you, too, we'll find another way to ruin him, but his days are numbered."

"No, no, so far things have been going smoothly. I just don't know if it's worth it."

"Wait, wait, wait," Ava said carefully, "you're not feeling his vibe are you?"

Lynds stopped her. "Of course she's not, but, Bri, is the kissing making you uncomfortable? Is he being too touchy?"

It wasn't that either. Lynds tried to understand, but she didn't quite get it. I wasn't repulsed by kissing or physical touch, I just didn't usually do it. I didn't usually see a point in doing it with someone I wasn't attracted to, and I'd yet to feel genuine attraction to someone. Kissing Shawn didn't repulse me, but it felt as meaningless to me as it probably did to him. I was just worried that it felt like something else to the others.

Well, not to Roxy. I wasn't worried about her. She seemed more in love with revenge than she had ever been with Shawn, but Lynds had really cared about Shawn, and Ava and Shawn had seemed really close. I didn't want to accidentally hurt either of them while trying to hurt him.

"That's not it. He actually kissed really respectfully."

"Shawn?" Roxy asked. "Shawn Parker? Shawny boy kissed you *respectfully*?"

"What does that even mean?" Gavin asked, and I was glad that he gave me a question to try to answer.

"He was sweet about it. Didn't try to shove his tongue down my mouth and didn't make it last overly long."

"Did you just describe him as sweet? Now I know you're not talking about the same boy that threw my ass against a tree and started stripping me."

"I mean he was always sweet with me when it came to stuff like that," Lynds said.

"Always?" I asked her. "How often did it happen?"

Ava was looking at her, too. Lynds blushed a little and said, "Just a couple of times after the party. We stopped talking after the pictures came out, though, I swear."

I looked at Ava, who said, "We weren't really like that. He was sweet to me, and I think our parents expected us to get together, and maybe he did, too, but I wasn't really into him like that. He wasn't really my type."

"What is your type?" I asked. I wasn't attracted to most people, but I couldn't imagine most girls wouldn't be attracted to Shawn.

"Well, I'm a lesbian, so, girls," she said simply.

"Girls?" Roxy asked from the front seat, and I tensed. Everyone was fine when I came out and Gavin was gay, but you never really knew how these things were going to go.

I was about to cut in and tell Ava that was great and I was glad she trusted us when she started laughing and said, "Okay, one woman in particular. It's new, though. I didn't want to jinx it."

"Ohhhhh a secret girlfriend?" Roxy asked. "Do tell."

I smiled at Ava encouragingly. Lynds still looked surprised, but Gavin didn't seem like this was news. *Interesting.*

Ava blushed, saying, "Well, she's bossy and beautiful, has really pretty eyes and dark hair, and can be really frustrating sometimes."

"Frustrating?" Roxy pressed.

"Yeah, she doesn't want people to know about us, which I totally get cause it's a new thing, but then I get put in these impossible situations where I want to just brag about her and how perfect she is, but I feel like my hands are tied. I respect the hell out of her and her right to want to keep things on the DL, but times like this drive me crazy."

"I'm sorry," I said quickly. "That sounds so difficult."

"Thanks," she said with a smile and a chuckle. "She has her reasons, but it feels like a lot sometimes."

"Can I admit something?" Roxy asked from the front.

"As long as it's something important," I said quickly in a tone that was almost snapping at her. I didn't like how she was acting toward Ava. This was a huge thing Ava was trusting us with, and Roxy seemed to be treating it as a joke. "Cause I'm not sure Ava was done yet," I said pointedly.

Roxy laughed at that. "Ava's my secret girlfriend."

"She's your what?" I exclaimed.

"No way!" Lynds cried out.

"Actually?" I asked, turning to Ava, who was beaming at Roxy through the rearview mirror.

"Really," she said, grinning.

"What? When? How?" Lynds asked.

I turned to her to tell her to stop asking questions, but she waved a hand at me. "I'm not trying to be rude, but we all grew up together. I've known them most of my life and now I'm finding out that the other two girls Shawn was involved with are involved with each other? I didn't even know you guys weren't straight!" She turned to me and asked, "Did you know?"

"You mean because we're supposed to be able to pick other queers out of a lineup?" I asked skeptically.

She elbowed me. "Quit being an ass. Obviously that's not what I meant. I mean, did they tell you?"

"I had no idea," I said. To be honest, I was still having a hard time wrapping my head around it myself. Not around them being queer, but around them dating.

"Thank our lord and savior Savannah Hollywood that you finally told them." Gavin exclaimed.

We all laughed at that before I asked Roxy, "So, how do you identify?"

"I'm bi-conic, and as mainstream as Savannah is, I adore her for embracing that term. In this car, we stan bi-con Savannah Hollywood."

I laughed at that. "I didn't peg you for a pop girlie."

"I'm not, but queer pop passes the vibe check."

I grinned at that, and Lynds asked to put on a Savannah Hollywood song. I was touched that Roxy passed her the aux chord. That was a whole new level of friendship. Ava snaked her left hand around the driver's seat to rest on Roxy's shoulder and squeezed it. Savannah Hollywood started blasting through the speakers and we all sang along at the top of our lungs and just like that, it felt like everything was right with the world again.

Laying on our towels on the beach, I rolled over to look at Lynds and asked, "Are you sure you're okay with seeing me with Shawn?"

She paused before scrutinizing me and asking, "It's not real, is it?"

I waved her off. "Of course not. Strictly revenge. Cross my heart, swear to lie, I'll do my best to make him cry, Shawn Parker must die."

"Oooh," Lynds said, smirking. "I like that. He deserves what's coming to him."

We understood what most of the rest of Harris High didn't yet, that when you idolize someone like they did Shawn, it made him into more than a boy. It made him larger than life, made him into a legend, and it was the legend of Shawn Parker, of the perfect football player who could do no wrong on or off the field, that needed to die. I couldn't continue to hear the school singing the praises of someone who had hurt my new friends. Whether or not they were still hurting, he had hurt them and he deserved to pay for it.

"Of course," Lynds said after a minute, "Roxy and Ava seem happy enough." She turned, laying on her back again, putting her sunglasses back over her eyes so I couldn't see them and said, "If you're just doing this for me, it's okay. You don't have to swoop in and rescue me."

"Is that what you think I'm doing?" I asked.

She nodded. "Of course you are, and I love you for it, but you don't have to."

I sighed. "It's not just for you, though. I mean, yes, it's mostly for you, and for Roxy and Ava, too, but you haven't been nearly as many places as I have, but Shawn Parkers are a dime a dozen out there. At every school I've been to, there's always a boy like him that has the school wrapped around his finger and all the girls at his beck and call. He can do no wrong. I mean seriously, the whole school knows he's unfaithful and yet they're still lining up to have a shot at him. It's mental if you ask me. I never understood it, and I've watched so many girls get hurt by guys just like him, and I'm sick of it. Those other times, I was never around long enough to help anyone, but this time is different. This time, he hurt you, and I'm here to stay, so mark my words, he's going to rue the day he hurt you."

She smiled softly at that. "I love you, too, and I'm glad you're stopping him hopefully before he has a chance to hurt anyone else. Before you stepped up into his line of fire, I really thought Grace was going to be next."

"Why do you care what happens to her?" I asked.

Grace hadn't so much as said a word to Lynds since the pictures came out. Lynds felt like she deserved it for breaking girl code since she had known Grace liked Shawn, too, but that was ridiculous. I had tried to tell Lynds time and time again that if the roles had been reversed, Grace wouldn't have thought twice about how Lynds would have felt about the situation if Shawn had been into her, but it didn't matter, Lynds still felt guilty.

"She was my best friend for a long time."

"A shitty one," I added.

She shrugged. "She wasn't the *best* friend, but she was *my* best friend."

"Was being the operative word. Why should you care about protecting her now?"

"Because I know she's still hurt by what I did, and just because she hurt me, doesn't mean I want to see her hurt. I tried reaching out to her to warn her about him, but she didn't bother responding."

That wasn't entirely true. They hadn't talked, but Grace had left more than enough vindictive comments about Lynds on the photos for it to be more than clear how she felt about her ex-best friend. She had left a good amount of similar comments on everything Tiger Shark Tea posted about Shawn with anyone, though, so I had been the target of quite a few of those now, too.

It was a little surprising that she would be bold enough to go after upperclassmen as a sophomore, though, but I supposed that was the benefit of having righteous indignation. She felt like the Lord was always supporting her, so it was easier to be loud about her nasty opinions and bigotry. People like her were the reason people like me felt like we couldn't live our truths and I hated that Lynds let someone like that get to her.

"Well, it's a good thing you have better friends now."

She looked back at me, saying, "It's a good thing I have the best cousin a girl could ever want. Cousin doesn't feel close enough, to be honest."

"We're basically sisters now. We share a room and everything."

She grinned at that. "Well, the best cousin, sister, friend anyone could ask for. I really don't know what I'd do without you."

"Without you, I'd still be on the road floating through school after school being a ghost. You guys gave me somewhere to belong to. I can't thank you enough for that."

I pulled her into a hug, and then Gavin yelled, "Let's hit the waves!"

Roxy and Ava disentangled from their towel where they were laying together, still holding hands. I grabbed Lynds's hand and Ava's, and Roxy grabbed Gavin's hand with her free one and together we ran screaming and laughing into the ocean.

# Chapter Twenty Four

"How was the lake?" I asked Shannon when I slid into my seat in English after the long weekend.

"It was fun!" she said, grinning. "Would've been better if you came, though."

"Would've been better if you invited me," I quipped.

She laughed. "Fair enough. Next time, you can come as my guest. That'll really show Shawn."

I grinned at her and was still smiling as class started.

"You ready for auditions, Shan?" Priya asked at lunch.

She smiled. "Ready as I'll ever be. I practiced a bit over the weekend. Sorry I missed you guys, though."

"It wasn't the same without you," one of the boys, Nate, said.

Shannon turned to me, explaining, "Us lifers always practice together before auditions. It's a ritual I ruined by being away for the weekend," she turned back to the table, "but I'll still be there for the last-minute night before practice sesh."

"Thank goodness, cause I'm sure you'll need it," Priya said while laughing at her own joke.

"Yeah, right," another one of the girls, Melissa, said. "We should just start calling her Juliet now."

I laughed with them, loving the ease they had with each other, but I couldn't help feeling a little left out. They had rituals with each other and a bond that I wouldn't ever have with any of them, and even though they weren't excited about doing Romeo and Juliet, it still sounded like it was going to be a lot of fun. I didn't want to miss out, but I was busy enough with actual school and planning with the gang for our Shawn revenge. I didn't really have time to take on another thing.

That didn't stop me from thinking about it all day, though. On the drive home, Lynds knew something was bugging me. When she asked, I couldn't lie.

"I think I want to try out for the school play," I said quickly, before I could change my mind about telling her.

"And you're nervous about it?" she asked slowly.

"Well, no. I mean yes, sort of." I wasn't sure how to explain that it wasn't the play I was nervous about. I was nervous about letting her and the girls down, but I didn't want to make her feel guilty either.

"We can practice your audition piece for the next couple of nights until auditions," she said, quickly. "I'm sure you'll do great!"

That wasn't really the reaction I expected.

"You think I should do it?"

"You want to, right?"

I paused before saying, "Yeah, I think I do."

"So why wouldn't I tell you to go for it?"

"It might keep me too busy," I said carefully.

"Do you think your grades would suffer? You're really smart. I wouldn't worry about that."

I couldn't believe she wasn't getting what I was trying to say. I took a deep breath and just came out with it. "I'm worried that I'll have less time for the Shawn plan or that he won't want a theatre kid who hangs out with his little sister and her friends."

She looked at me and shrugged. "If that's the case, then it is what it is. I'm mostly over it and you know Ava and Roxy are fine now, too."

I couldn't believe she was okay with me abandoning the plan. "You can't be serious?"

"Of course I am. You're family and I love you. I want the best for you, and I want you to enjoy your time here. You don't have to do everything for me, you know. You can do something for you."

"But we've put so much time and effort into this. If I don't go through with the plan, what was it all for?"

She rolled her eyes. "Yes, whatever will we do with the new friendships we've built? However will we live with all the wasted bonding time? How dare you do something for yourself."

I laughed. "Okay, okay, fine, but you think the others will feel the same?"

"Only one way to find out."

"Group meeting?"

"Group meeting," she agreed, and the "Shawn Parker Must Die" group chat dinged on my phone.

It dinged again almost immediately.

"Roxy said they're all in, meeting them at our diner for dinner."

Well at least that only gave me a couple of hours to be nervous about it.

# CHAPTER TWENTY FIVE

I waited until the food was eaten and we were almost ready to leave to finally come out with it.

"I think I'm going to try out for the school play."

I looked around their faces, waiting for a reaction. I was expecting some sort of outburst or annoyance, but Ava grinned, Gavin said, "Cool!", and Roxy looked puzzled before asking, "That's it?"

"What do you mean?" I asked.

Gavin elbowed her, and she quickly amended, "No, no that's super cool. It's just Lynds had us worried. We thought it was something serious."

"So you guys are okay with me trying out?"

"Of course!" Ava said.

"Definitely," Gavin confirmed.

"Why wouldn't we be?" Roxy asked.

It felt like déjà vu as I told them I was worried about it taking away from the plan with Shawn, that I was worried he wouldn't want a theatre kid and that I would ruin things, and just like Lynds, none of them were concerned about it.

"If that's how things work out, then so be it," Ava said, shrugging.

"Really?" I asked, looking at Roxy.

"Really," she agreed. "I think you've put in enough work that he'll still want you." Ava narrowed her eyes at Roxy, who laughed. "I know, I know. Just thinking out loud, but Aves is right, that's not the point. Shawny boy's awful and deserves to get karma-ed, but not at your expense. If we don't do it, I'm sure life'll take care of him, eventually."

"Besides," Ava added, "he brought us together, and that's not nothing," Ava said, squeezing Roxy's hand.

"Definitely not nothing," Roxy said, kissing Ava on the cheek before smiling at the rest of us, "but if you're asking me to be grateful for him, that's not happening. We happened despite him, not because of him. We all made this happen, not him, but," she said, turning her attention just to me, "if you don't want to keep going with the plan, I don't blame you. He'll get his, eventually. I care more about you being happy than him being unhappy."

I couldn't stop my eyes from tearing up at that. They all looked at me, concerned. Ava reached across the table and squeezed my hand. "What's wrong?"

"You guys are too much in the best way. I've never had anything like this before."

"Well, too much or not, you better get used to it cause you're stuck with us," Gavin interjected.

"Too much in all the right ways," I said. "Roxy, I can't believe you care about me more than getting revenge on Shawn."

The others burst into laughter at that.

A few moments later, she asked, "Have I been that obnoxious about it that it's that hard to believe I'd be willing to let it go?"

"You haven't been obnoxious," I said quickly, but Gavin said, "Of course you have," at the same time.

Ava piped up and said, "You've been a *little* obnoxious, but in the best way for the best reasons."

Roxy laughed at that before saying, "Okay, okay, I'll cool it a bit." She turned to me and said in a serious tone, "The council of vengeance has convened, in the matter of Bri vs the Shawn Parker Must Die group chat, the council rules in favor of Bri."

I threw a cold fry at her as we all laughed.

"So I'm really doing it?" I asked.

"You're really doing it," Lynds said.

"If you want to," Ava added.

Lynds elbowed me. "She does, she's doing it."

"Let us know if we can help?" Ava half asked, half told me.

"Thank you, guys. I might not even get in, though."

"You definitely will," Roxy said with such confidence it confused me.

"What makes you say that?" I asked.

"The way you've been walking Shawn like a dog tells me how good of an actress you are."

We all laughed at that, and that night I slept the best I had since school started.

# CHAPTER TWENTY SIX

The auditions snuck up on me. I was grateful I had only given myself a couple of days to stress about it, though. Shannon and the rest of the drama crew had been worried about it way longer.

Lynds practiced with me and told me I was ready, but I was still nervous. I had considered telling Shannon and the others that I was trying out, but ultimately decided not to. Part of me worried they wouldn't be supportive of competition and another part of me worried I wasn't good enough to get in and didn't want them to feel bad for me.

I was pacing around the parking lot rehearsing lines in my head when I heard a voice call, "Bridgette! hey!"

I looked up and saw Shawn jogging toward me. He grinned and pulled to a stop in front of me. "Glad I caught you. You're coming to the game tomorrow, right?"

I didn't really have time for him or any mind games, so I just shrugged and said, "Yeah the whole school'll be there, so I might as well."

He grinned, "Cool, cool," and raked his hand through his hair. "And you'll be at the party after?"

"Is that you asking me?" I asked, raising an eyebrow.

He chuckled at that. "Apparently my annoying little sis was right; I've lost my touch. Yes, this is me asking you. Please come to the party. I want to see more of you."

My phone buzzed and, happy for the distraction, I pulled it out quickly and saw a string of good luck texts coming through the group chat. I smiled at it, checking the time and seeing I really didn't have time to keep standing here.

"Sorry, I have to go," I said, moving to head to the school.

He grabbed my wrist lightly, stopping me as I walked by. The moment I stopped, he let go, seeming to realize he might've overstepped by grabbing me.

"Say you'll come?"

I looked between him and the school. I didn't have time for this.

"Yeah, I'll be there," I agreed.

He grinned.

"It's Shannon's house, too. She already invited me."

He deflated a little just like I wanted before shrugging. "Whatever gets you there. I suppose it's lucky for me I have an in with you, if that's what it takes."

"I have to go. See you around." I took a step before adding an afterthought. "Good luck at the game tomorrow."

He grinned. "I'll play better knowing you're watching."

I didn't respond, just took off in a jog toward the arts wing of the school.

"Catch ya later, Bridgette," he called after me.

# Chapter Twenty Seven

I hung out around a bend in the hallway, out of sight of the others, waiting until Shannon went in.

I was glad I waited because Priya squealed when she saw me. "You're here!"

The others turned to me and Nate asked, "Are you trying out?"

I fought a blush and tried to push away my nerves. "Maybe."

A chorus of excitement was thrown at me that made me grin. I was really glad they weren't upset. Nate immediately passed me the signup sheet. I grabbed my purple pen from my bag for luck and put my name down.

The sheet was immediately taken away by Priya saying, "You've signed the blood oath, no take backs now."

I laughed at that. "If I get in, I'm in, don't worry."

"You might regret saying that since you're up next."

I paled at that. I really thought I would have more time.

"Shannon went last?"

One of the girls nodded.

"So what are you guys all still doing here?"

Priya raised an eyebrow at me, saying, "Being good friends, and we're going out for ice cream after if you wanna come?" she offered.

"I'd love that. I'm so nervous I could use the sugar."

"You're one of us already," she said, grinning.

The others quieted, letting me mentally rehearse my lines while we waited for Shannon.

When she burst through the door, a whirl of nervous energy, the others surrounded her.

"I don't know how that went," she said.

"Amazingly I'm sure," Priya offered.

"I'm sure you did great!" one of the girls said.

"Guess who's next?" Nate asked her.

I could hear the confusion in her voice. "I thought I was last?"

"Nope. Someone squeaked in just under the wire."

They pulled out of their group hug, letting Shannon see me. She beamed and rushed to me, pulling me into a hug. "You're here! Ohmygosh you're going to do great! I'm so excited you're joining!"

She was squeezing me hard enough it was hard to respond.

"Easy there, Shan," Priya said. "You're crushing the girl." She laughed and loosened her grip.

"I'm here. Really nervous, though. I doubt I'm good enough."

"You're definitely good enough!" she said quickly. "Go ahead and get in there!" she said, pushing me toward the door before pulling me back a moment later. "Wait, are you coming with us for ice cream?"

"Definitely!"

Her smile widened. "Perfect. See you in a bit! Good-" She was elbowed by Nate, who hushed her and she immediately corrected, "Break a leg!"

I was confused before Priya explained, "The duck with an L word is bad juju in theatre, but you've got this!"

"You really do," Shannon said again, pushing me toward the door.

Mr. Hayes and a couple other adults I didn't know were there to watch and judge the auditions. I read for Juliet like all the girls did, but I was just hoping to be cast. I didn't care who, but I had made such a big deal about auditioning that I really hoped I would get in.

Shannon was the first to pull me into a hug when I opened the doors. A moment later, the others' arms were around me and Priya started chanting, "One of us, one of us," and the others picked up the call.

I started laughing and was sure I was grinning like a madman.

Shannon hitched a ride with me, and I let her have the aux chord, curious what she would put on. She looked at me when she hit play and a lesser-known Savannah Hollywood song came on. It felt like a test of some sort, but whatever it told her about me, I knew every word, which made her really happy. I was thrown off by her voice, though. She was good. Not just good, but 'could go professional' levels of good.

When I told her that she just laughed. "My singing is better than my acting. That's why I was so nervous about today."

"I'm sure you did great," I said quickly.

She laughed. "Thanks, but you're new here; you wouldn't know. You haven't seen me act yet."

"No, but I feel like I know you."

"And that implies I'm a good actress?"

"No, but your friends think you are."

"And you think they're right?"

"I trust your judgment and know you well enough to know you wouldn't suffer fools or flatterers as friends."

A surprised laugh flew out of her at that, and I felt a little burst of pride at having surprised her to laughter.

# Chapter Twenty Eight

Shannon and the others argued over who was buying my ice cream. According to Shannon, it "brought good duck with an L to whoever bought the newbie their post-audition treat."

To the teasing of the others, Shannon ended up buying mine even though everyone insisted she didn't need the luck.

I gave Shannon a ride home to the Parker Palace. She invited me in and laughed when I made a face at the suggestion. "I know, I know," she said. "Probably better to avoid him."

"He already cornered and persuaded me into going to the game tomorrow."

Her eyes widened in surprise. If he didn't run screaming if I turned into a theatre kid, she was going to be dealing with a lot of surprise when it came to me and her brother. I could only hope that if the revenge plan worked that her dislike of him was strong enough that she would take my side.

"Are you going?" I asked hopefully.

"Nah, it's not my thing."

"I figured, but he said everyone would be there."

She rolled her eyes. "When Shawn says *everyone*, he means his crew and little clique, the people that matter to him."

"Could you be convinced?" I asked.

She considered a moment before saying, "By you? Normally? Probably, but the first game of the year where they're going to hero worship my brother before he even proves himself, I'd rather not."

"Makes sense. Would've been nice to commiserate with you, though."

She laughed at that. "You don't have to go, you know."

"I know, but I promised Ava I'd be there to cheer on her cheering."

"You're a good friend. I'm really glad I met you," she said, hopping out of the car before I could return the sentiment. I rolled down the window to call out to her, but she was already dashing to her door, calling out, "See you tomorrow," over her shoulder.

# Chapter Twenty Nine

As I pulled up to the school for Friday night's football game wearing green and gold, I was cursing myself for not making more friends.

Ava was cheerleading at the game tonight, Lynds was with the band, and Shannon wasn't coming. Roxy and Gavin would be here though, which would have surprised me if I was still in the dark about her and Ava. Now I knew that, secret or not, she wouldn't miss her girlfriend's first game. Roxy had surprised me even more by agreeing to go to Parker's party after. Lynds was going out with some of the band after the game and told us to have fun without her. I was pleasantly surprised Roxy was coming with us this time, though. The party was sure to be more fun with her there.

I found an empty spot to park in and texted Roxy.

> Just got here. Do you know anyone I can sit with?

Her response was near instantaneous.

Roxy

> What? Did I offend you?

Course not

Roxy

You don't want to sit with me and Gavin?

She had to be messing with me, so I texted back.

Course I do. Just figured it was violating the 'keeping our distance' rule.

She started and then stopped typing and then started again. This happened a couple of times before I read,

Roxy

That's a lunch time rule. Game nights are different.

Thank goodness. I turned off the car and headed toward the field.

I was shocked to see Gavin decked out in green and gold with a large green foam finger.

"What's with the get-up?" I asked.

"Please, I'm a big sports ball fan," Gavin said with a forced straight face that I couldn't help laughing at.

"He likes to dress up," Roxy explained.

I devolved into another fit of giggles and was glad Gavin was laughing, too.

"We get to cuss out the other teams," he said conspiratorially.

"He learned real quick the more team spirit he's dressed in, the worse language he gets to use," Roxy said with a laugh.

I took a look at him and said, "So you're really pushing the limit today?"

He looked down and said, "No. Actually, this is pretty tame. I ramp it up further into the season."

It didn't look like he was joking, but he had to be.

"He's joking, right?" I asked Roxy.

"Oh, you sweet summer child, unfortunately no," she said, laughing at the shock on my face.

I settled in and as the game got underway, I realized just how shockingly little I knew about football.

It was hard to keep track of the players, too, not that it mattered. It wasn't like I actually had to be watching Shawn. I cheered when other people did and joined in a lewd chant Gavin started about the other team's mothers Gavin had to have invented.

Against all odds, I was having fun.

I would've been miserable sitting by myself, but I was still confused why it was okay to be sitting with them now.

After a while of wondering, I finally asked Roxy, "So what makes the seating at games different?"

"Easy," she said. "We're packed in enough that you can hardly control who you're next to. Plausible deniability. Besides, Shawny boy and all his friends are a little too busy to pay attention to us."

She was probably right, but I had to ask, "What if they notice?"

She grinned. "Well, then Shawny boy's not gonna sleep so well wondering what I could be saying about him." I laughed at that. "But seriously, odds are low he'll notice."

She was wrong, though. During half-time, the players all whipped off their helmets while running to the sidelines and I found Shawn's mop of blond hair. As I watched, he scanned the stands with his eyes, stopping when he saw me and gave me a wink and a wave.

I blushed as people turned around to see who the girl was that had caught his attention. He looked over, noticed Roxy, and a confused frown hit his face for a moment before he winked one more time in case I or anyone else had missed the first one.

"Parker!" the coach yelled loud enough that his voice floated into the stands. "Get your head in the game!" He shrugged and loped over to the others.

There were quite a few girls glaring at me jealously, but the worst was coming from a brunette I recognized. Grace, Lynds's ex-best friend. I couldn't help myself. I gave her a little wave and a smirk. She crossed her arms in disbelief before whirling back around.

Roxy had been watching and said, "She's the worst."

"Seriously though."

"But dude," Roxy said, refocusing, "Shawn's never singled out a girl at a game before."

"Really?"

"Really," she said, bumping her shoulder into mine. "Why do you think everyone's so confused about it?"

"So, you think our plan still might work?"

She grinned. "I think we've got him right where we want him and I don't think anything could change it."

# Chapter Thirty

They won.

It was pandemonium.

Roxy followed me to my house to drop my car off and drove me to the Parker Palace.

We had to park even further away this time. Apparently, Shawn hadn't been kidding when he said the whole school would be here. Well, the upperclassmen anyway. There had to be at least three times the people that were at the last party. The party had expanded from inside the house to the front lawn. There was a table set up for beer pong and people already seemed trashed. I had no idea how that was possible when we had basically come right here from dropping my car off. We weren't the first ones to leave the school, but we weren't anywhere near the last.

The team hadn't even made it here yet.

"How's the party already going without Shawn and the rest of the team?"

"They always do that," Roxy said. "Don't know why the Millionaire Mayor puts up with it, but they almost always throw parties after home games."

"Without anyone home?"

I knew Shannon wasn't the one throwing them. I doubted she was here tonight, since she hadn't even wanted to go to the game. The afterparty, where everyone was sure to be celebrating Shawn even more loudly and proudly, seemed like a more unlikely place to find her.

"They pick a few party ambassadors to come set up the house after each game, and I wouldn't put it past the mayor to have staff for that sort of thing."

"So, how long are we staying?" I asked, surveying the already chaotic scene in the front.

"Not sure. We'll play it by ear, but assuming you still want to give the plan a shot, you should probably get some face time in with Shawny boy," Roxy suggested.

She wasn't wrong. Apparently, I had my hooks in him pretty deep if he was singling me out during the game. Even if I was breaking out of my role a little by trying out for the fall play, I still wanted to give the plan my all until it was proven it wasn't going to work.

"Let's try to stay awhile," Gavin said. "Since I'm not recon this time, I wanna enjoy myself."

"Should we not be seen together once we're inside?" I asked.

"Doesn't matter here either," Roxy said, grinning. "It's a party, anything goes."

We got swept into the music and the noise the moment we entered. The party was in full swing. You would never be able to guess that a lot of these people had just arrived; a lot of them were already halfway to passed out.

I wondered if anyone would still be up and going by the time the team got here.

I did a lap with Gavin, looking for familiar faces. I saw a few, but most of the people I knew would be here were on the football team or cheer squad, none of which had arrived yet.

I slid outside and was dismayed to see the backyard that had been an oasis last time was overflowing with people. There were people packed like sardines into the pool and people yelling and dancing out there, too. It wasn't until my eyes fell on the pool house pub that I realized I had been looking for Shannon. I didn't really expect to see her, but it hadn't stopped me from looking just in case. Not only was she not there, but what had been an open window over the counter last time was closed up.

Not only was she not here to provide an escape, but it didn't look like I could hide in her fort, either. After a few minutes and dodging a few boys that tried to pull me into the pool and into conversation, I figured inside was the lesser of two evils. At least in there, people couldn't talk to me.

I tried to open the sliding door, but it wouldn't budge. I knocked on the glass, but no one came to open it. I tried waving down some people who looked my way, but they just waved back at me. After another minute of making no headway with the door, I gave up and made my way to the front of the house. I weaved through the people packed on the front lawn, heading for the front door, when a school bus roared onto the street, slowing to a stop in front of the house.

I stared in shock as the door opened, and the team came spilling out onto the lawn towards the house. I thought about making my escape back to the backyard, but knew there was no real point. I was almost positive Shawn had already seen me, anyway. Trying to hide from him at his own party would be pointless. I stayed there, frozen to the spot, waiting. He was one of the last people to get off the bus. It surprised me that he stopped to thank the bus driver. It was crazy to me that there was a school bus here at all, that the mayor was able to swing letting the team use the bus for transport to the party. I wondered if the cheer squad would be showing up soon in a different bus.

When Shawn got to the lawn, he scanned the area, and, locking eyes with me, he broke into a grin yelling, "You came!" He ran over to me, picking me up and spinning me around while letting out a victory cry.

A moment later he set me down, but he yelled out for anyone to hear, "We won the game, and I'm going to win the girl!"

I just rolled my eyes at him and asked, "Did you already start drinking?"

He grinned. "We have a locker room stash for wins."

"What about for losses?"

"An even bigger stash. Come on," he said, taking my hand. "It's a million degrees. I could use a dip in the pool."

He didn't ask how I was doing or if I wanted to join him, just dragged me along. If that was how tonight was going to go, I wasn't sure how long I could manage it here. He got around to the back of his house and saw the pool was packed and frowned, before yelling out, "Parker says 'senior swim time.'" A bunch of people grumbled, but over half of them scrambled out of the pool. After a few stragglers left, there was more than enough room in there for us.

"Are you always this bossy?" I asked.

"It's my house, I can be." He shrugged. "I can't help that I know what I want and go for it. Like right now," he said, looking me up and down, "I want you to strip off anything you don't want getting wet."

"What?" He couldn't be serious, but just in case, I took off my mesh sweater, revealing my tank top underneath. Next, I slipped off my flip-flops and pulled my phone out of my shorts' pocket, tossing it onto my sweater on the ground.

"Really?" he asked.

I shrugged. "You're gonna have to try harder than that to undress me."

He smirked, "I do like a challenge," then he tossed down his own phone, tore off his shoes, and peeled off his shirt.

I took the moment to look around for Roxy or Gavin, but neither of them were in sight. When I looked back at Shawn, he had on a cocky grin. The moment my attention was back on him, he moved his hand from his washboard abs to the waistband of his shorts. I was sure from the disappointment that flitted across his face that he was expecting me to look more interested. I could've faked it, but the truth was, I wasn't impressed.

I knew he was objectively handsome, but as far as I was concerned, he was ugly on the inside, so I would never be able to find him attractive. Not that he knew that, and from what the others had told me, he certainly wasn't used to not impressing girls.

Well, there was a first time for everything and if he was going to continue spending time around me, he was going to have to get used to it.

He lunged for me, and I jumped back with a squeal, but it was too late. He scooped me up in his arms and in two bounds, we were at the pool, and then we were flying through the air. We hung suspended for a moment before hitting the water. It was refreshing and, as much as I wanted to be annoyed, it had been a good idea.

We popped up to the surface, and he grinned at me. "Just what I needed."

A minute later, some of the other guys from the team came roaring into the backyard with some of the cheer squad in tow. I was relieved to see Ava was with them. The guys started jumping into the pool and Shawn pulled me into him, hugging me to him. I couldn't decide if I should be happy he was keeping me out of the way of the guys jumping in or annoyed he was taking advantage of the situation by pressing my body to his.

I watched Ava, thrilled when she finally looked over. Her eyes widened as she took me in and I gave her a little wave.

"Jer-bear!" she called out. I looked over and saw Jeremiah was one of the people in the pool with us. "What do you say we challenge Parker and Bridgette to a game of chicken?"

I didn't know whether to be thrilled at the situation or annoyed with Ava, but it was a good idea, especially drawing in Jeremiah. She was basically begging for us to be on Tiger Shark Tea again, though. With Shawn, Jeremiah, and me, it seemed inevitable.

Before checking with me, Shawn ducked under the water and grasped my legs, pulled me onto his shoulders, and then started to come up. I wavered a little before grabbing his hair to steady myself.

When he was fully standing he said, "Damn, I like it when a girl gets a little rough."

I was tempted to release my grip on him and topple over, disqualifying us, but he had a tight grip on my thighs, and I wasn't sure I'd be able to get away that easily, so I stayed where I was. He walked us over to where Ava was now perched on Jeremiah's shoulders.

A junior I recognized from a couple of my classes, but didn't really know, ended up playing ref and the boys went at it. Ava and I were gentle and mostly giggled about them fighting it out. Shawn was going a lot harder than necessary and kept trying to dunk Jeremiah under the water instead of push him off balance. Eventually Shawn managed to get the upper hand on Jeremiah, and Ava went down.

We went two more rounds, with Jeremiah and Ava winning one while we won the final round. By the time we were done we were all soaked. To my relief, Ava said she was calling it a night. I quickly agreed and was going to say goodbye to Shawn when he asked, "Want some dry clothes?"

I was surprised he offered. I thought for sure he would've taken every minute he could to ogle at me in my now skintight tank top clinging to my chest. I leaned down and grabbed my phone and sweater and slipped my shoes back on. "Do you have something I can wear?"

"I'm sure Shannon does. Come on."

I thought about objecting. I was pretty sure if I were anyone else, she would mind that he was offering her clothes up, but I was starting to get chilly and Shannon and I were friends, I was reasonably sure she would be okay with me borrowing some of her clothes.

He took my hand and led me into the house. The door stuck for him, too, but either it needed more brute strength than I had applied or there was a trick to it since, after cursing at the door, it opened on his second try.

He brought me up the stairs and opened a door to what had to be Shannon's room. He shut the door behind me, blissfully closing out some of the noise. I looked around, my attention instantly snagging on the ivy covering a portion of her wall and the wisteria draped from the ceiling. I went over to her dresser and noticed she had what looked like a collection of old vinyls that I was dying to look through, but it didn't feel right looking through her stuff without her here. I debated whether to grab something from her dresser or her closet.

I figured the bottom drawers of the dresser probably had the comfort clothes I was looking for, but when I got closer to the dresser, the mirror grabbed my attention. She had it lined with photos and what looked like notes of song lyrics and tucked up in a corner, I was surprised to see my familiar writing. I looked closer and saw she had saved one of our notes. It was so adorable that I couldn't help but smile.

I heard a knock on the door and yelled over, "Not ready yet." I doubted very much that I was heard, though. Feeling short on time, I abandoned the dresser and went over to the closet. It felt less invasive looking through it, since there wasn't a door on it. I grabbed a Lake Tahoe sweatshirt that smelled like her strawberry and coconut scent and a pair of yoga pants.

I quickly stripped out of my wet clothes and put them on.

They were cozy, and all of a sudden the day caught up with me. I was exhausted and even more glad to be leaving. I shot a text to Roxy to see if they were leaving soon too or if I should catch a ride with Ava.

Roxy texted back almost immediately that they had looked everywhere for me and were ready to go, too.

I rushed out before Shawn could find me again and met them on the front porch.

When I told them I had been upstairs, they made jokes the entire ride back to my house about how I was going above and beyond for the plan and that I hadn't needed to see his room. I just rolled my eyes at them and let them have their fun. I felt extra cozy in Shannon's sweatshirt and couldn't wait to get to bed.

# CHAPTER THIRTY ONE

I woke up at what I considered to be far too early and was surprised to see I had a text from Shannon.

The Better Parker

So we're on the clothing stealing level of our relationship?

It took me a minute to remember what she was talking about. I had taken her sweatshirt and yoga pants and was still wearing them. I hadn't even bothered changing when I got home, just collapsed into bed.

Sorry! Shawn said it was fine - normally I wouldn't have, but I was freezing. I figured since it was me, you'd be okay with it.

I'm sorry. I should've texted and asked.

The Better Parker

No worries! Don't stress, you were right, because it was you, I don't care, but he better not be handing out my clothes to any of his friends.

Glad he told you - sorry I would've told you sooner, but I just woke up.

She texted a string of laughing emojis and then,

I wondered for a moment how she knew then before realizing that must mean I took something she missed immediately.



Another string of laughing emojis came my way, and she added,



She attached a link to the Tiger Shark Tea page.

I groaned. It was far too early for this, but I couldn't ignore it now. I clicked on it and read:

---

### Tiger Shark Tea

---

*Bridgerella strikes again except this time, instead of leaving part of herself behind, looks like she's leaving with more than she came with.*

*Spotted: Bridgette Tanner coming down from upstairs, leaving the Parker Palace with damp hair in clothes that aren't hers, and a few minutes later, Shawn coming down those same stairs damp with rumpled hair. Looks like Harris High's star player might've gotten lucky on more than just the field.*

I was worried, but to my surprise, later that day there was an update with pictures of us playing chicken.

| Tiger Shark Tea |
| --- |

*Update: it's not often I'm wrong, but apparently things were getting hot and steamy in the backyard pool, not in the upstairs of the Parker Palace. Bridgette was seen on Parker's shoulders while her and his ex, Ava, and his teammate, Jeremiah, went at it in the tensest game of chicken that's ever been played.*

*Sources say after the players called it quits, they were all quick to leave.*

*Bridgette, if you're reading this - I'm sure everyone would love to know whose clothes those are if nothing happened with Shawn - my DMs are open.*

I rolled my eyes. Yeah, right. I was glad they had retracted the implication that I messed around with Shawn, but they weren't fooling me into thinking they had my back. I didn't have to know who they were to know I couldn't trust them and wouldn't be messaging them anytime soon.

# Chapter Thirty Two

After the final bell Monday, I headed to the theatre wing. Our table had spent all of lunch talking about how the cast list was going to be put up today.

No one doubted that Shannon would be Juliet, but no one was sure about Romeo. There were only a few guys in theatre, so it was highly possible Romeo could be a woman. It was pretty common for Shakespeare to really test people's acting abilities in that way. I wondered who would get to be the romantic lead to Shannon's Juliet. We hadn't seen each other's auditions, of course, so no one agreed who would be right for the role. I was just hoping to be cast in any sort of role. I had been pretty nervous, though, so it wouldn't surprise me if I hadn't made the cut.

I turned the corner and ran into Shannon, who was standing there with the rest of the group. My phone buzzing in my pocket told me my friends were wishing me good luck. I smiled at Shannon, who reached for my hand and squeezed it.

I looked around for the cast list, but didn't see anything.

"Nothing yet," Shannon said, tracking my movement.

"Should be any minute now though," Priya said.

Before anyone else could respond, the doors burst open, and Mr. Hayes walked out. He had a paper in hand that had to be the cast list.

"Now, now," he said, "before I post this, I need you all to know these weren't easy decisions and the decisions aren't done being made. We were able to decide on everyone except for our dear Romeo. Our dear Romeo has alluded us, so there will be callbacks on Wednesday for his role. Those picked for the callback will read with our Juliet for the part. We ask that you truly ask yourself, as Juliet did, 'wherefore art thou Romeo?' Ask yourself, as Juliet did, what makes Romeo Romeo and embody it. Romeo and Juliet is one of the bard's most performed works for a reason, and I want each and every one of you to do everything you can to truly make this show shine."

With that, he turned and, with a flourish, put up the cast list. We all rushed in to see it. Shannon's name was at the top for Juliet, which was surprising to no one. She was still holding my hand, so I gave hers a squeeze. We all knew she had the role, of course, but I was happy for her.

I had wondered if I might feel a little jealous, but I didn't. I wouldn't have been suited to Juliet the way that she was. Romeo talked about Juliet as the sun, lighting up his world, and the way sunny haired

Shannon was beaming at seeing her name up there, I couldn't think of anyone who would make a better Juliet.

I was still looking at Shannon when her face fell and she looked back at me, frowning, and squeezed my hand hard. I hadn't really expected to make it into the show, though. I looked back and trailed down the list and sure enough, my name wasn't on it.

"I'm so sorry," Shannon said softly while all around us, the others squealed in delight and celebrated.

"That's okay," I said, surprised to find I meant it. "I'm excited for you, and I'll be front row at the first show cheering you all on."

She examined me a little longer, searching for something in my face. Whatever she found made her smile softly. "Promise?"

"Definitely."

After some of the fanfare died down, Mr. Hayes continued, "And for our potential Romeos, there are but two. One will be our dear Romeo and the other our merry Mercutio." He tacked up the other piece of paper.

I hadn't seen the names yet when I heard Shannon's sharp inhale and felt her squeeze my hand hard. I quickly turned to look at her and she squealed and started jumping up and down. I joined her, confused but happy she was happy.

"I can't believe it!" she squealed.

"Why are we jumping?" I asked, giggling at how giddy she was. From the way she was squealing, I figured it had to be someone she had a thing for, and I wondered who it could be, who I was going to get to watch her with at the show.

She stopped and looked at me surprised. "You didn't look?"

"You beat me to it," I said with a shrug, "but I'm happy you're happy."

She just looked at me dumbfounded before saying, "Of course I'm happy! You did it!"

I couldn't have heard her right.

"I did it? Did what?"

She just huffed and pulled me to the wall and pointed at the second name on the list. Right after Stephanie Rollins, it read Bridgette Tanner. I blinked at it, waiting for it to change, for the world to make sense again, but it still said my name.

"I got cast?" I asked.

"You got cast!" Shannon exclaimed.

"I got cast!" I cried out, and we both started jumping up and down squealing again. I couldn't believe it. I had no idea what they saw in me at my audition, but I was going to be Mercutio to Steph's Romeo and I was so excited for it.

The next day and a half, I ate, slept, and breathed Shakespeare. Shannon and the others agreed that we would celebrate Friday since apparently it was also bad luck to celebrate before the entire show had been cast. Callbacks were Wednesday and the final casting would be posted on Friday. I wasn't sure why anyone was unsure about it, though. Stephanie was a senior who had done theatre every year. I was the new kid with no acting experience. It was a miracle I was cast at all, nevermind as Mercutio. It was nothing short of a miracle if I was being honest.

I practiced hard, though, not because I thought I had a chance at Romeo, but because we'd both be reading in front of Mr. Hayes with Shannon and I wanted to impress Shannon, and I didn't want to give Mr. Hayes and the others any reason to question their decision to give me a chance.

# Chapter Thirty Three

Callbacks were over before I knew it. Even though it was incredibly nerve-wracking, running lines with Shannon had been more fun than I thought. Getting to court her as a lovesick Romeo had been a good time. The others had said she was a good actress, but seeing her perform, they had undersold her.

She was flawless. It was so easy to see her as a love-struck teenager pining over a boy who circumstance and her family were keeping from her. When I kissed her hand, she was even able to manufacture a blush and giggled a little. I didn't remember Juliet giggling in the script, but it was authentic and felt real. I was in awe of her and told her so after and again in class on Thursday and at lunch until she was finally sick of it and told me that I was acting a bit too much like Romeo.

I grinned at that and said, "Well I'll have to stop then, because I'm sure Mercutio wouldn't be making moves on Juliet."

Shannon laughed at that and said, "Don't be so sure about casting. I think you have a real chance at Romeo."

"Thank you," I told her. She was incredibly sweet, but she was biased. We were friends. Of course, she thought I was good. I was decent. I had to have been to have made it to the callback, but I wasn't better than Stephanie.

Apparently Mr. Hayes and the others disagreed. They didn't even make us wait until after school Friday; they posted the announcement Friday morning.

I was *Romeo*.

*I* was Romeo.

I couldn't believe it.

It was all we could talk about at lunch. We were going out to dinner tonight to celebrate, and I couldn't wait.

When Shawn managed to find me after last bell and asked me if he would see me at the game that night, I was excited to have an excuse to say no.

"I'm sorry, I already have plans."

"You're not gonna be there?" he asked, deflating.

I shook my head. "Sorry, Shannon and I have plans."

He raised an eyebrow at that. "You're skipping the game to hang out with my little sister and her group of theatre geeks?"

I wasn't sure if it was my anger at the comment or the want to get the charade over with, but I told him, "Yup, you're looking at Shannon's co-lead theatre geek."

He paled and rushed to say, "Come on, I didn't mean it like that. I didn't know you were into theatre."

I shrugged. "Sounds like you don't know a whole lot about me, then."

"Maybe I don't, but I'd like to."

"You want to get to know a theatre geek?"

"I shouldn't have said that. If you like theatre, there's probably something cool about it. I'm just used to my dorky little sister talking about it. I didn't mean to upset you. I'm sorry."

"She's my friend," I said. "I know she's your little sister, but she's my friend."

"Got it. She's still a dork, though," he said, but this time, the inflection was different. It felt like more of an endearment than an insult like it had before.

I gave him a break and gave him 3 more digits. He was grinning like a fool and pumped his fist in the air, John Bender from the Breakfast Club style, when he walked away, leaving me giggling.

# Chapter Thirty Four

Dinner was so much fun. I spent lunch with them, but this was different. Now I was really one of the crew and apparently, I had signed up for a lot more than just the actual rehearsals. There were meet ups on non-rehearsal days and practices outside of drama club. I knew I was going to be busy, but I hadn't really understood how much of my time it would take up.

At least I had already talked to the others about it, and if it made Shawn's head turn elsewhere, they were okay with it. Although I wasn't discouraged yet. He hadn't been horrible about me joining theatre, so maybe there was a chance I could do the play and still continue with the plan. Maybe I really could have it all.

Shannon asked to hitch a ride home with me after dinner. We had stayed out late and by the time we got to her house, the party was in full swing. She halfheartedly invited me in, but I couldn't have been paid enough to brave the party right now.

I felt horrible looking at how tired she looked, though, as she rallied herself to go inside.

The idea came out of my mouth the moment the thought formed. "Do you want to sleep over tonight?"

She looked at me in surprise. "Really?"

I shrugged. "Yeah, why not? I doubt you wanna be here anymore than I want to."

She smiled a little, saying, "Thanks, but I don't want to impose. I'm not sure your family would be okay with it."

I knew Auntie Jen and Uncle Cam would be fine with it, and I was pretty sure Lynds wouldn't mind, but Shannon was right, I should probably check.

I pulled out my phone and texted Lynds.



I didn't have to wait more than a few seconds for her response.



"My aunt and uncle couldn't care less and Lynds said you're welcome as long as we stop for ice cream."

"Really?" she asked, her smile growing.

"Yeah. Why's that so surprising?"

She shrugged. "I mean I'm Shawn's sister and after how he treated her, I wasn't sure Lyndsey would want to be near me."

I waved away her concerns. "Please, she doesn't blame you for that." She still didn't look convinced though, so I added, "If she was still holding a grudge about that, I for sure wouldn't be caught dead talking to Shawn."

"Good point, but if I know him, which I definitely do, he's not giving you much of a chance to get away from him."

"You're not wrong," I said, laughing. "So, are you gonna go pack?"

She sighed, looking at the house and then back at me. "You still have my Tahoe sweatshirt and yoga pants, right?"

I did. I had kept meaning to return them, but kept forgetting. If I was telling the truth, though, they were so comfy I didn't want to give them back. "I was hoping you'd forgotten."

She laughed. "Keep them if you want as long as I can borrow something of yours."

"Sounds good," I said with a grin. "Between me and Lynds you should be able to borrow whatever else you need."

"Great, cause I really didn't want to go in there."

"I don't blame you."

I sat in between Lynds and Shannon on the couch as we polished off the ice cream and watched The Breakfast Club. Shannon and Lynds had both seemed nervous, but throughout the movie, they were laughing at the same parts which quickly broke the ice. I loved seeing them getting along. Lynds could use more friends, and I really liked Shannon, too.

I offered to get Shannon the air mattress, but she didn't want me to go to the trouble and said she could just share with me. With Shannon and me in my twin bed, it was going to be a tight squeeze, though.

When she laid down on the edge of the bed, there was more space between us than I expected. Then I noticed it was because she was perched on the edge of the bed, basically falling off. She couldn't have been comfy.

I moved back a little, pressing my back against the wall, and whispered, "There's more room if you want to get closer."

"Are you sure?" she asked quietly.

"Absolutely. Come cuddle your Romeo, Juliet."

She giggled and moved back a little, but she still didn't look comfy and there was more room.

I whispered in her ear, "There's more room if you want to get closer."

She shuttered. I must have surprised her with my closeness.

"Are you sure?" she asked again.

"Absolutely. Quit being stubborn. We're gonna have to kiss plenty for the play. I think you can deal with cuddling with me."

She didn't say anything, but she scooted closer to me until her back touched my front. My left arm was under her pillow, but I didn't know what to do with my right. I tried tucking it at my side, but it wasn't remotely comfy and didn't feel natural. After a minute of Shannon still being incredibly stiff and me not being all that comfy either, I figured it wouldn't hurt to try actually cuddling. I wrapped my right arm around her middle and pulled her tighter to me, so she wasn't in danger of falling off the bed.

She let out a little squeak when I grabbed her before stifling it quickly. I was glad since I didn't want to wake Lynds up. She was probably already sleeping.

"Is this okay?" I asked.

She nodded.

"Comfier?" I asked.

Again, she nodded.

As she began to relax, I found my thumb tracing the bottom hem of the tank top she was wearing. Feeling her warm skin and her soft tank top was comforting. A few minutes later, her breathing settled into a rhythm that told me she was likely asleep. I fell asleep shortly after that.

# CHAPTER THIRTY FIVE

If Auntie Jen and Uncle Cam were surprised or upset to have company at breakfast Saturday morning, they were kind enough not to say. They embraced and welcomed Shannon like they had Roxy and Gavin. The little things like that took me from feeling like a visitor to feeling like I was home. I never used to have friends to invite to sleepovers, but even if I had, I never would've been able to with my mother. Things at our place were always too unpredictable; she was too unpredictable. It was so nice being somewhere normal where I didn't have to worry about what sort of mood Auntie Jen or Uncle Cam would be in. They were always loving and welcoming to me and anyone I brought home, and I was so thankful for that.

Shannon seemed to love their attention, too. She was more than willing to answer all their questions about school, and they were thrilled to find out her and I were co-starring in the play together.

I offered to bring her home after breakfast, but she suggested we run lines instead.

"What if we all help out?" Lynds offered.

I was about to tell her, Auntie Jen, and Uncle Cam that they didn't have to, but Shannon beamed at the suggestion.

"Like a table read?" she asked.

"Yeah, just like that. What do you say, Mom? Dad?"

Auntie Jen looked at Uncle Cam and said, "I always thought I would make a good actress. What do you say?"

"Spending a Saturday with the bard? I'm in."

We cleared the breakfast table and Uncle Cam went to his office to print more copies of the script while Auntie Jen brought me, Lynds, and Shannon to their room. "I think I have some fun costume pieces in here somewhere," she said, gesturing for us to sit on the bed while she went into the walk-in closet.

A moment later she popped out with a dress that looked straight out of a ren faire. It was a deep purple with poofed up then draped sleeves and a cinched waist with ties in the front. "What do you think for Juliet?"

Shannon's eyes lit up. "Absolutely yes! It's probably better than anything the costume department will be able to whip up for the actual play."

They had been asking for donations of old clothes that could be turned into new pieces for the show, but it wasn't looking promising yet and only period dresses the costume department still had seen better days and desperately needed a refresh. Even in their heyday, though, I was sure none of the dresses they had were as pretty as this one.

"Well, if it fits well enough, you're welcome to wear it for the actual show," Auntie Jen said.

Shannon gasped. "Really?"

"Of course!" she said. "Now come here. Let's see if the costume gods are on our side."

It turns out they were, since it fit her perfectly.

"You look incredible!" I marveled.

Shannon grinned. "Spoken like a true Romeo."

I laughed. "That was coming from Bri. I mean it, that dress was made for you."

"It really was," Lynds said.

Shannon blushed, looking guiltily at Auntie Jen, but Auntie Jen looked delighted. "Give us a twirl," she told Shannon.

Shannon twirled, grinning and giving us a cute little curtsy.

Auntie Jen was able to scrounge up some oversized shirts for me and Lynds that looked like poet shirts. I could've easily pictured the bard himself in something similar, so it seemed fitting for Romeo.

Uncle Cam called in that the scripts were ready. Auntie Jen went out to the kitchen and told him to sit at the table. When he sat, she called out announcing Lyndsey as Benvolio, me as Romeo, and lastly Shannon as Juliet. He clapped when each of us entered, complimenting our outfits, and we sat down and read lines. I stuck with Romeo and Shannon with Juliet, while the others filled in the rest of the cast. Auntie Jen did a hilarious job with Juliet's nurse and Uncle Cam made a very dramatic Mercutio. Lynds took to Tybalt better than I would have imagined, waving around an imaginary sword and gleefully fake stabbing her father.

The hardest piece of acting was not cracking up every five seconds at how ridiculous my family was. I loved them all so much and I was thrilled that Shannon was enjoying herself, too. She didn't seem as distracted by them as I was, though, since she was still able to act well enough to produce a blush on her cheeks when I kissed her on the cheek.

Lynds had booed at me for going off script, but Auntie Jen and Uncle Cam had just laughed. My aunt said, "I'll allow it," and so I stuck to her cheek for the other kissing scenes, too.

We were going to have to practice the kisses at some point, but even if they were just stage kisses, I certainly didn't want the first time to be in front of my family. I was sure the first time was going to be awkward, and I didn't want any more witnesses than necessary.

# Chapter Thirty Six

Auntie Jen and Uncle Cam insisted Shannon stay for dinner after. I told her she didn't have to, but she assured me she didn't have anywhere else to be and that she was having a good time, so she stayed.

After dinner, we watched another movie, this time as a family. We picked out Romeo & Juliet, pausing the movie every few minutes to laugh about how we had done this or that better.

After the movie, I drove her home. When I got to her house and stopped the car in front of her house, she made no move to get out. Sensing she wanted to talk, I put the car in park and reached over to her. I intended to pat or squeeze her shoulder to offer moral support, but was surprised when she turned to me and grabbed my hand, squeezing it. I hadn't noticed that she was this touchy feely with her other friends, but she always seemed willing to touch me. I was touched that she felt so comfortable with me.

It was then I noticed why she had been so quiet on the ride here. There were tear stains on her face.

"What's wrong? Are you okay?" The moment I asked I started mentally berating myself for asking that stupid of a question. Of course, she wasn't okay. People didn't cry for no reason.

She nodded and then shook her head. "I'm sorry. We had such a great day. I had a really good time, I promise," she sniffled.

I wasn't sure what to say but sensed she wasn't done yet, so I waited.

After a little more silence, she said, "I love your family so much. It's just your aunt reminds me so much of my mother, and I miss her a lot."

I wracked my brain trying to remember what, if anything, I had heard about Shawn and Shannon's mother, but came up blank. I'd heard plenty about the Millionaire Mayor, but nothing about his wife.

"What happened?" I asked, squeezing her hand.

"Cancer, a few years ago," she said quietly. "She would've really liked you," she said before adding, "Today was great, but it still hurts that my mom isn't here, that her and I don't get days like that anymore."

Now I could feel my own eyes starting to water. "I know what you mean."

"Is your mom-" she started before trailing off, but I knew what she was asking.

I shook my head. "She's alive, but things are complicated. She's complicated."

I wasn't sure what else to say, but Shannon squeezed my hand comfortingly and waited silently, allowing me to choose whether to continue, so I told her. "My mom's an addict. That's why we used to move around as much as we did. I'm not actually supposed to be here. We were supposed to stay with my uncle and aunt, her sister, for a couple of days in between places, but when Auntie Jen saw how bad Mom had gotten, she gave her an ultimatum. Either she stayed here with me and got clean, or she left."

I felt my own tears come when Shannon asked, "And I'm guessing I didn't meet her because she made the wrong choice?"

I swallowed past the lump in my throat, wiped away some of my tears with my sleeve, and nodded. "I miss her sometimes, but I'm happier here. I feel guilty for that sometimes, but I couldn't keep living with the stress of having to take care of her, of worrying if this time was going to be the time she didn't make it. I feel guilty about it, but I can't stop myself from wishing sometimes that Auntie Jen and Uncle Cam were my parents."

Shannon squeezed my hand and said, "Thank you for telling me that. I knew you were brave, I just had no idea how brave."

We shared sad smiles while trying not to cry. I fanned my face with my free hand, and she let out a little laugh. "I'm sorry. I didn't mean to make things so deep."

"No, no, you're fine," I said, pulling her toward me. I let go of her hand and looped my arm around her shoulders. She rested her head on my shoulder. "I'm glad we talked. I hope you know I'm always here if you need someone, and I feel confident speaking for the rest of the family that the Matthews household is always open to you whenever you need anything."

She sniffled some more at that before saying, "Thank you, so much. I'm so glad you're here."

"I am, too." As guilty as I felt, I was happy here. I was at the point where I couldn't imagine my life without my new friends and Shannon in it.

# CHAPTER THIRTY SEVEN

Sunday morning before I could even say good morning to Lynds, my phone was ringing. I picked it up with a groggy, "Hello?"

"Did you see what that hoe did?" Roxy yelled instead of a greeting.

"What hoe? What's going on?" I asked.

I heard Gavin in the background say, "You have to give her more context than that. Besides, he's not a hoe, he's a man hoe."

"Well, him too, but I was talking about her. Is Lynds up?"

I looked over and saw she was sitting up in bed, looking at me questioningly. "She's up," I told them.

"Put us on speaker. I gotta know if she's seen it," Roxy said.

I put her on speaker, and Roxy immediately asked, "Did you see it?"

I expected Lynds to be confused, but she wasn't. "I did. I'm sure she's thrilled."

"Okay, someone fill me in. What happened?"

"Lynds, you wanna take this, or should I?" Roxy asked.

"There's a picture of Shawn with Grace at last night's party. They're just hugging, but Tiger Shark Tea is saying that Shawn must have caught another case of the wandering eye."

"I'm going to make his case of wandering eye terminal if he keeps treating people like garbage," Roxy said.

"So, what do we think?" I asked.

"It's probably still salvageable," Roxy said after a long pause.

"He'll lose interest in Grace real quick. She's too holy to do much with him," Gavin said.

"I haven't done much with him," I pointed out.

"Yes," Roxy said slowly, "but Gavin's right, you're still a challenge. He knows Grace and how far she's willing to go."

"Which isn't far," Gavin interjected.

"But you're still a mystery," Roxy said. "You've got this. He'd have to be an idiot to go for her over you."

That didn't fill me with the confidence it maybe should have. He was an idiot for how he had treated Lynds, and Roxy, and Ava. I had no hope now that he wouldn't do the same to me. It just came down to whether or not we could get the jump on him and humiliate him first, or if the game was already up.

Shortly after we got off the phone, a text came through from Shannon.



I stared down at the message, not sure what to say. I hated having to lie to her, especially after this weekend when she opened up so much to me. I decided not to confirm or deny.

The Better Parker

You're right - he's really not. Besides your Juliet adores you, you don't need him.

I laughed at that, sending her some hearts.

If you're the sun, my dear Juliet, he must be the moon, since he tries and fails to outshine you.

Shannon sent some laughing emojis and a 'I'm glad you're okay' with a heart.

# Chapter Thirty Eight

Lynds, Ava, Roxy, Gavin, and I were sprawled out on Ava's bedroom floor. After lounging by her pool for most of the day, we wanted a change of pace. Ava suggested makeovers and Roxy agreed if she could give Ava her signature cat eye smokey eye look, which led to Ava insisting she get to make Roxy up like her and now we were all raiding each other's makeup stashes and wardrobe options. Gavin, per usual, was sitting around cracking jokes.

I was glad to get to relax and spend time with them. Taking a break from schoolwork, and rehearsals, and from dealing with Shawn was nice, but I was starting to worry the plan was falling apart. Finding out I was in theatre hadn't seemed to upset him initially, but since their loss last weekend, Shawn hadn't tried to talk to me, and I hadn't seen much of him.

Maybe Tiger Shark Tea was right, and he really was moving his attention to Grace.

"Should I be worried Shawn isn't trying harder?" I asked.

"You mean should you be worried that he's too much of an egotistical jackass to date a girl with substance who has more interests than him?" Roxy asked.

I laughed. "I more meant should I be trying harder? Maybe stop pushing him away as much and make one last ditch effort to continue with the plan?"

"Do you want to?" Lynds asked.

I shrugged. "I mean we've come this far, and seeing the pictures of him and Grace has me wanting to teach him and her a thing or two." I turned to Lynds. "I can't believe she'd do that to you."

Lynds shrugged. "As far as the rest of the school is concerned, my own cousin did it to me first."

"Fair point," I conceded.

"Besides," Lynds continued, "I'm sure she's looking at it like I did it to her first. I knew how she felt, but I don't think she knew how I felt. At least, I never mentioned it to her. I didn't bother cause I didn't think it would matter. He wasn't going to look twice at me anyway, especially if he was overlooking her."

"You're worth so much more than her," I said quickly.

"Way better," Roxy agreed.

"And hotter," Ava said.

Roxy raised an eyebrow at her, and Ava laughed. "What? What good is being out if I can't hype my friends? Besides," she said, pulling Roxy into her lap, "you know I think you're the hottest." Ava pulled her into a kiss that lasted a few seconds longer than was comfortable to watch before Ava pulled away.

"You're hot, too," Roxy said, smiling at her. "Now stop distracting me or your eyeliner's gonna get messed up."

We laughed at that and Roxy maneuvered them so she was straddling Ava and continued with her eyeliner.

"If you want to keep trying, I say go for it," Roxy continued. "You know he deserves it, and I wouldn't be upset to see Grace taken down a peg or two."

"Or three," Gavin said, nodded.

After a moment Ava said, "If you want to make one more play for him, you'll have to go to the game and the party next weekend. You'll have to get his attention back before he asks someone else to Homecoming. I'm sure the team's going to start lining up dates this week."

"Alright," I said. "I'll give it my all this week, and if that doesn't work, we scrap the plan?" I asked.

They all nodded in agreement, and I felt some relief at that. I could do that. I could give the week my all and if it didn't work out, if he wasn't interested, then I didn't have to worry about it. I wasn't sure whether I hoped he was or wasn't, but I was glad that either way after this week I wouldn't have to wonder and worry anymore. Either it would be full speed ahead destination revenge, or I'd get to ditch Bridgette for good and not have to worry about Shawn. Things were looking more up by the day.

# Chapter Thirty Nine

By Thursday, when he still hadn't said anything to me, I gave up waiting for him to approach me and waltzed up to his lunch table. This was for all the marbles. If this didn't work, the plan was dead.

His table was mostly other football players, but Grace and a few other girls were sitting there, too. They all looked up at me when I stopped in front of the table. Grace glared at me, but I turned my attention to Shawn. "Hey stranger. Heard you haven't won a game since the last time I was there. Can't perform without motivation?" The guys ooohed and Grace's eyes narrowed further when Shawn grinned.

"No one's ever complained about my performance."

"First time for everything."

"Ouch," he said, still grinning. "What do you say you come this Friday and we test that little theory?"

"What's in it for me?" I asked, like this wasn't the outcome I was trying for in the first place.

"I bet I'll think of something. Say you'll come?"

I paused, pretending to consider it, before saying, "You better make it worth my while, Parker."

He was still beaming when I turned and walked away. I felt like everyone's eyes were on me as I walked back to the table.

Shannon and the others watched my approach and when I sat down, Shannon asked, "What was that all about?"

"Had to go put your brother in his place."

"And did it work?" Priya asked.

"Doubtful," Shannon said. "He has more ego than sense."

"You can say that again," I said, chuckling.

The others moved back to their conversations, but Shannon leaned into me and said quietly, "You're too good for him."

"Thank you," I said, wishing not for the first time that I didn't have to lie to her.

Shannon had invited me out Friday night with the rest of the drama club, but I had to go to the game and see what Shawn had planned. If he continued to ignore me for Grace after today, I was done with him, but I had to give it one last try.

Roxy had saved me a seat in the bleachers with her and Gavin. It took me longer to find them than it had last time since they were a lot closer to the field this time. When I squeezed in next to Roxy, she explained, "Figured whatever Shawn had planned would be easier if you were more front and center."

"What do you think he has planned?" I asked.

"No clue, so be ready for anything."

I was on edge for a lot of the game. During halftime, Shawn saw me in the bleachers and shot his fist in the air, grinning like a fool. I smiled back.

The game was close, but they just barely managed to squeak out a win. The moment the game ended, Shawn whipped off his helmet and ran toward the announcer. People were still standing up cheering and the team was celebrating on the field, but Shawn came back out onto the field with a microphone.

"Thank you all for coming tonight, but I wanted to give a special thank you to someone special. She's my good luck charm and I couldn't have brought home this win without her." Roxy elbowed me. I couldn't believe he was doing this, whatever this was. "She makes me want to be a better man. I promised her I'd make coming out tonight worth her while, so Bridgette Tanner..." He paused as he came over to the bleachers and made his way to me. People parted around him as he did. When we got to me, he finally continued. "...will you go to Homecoming with me?"

"Definitely!" I squealed, not even having to fake my excitement. I couldn't believe that the plan was somehow still working. I let him wrap his arms around me and kiss me to the hoots and hollers and cheers of the fans. He was hot and sweaty from the game and didn't smell the best, but thankfully, he didn't try to draw the kiss out.

He let go of me and flipped off the microphone. "Come to the party tonight? We've got a lot to celebrate."

# CHAPTER FORTY

There was no hiding at the party. Shawn singling me out as the team's good luck charm meant that everyone was trying to get a drink for me, pull me into a game, or talk to me. I ended up in the front yard, since the backyard was overflowing with people and it was too loud inside. Even the front yard wasn't calm, though. Shawn found me out there and got me roped into beer pong with a couple of his friends.

I told them I didn't drink, and they assured me I didn't need to.

"You're good enough luck that you can just stand there. I'll do all the work," Shawn assured me.

I wasn't sure if the guys let him win or not, but he made quick work of it.

He was crowing about his win when Shannon found us. "Shan!" I called out to her. I didn't need to, though, since she was already heading our way.

"I heard Shawn talking a big game over here," she said, grinning, pulling me into a hug. "I bet you carried the team."

I laughed at that. Shawn had only let me get a couple of throws in and only one of them landed.

Shawn was still yelling about how he was undefeated when Shannon turned to him and said, "I bet I can take you."

There was a chorus of oooohs at that. Shawn smiled good-naturedly at her. "Sure you can, little sis."

"You scared?" she egged on.

"Not even a little, but it wouldn't be fair for me to destroy you like that."

"I'll live. Come on."

"What's in it for me?"

"How about if Shawny boy wins Bridgette kisses Parker?" Roxy called out. I hadn't even known she had found us until she said that.

There was a lot of commotion over the suggestion. I looked at Roxy, but she just smirked at me.

I wasn't sure if Shannon would win, but as Shawn's homecoming date, I was going to have to kiss him again sooner or later. If we lost, it would just be a lot sooner than I planned.

"Sounds fair to me," I said.

"Hardly fair," Shawn said. "Bridgette, why don't you help give my sis a fighting chance? Wouldn't want anyone saying I stole a kiss from you."

"So sure you can win that you're going solo?" Shannon asked.

"I've got this," he said, grinning. "I've got a girl worth fighting for," he said, winking at me.

He gave us our turn first, and unlike him Shannon let me play more than just a couple times. It turned out it wasn't to our benefit, though. I wasn't bad, but Shannon and Shawn were both really good. If I wasn't playing, they might've been evenly matched, but I was holding her back.

"You should take my shot," I told her halfway through, trying to hand her the ping-pong ball, but she refused. "You should play, too."

No one was even drinking the beer this time. Shawn was too focused on trying to win, and Shannon on defending me. I was glad no one was getting drunk on my account.

It became clearer and clearer that without me holding her back, Shannon would've won, but she refused to stop me from playing. Shawn had to have known his sister would've won without my help. His smirk grew as the cups dwindled.

When there was one left, he called out to me, "I hope your lips are ready for me." The ball hit the cup at an odd angle and circled the rim, once, twice… I held my breath, waiting to see if it would tip out, but unfortunately on the third pass, it fell into the cup.

As the yard cheered for Shawn, their conquering hero, I stood there frozen. Shannon quietly told me she was sorry she let me down. I looked over at Roxy, who pointedly looked at Shannon and then back at me. Whatever she was trying to communicate, I was missing it.

"Looks like I won," Shawn said loudly. "Come over and give me my prize."

I shot a look at Roxy, who said loudly, "Well, Bridgette, you did agree to kiss Parker."

She raised her eyebrows at me and the meaning of her words finally crashed in. Parker, not Shawn. She hadn't ever actually said Shawn, and neither had I. Shawn wasn't the only Parker. To everyone else Shannon might have been just the other Parker, but to me she was the better Parker.

I had a choice, and it wasn't even a question. When it came to a choice between Shannon and Shawn, I would pick Shannon every time. Besides, I was going to have to kiss her a lot for the play, anyway. I pulled away from her, caught her eye, and meaningfully looked at her lips. She looked confused a moment before her eyes widened, and she gave me a smile.

That was all the permission I needed. "Alright, alright, you're right," I told Roxy loudly. "Shawn won fair and square, so I'll kiss Parker."

I closed the distance between me and Shannon and pressed my lips to hers. Her lips were soft, and she tasted like cherries. It was a nice kiss; far nicer than the ones I'd shared with her brother. We were being cheered and catcalled so loudly it was hard to think. I held the kiss for a count of five before letting her go.

I hoped I hadn't made things awkward between us, but she grinned at me. I looked at Shawn, whose jaw was on the floor, and winked at him.

I leaned closer to Shannon and said, "Thanks. I owe you one."

"Anytime, Romeo," she said, still grinning at me.

Shawn managed to compose himself and walked over to us. He slung his arm around my shoulder and said, "Hey sis, don't be trying to steal my Homecoming date."

She raised an eyebrow at me. "You're going to Homecoming with him?"

When I didn't say no, even more confusion settled on her features. I had never disliked it more that I couldn't tell her the truth. I knew she had to be worried about me and hated that I was putting her through that emotional turmoil for nothing. He wasn't going to hurt me, but I couldn't explain that to her without telling her about the plan, and I couldn't do that.

I knew she didn't like the way her brother treated girls, and she had to be worried about me, but he was her brother. As close as I was growing with her, I couldn't count on her picking my side, on her letting me hurt her brother.

So, I just shrugged and said the only thing I could think to, "He asked."

"And she said yes," he said, grinning. "Let's go get a drink," he said, pulling me toward the house. We left a confused-looking Shannon in the yard.

I got away from him a few minutes later when someone stopped him on his way to the kitchen to congratulate him on the team's win. I retraced by steps back to the front yard, but Shannon wasn't there. I looked for her in the backyard, too, but couldn't find her.

I thought about trying her room, but that felt too invasive. If she wanted to find me, she would have and if this was her wanting a little space from me; I felt like I had to give it to her.

I found Roxy who was luckily as ready to leave as I was, and she took me home.

Before I fell asleep, I texted Shannon.

> Hey sorry if I made things weird, I tried to find you before I left but I couldn't.

Her answering text took a while to come through, worrying me further.

The Better Parker

> No worries! Things aren't weird. I was just surprised. Lynds is okay with you going to HoCo with him?

I hated this so much, hated what she must be thinking about me, but at least I didn't have to lie about Lynds's feelings.

> Yeah she's fine with it. She says she's over him.

The Better Parker

> And you believe her?

I stopped to think about it a moment, looking over at Lynds's peacefully sleeping form, and found that I did. She might not be all the way over him, but she was doing so much better than she had been a month and a half ago when this all started. I was so proud of her.

I do

The Better Parker

I'm glad, but why do YOU want to go with him?

This was trickier. I gave her a half truth.

He's pretty enough, and I wasn't sure anyone else would ask.

I had never had a date to a dance before at my other schools, so it was true enough. I hadn't cared then, but going with a date this time, even if it was Shawn, could be fun.

The Better Parker

You're ridiculous. You're gorgeous - someone else would've asked for sure.

I mean he asked me at the game in front of everyone. Was I really supposed to say no?

Even if it hadn't been exactly what I wanted, I would've had a hard time turning him down in front of everyone.

The Better Parker

I saw the video. I can't believe he did that!

Seriously though! It was a lot

The Better Parker

At least he knows you're special though. He doesn't normally chase people.

I didn't know what to say to that, but luckily she sent another text.

The Better Parker

> Just promise me you'll be careful - my idiot brother has hurt a lot of girls, and it would kill me to see you be another one of them.

I was glad to be able to tell her the truth, that she wasn't going to have to worry about me getting hurt. My heart wasn't on the line. Besides, if I had anything to say about it, he would be the one getting hurt.

# Chapter Forty One

I wasn't surprised in the slightest to find in the morning that I was again being featured on Tiger Shark Tea. When I woke up, I instinctually went to check on the page before it could come through on the group chat. I knew there would be something there, and there was. I wasn't surprised that I was featured in yet another story, but I was surprised at the direction it went.

Tiger Shark Tea

*New Girl has a thing for Parker, but which one?*

*To no one's surprise except maybe Grace's, Shawn asked new girl Bridgette Tanner to Homecoming and of course, because no one turns down Harris High's golden boy, she said yes. They celebrated together at the Parker Palace party later that night, but instead of sealing it with a kiss with Shawn, Bridgette was seen locking lips with the other Parker, Shannon.*

*Word on the street is that we'll be seeing a lot more of that, too, since Bridgette and Shannon have been cast as Romeo and Juliet in the fall play. Hope Shawn doesn't mind sharing.*

# CHAPTER FORTY TWO

It had felt like everyone's eyes were on me all week, whispering about me and the Parkers. I was overjoyed it was the weekend again so I could get a break from it. It might've been naive of me, but I hadn't expected anyone to make anything out of my kiss with Shannon. Although they probably only were because of Tiger Shark Tea. I wondered for the millionth time who was running the account and why they were so interested in me, but it didn't really matter.

Besides, Tiger Shark Tea wasn't wrong. I was going to be kissing Shannon a lot more in the play, so people were going to have to get used to it.

I was surprised, though, that Shawn already seemed used to it and that people were congratulating him on having a hot homecoming date who was willing to put on a show for him.

It boiled my blood that people were saying I kissed Shannon for his benefit, when I really did it to avoid kissing him, but I couldn't exactly argue with people about it, so I had kept quiet and it had been a long week.

I got lucky with the weekend, too. The Friday game was an away one, so I wasn't expected at the game and there wasn't a party I was expected at. Lynds and I had a quiet night in, and Saturday Shannon texted me to meet up with her to run lines. Shawn and her father were both out for the day, so she invited me to the Parker Palace.

I was glad to have an excuse to see her. She'd been a little distant, understandably, but I missed her and wanted to get to talk to her more.

Unfortunately, Shannon was all business, ushering me into the living room and immediately launching into rehearsing our lines. To her and my mounting frustration, we both kept messing up on our first scene together. I knew we both knew the lines and could do better than this, but I was distracted, and it seemed like she was, too.

After the fourth time we couldn't get through the scene with Romeo and Juliet meeting at the party, I finally suggested, "This might go smoother if you tell me what's bothering you?"

I was pretty sure I knew, though. She had been weird since I accepted Shawn's offer to go to Homecoming. I hated the distance it had put between us. I couldn't give her an explanation, though, so the least I could do was give her space to talk about her feelings.

She sighed. "It's just Shawn always does this."

"Always does what?" I asked not sure what she was implying.

"He always tries to ruin things for me." She sighed, collapsing on her bed in frustration. "The worst part is that it's hard to really blame him. We've all been a little messed up since Mom died. Me, him, and my dad. But Shawn continually tries to get between me and anyone I'm f-" She stopped herself and instead said, "I'm sorry I'm being really dramatic, this is ridiculous. All you did was agree to a date with him. You didn't sign up for our family drama."

"It's okay. If I did something to hurt you, I want to know. That was the last thing I was trying to do." That at least was a complete truth I could give her.

"I know you weren't, and I don't think he was either. He's just always been competitive, but it's gotten worse since Mom died. I think he's worried about losing others now, so he finds ways to push them away first. It's been a while since he's gone after a friend of mine, though. I was hoping he wouldn't do that again."

"I'm really sorry," I said.

"It's not your fault," she said, sighing. "I'm just worr ied... about you, about him, about our friendship... It's just a lot," she looked up quickly and added, "but it's really not your fault. I just don't want to see anyone get hurt."

That hit me like a gut punch. After all, I was doing all this because I was trying to hurt Shawn. He deserved to get put in his place, but Shannon talking about where his pain came from was humanizing him to the point where I was starting to feel some guilt for the first time about wanting to hurt him. Now that Shannon said it, I wasn't sure how I had missed it. Shawn was clearly hurting, too. I didn't think that was enough reason to change my plans, though. Just because he was hurting didn't mean he got to hurt others without repercussions.

"I'm sorry you guys are going through so much. I don't want to come between your family," I said carefully. I didn't, and I really liked Shannon, but if it came down to choosing between Shannon and the plan, between Shannon and Lynds, Roxy, and Ava, I didn't think I would choose Shannon.

Thankfully, she didn't ask me to.

"It's okay and you're not. I just didn't really expect you to say yes."

I was about to remind her he didn't give me much of a choice when she said, "I think I know what's not working."

"About Shawn?"

"No. Screw Shawn. About us. Why we're tripping up so much practicing."

"I figured we were both distracted."

She shrugged. "I mean maybe, but I think it's that we're not committing enough."

"What do you mean?" I knew we both had been spending most of our free time studying and working on our lines for the play. The full rehearsals didn't even start until the week after Homecoming, partly to give us time to learn our lines, but also because Mr.

Hayes acknowledged we would all be too distracted by Homecoming to be of any real use until after it.

It was turning out Mr. Hayes wasn't wrong; Homecoming wasn't even until next weekend and it was all anyone was talking about.

"I mean to practicing right now, we're still just line reading. I don't think we're acting it enough."

"So, you want to really go for it?" I asked, making sure I understood.

"Exactly. No half assing or half acting."

"Where from?" I asked, glancing down at the script. I was mostly off script at this point, at least for the first half of the play.

She took a breath, before looking at me with wide-eyed hope that bowled me over, and saying, "Good pilgrim, you do wrong your hand too much..."

As she continued with her line, I realized what she was really saying. She didn't think I was dedicated enough because I was kissing her on the cheek. She was worried about the kissing and wanted to practice.

There was a pause, and I delivered my line, "Have not Saints lips and holy palmers, too?"

Maybe she was right, maybe that's why things had been weird in practice. I thought the kiss at the party would've been fine, but maybe it made things weird, and this is what we needed to fix it.

I gave my next couple of lines on autopilot before she gave her last before the kiss.

"Saints do not move, though grant for prayers' sake." She managed to deliver the line while looking a perfect mix of hopeful and scandalized, a perfect Juliet.

"Then move not while my prayer's effect I take," I answered and leaned in to kiss her. She stood still as I kissed her gently. It was sweet and endearing, a perfect first kiss for Romeo and Juliet, but I couldn't help thinking it felt like something was missing. It felt a bit lackluster.

Shannon pulled away, groaning, "It's still not right. Something's still missing."

"Are you sure?" I agreed the kiss itself was boring, but it felt right for the play. "I always read it as chaste like that."

"It is, but maybe that's the problem. Juliet should really be taking what she wants. Juliet shouldn't be standing there waiting for Romeo," she said, throwing her hands up in the air and turning back to me. "Juliet should be seizing Romeo," at that, she grabbed the neckline of my sweatshirt and pulled me to her, "and showing him exactly why she's worth the trouble." With that, she pulled my lips to hers roughly. I let myself as Romeo go along with her lead. I wasn't sure about her stage direction, but I couldn't argue with her that this kiss was certainly more exciting, more enticing. It was a kiss that would make a boy love-struck, a kiss he'd be willing to die for.

She pulled away after a few more moments. She was breathing heavily and whispered, "Something like that, to really show Romeo what he's been missing."

"That would do it," I said, matching her quiet intimacy. "Romeo wouldn't be able to resist."

That seemed to pull her back to herself as she said, "Too bad Juliet wouldn't do that. She was raised to be a proper lady."

"So the stage kiss should stay chaste?" I asked, making sure I understood her right.

She sighed. "Probably, although I still think that kiss would make a better play."

I couldn't help agreeing with her. Juliet having more agency and taking more initiative would've made it more entertaining for sure.

# CHAPTER FORTY THREE

The next week rushed by and before I knew it, it was Friday night, and I was cheering in the stands with Roxy and Gavin for our team again. They made quick work of the opponents. I was sure the party would be insane at the Parkers' house, but we weren't going since tomorrow was homecoming.

Roxy and Ava were staying over with me and Lynds tonight, so we would all be in one place to get ready tomorrow. Even though I was going with Shawn, I couldn't help being really excited about homecoming. Auntie Jen's magic closet had the perfect dress for me that only ended up needing minor alterations to fit right, and I was so excited to show it off and dance the night away with my friends.

I felt some guilt seeing the party all over socials, though. It looked even more wild than the others had been, which I hadn't thought was possible. I felt bad knowing Shannon might be stuck there. I wished I could've invited her to the sleepover, but since I knew we would be spending most of the night talking about different ways to destroy her brother, it wasn't an option.

When we woke up well into the morning, almost afternoon, Auntie Jen had breakfast ready for us. She went around the table asking us about our dates. Apparently, I hadn't been paying enough attention to my friends with the play taking up a lot of time, since it was news to me. Ava was going with Jeremiah, which was surprising but made some sense, if I didn't know she was with Roxy. Of course, they were still keeping things a secret, though. I wondered if Roxy was okay with it. Roxy was going with Gavin, but apparently Lynds also had a date.

"Who's Nick?" I asked, turning to Lynds.

She blushed a little. "Just a guy from my history class."

"He's friends with Gavin," Roxy interjected, seeing me gearing up for twenty questions.

"That's great!" Auntie Jen said, grinning. "I like Gavin. I'm sure his friend is a nice boy."

"Gavin has friends?" I asked Roxy, who cackled.

"Seriously, he's always with you," I said, trying to soften my surprised outburst a little.

She was still laughing. "He has friends besides us, and I like Nick. He's a good guy."

That made me feel a little better, but I still turned to Lynds and said, "I can't believe you didn't tell me!"

She shrugged. "He only asked yesterday, and it didn't come up."

I narrowed my eyes at her. "Well, I'm going to have to start asking way more questions now if that's how things are."

She rolled her eyes. "Quit being dramatic, I would've told you."

"When? When he showed up for pictures with everyone else?"

She laughed and admitted, "Probably."

Auntie Jen turned to me and asked, "Is Shannon wearing green, too?"

I couldn't understand the conversation switch, but said, "I'm actually not sure."

"Oooh! A surprise, how cute! Is she coming to get ready with you guys, or are you making her show up with the rest of the dates?"

I looked around the table, trying to see if anyone else understood what was going on, but they looked as confused as I did.

"Shannon's not my date," I said slowly.

Auntie Jen looked confused for a moment, before saying, "Oh I'm sorry, I just assumed-" She stopped herself before whatever else she was going to say and asked, "Well nevermind. You know what they say about assuming, so who are you going with?"

I looked at Lynds quickly in my alarm, but she looked calm enough. I hadn't really thought this part through either that I was going to have to introduce him to Auntie Jen and Uncle Cam. I didn't think Lynds had told them the name of the boy who upset her, though, hopefully.

"I'm actually going with Shannon's brother, Shawn."

She looked confused a moment before recovering and saying, "That's great. I'm sure you'll all have a great time."

She moved on to talking about everyone's hairstyle plans and makeup looks, but I couldn't shake her odd assumption from my mind, and couldn't stop thinking about Shannon. The thought of her getting ready alone at her house made me pick up my phone before I could think better of it.

> Do you want to come over and get ready with us?

The Better Parker

> You're the sweetest! I'm actually at Priya's, a bunch of us are getting ready together.

It was better that way, but it still made me sad that she wouldn't be coming over.

> Oh cool! excited to see you later!

She sent me a goofy selfie of her, Priya, and some of the other girls from drama. I was surprised to realize I missed her.

I got everyone to pose for our own selfie and sent it back to her before putting my phone away.

# CHAPTER FORTY FOUR

Auntie Jen spent all day with us, helping us get ready. She was a whiz with a curling iron and even better with a lash curler. Ava and Roxy kept thanking her and telling me and Lynds how lucky we were. Neither of us had to be told. Lynds and I both knew how lucky we were. I felt lucky just to be here, experiencing a normal school year at the same school with actual friends. It was the first time I wasn't getting ready for a dance alone.

Our dates were supposed to get there at six, but by Gavin's tenth 'I'm bored' text around three, we let him come over early. Of course, this just meant he was telling us in person how bored he was instead of through text.

He was wearing a lavender shirt with a floral dark purple tie and dark purple pants. It wasn't until we all were dressed that I realized he had managed to marry together the colors of both Ava and Roxy's dresses. It was a really cute touch that I knew they appreciated.

I pulled Ava aside before the others got there and asked, "How much does Jeremiah know?"

"He's a good friend. He just knows the person I wanted to go with didn't want to go with me," she said with a sad smile.

That threw me off. "Wait, Roxy didn't want to go with you?"

She waved off my concern. "Not like that. Of course she did, but when we talked about it, she said she didn't want to make it everyone's business."

"That's so weird," I said slowly. It didn't sound like the Roxy I knew. The Roxy I knew wouldn't have cared what anyone thought and did what she wanted to.

Ava shrugged. "The stuff with Shawn was tougher on her than she let on." My eyes widened in alarm and Ava quickly said, "No, not like that. She's not upset about him but about what people were saying about her after."

"But she seemed so cool about it," I said slowly.

"I mean she was, but it's hard hearing people say vile things about you. It was different for me and Lynds thankfully, but Roxy got the worst of it and she's worried that things would get bad again if people knew she's bi."

It hadn't occurred to me that she could be worried about her sexuality being weaponized to slut shame her. I had actually assumed that Ava was the one that didn't want people to know yet. "I know we already decided to ruin him, but now I'm even more impatient."

She chuckled a little, saying, "I know. I wasn't invested in Shawn really, but he hurt Roxy and Lynds, and he deserves to be miserable."

"It's really gonna suck seeing him crowned homecoming king tonight, huh?"

She rolled her eyes. "No different from every other year, but yeah."

"Are we sure I can't dump his ass tonight when he gets crowned?"

She laughed at that before saying, "You're being rash. Besides you're not together together yet. You'd be letting him off too easily in the humiliation department."

"Point taken," I said. "I just wish there was something we could do to steal the spotlight from him."

She laughed. "If anyone will come up with something for that, it'll be Roxy and Gavin."

I laughed at that, and we rejoined the others.

Lynds's date Nick showed up ten minutes early with flowers, both for Auntie Jen and for Lynds. Lynds was blushing like crazy, her cheeks burning as red as her hair when he told her how amazing she looked. In her sequined blue dress that fell just above her knee, she looked a lot like a poised, beautiful figure skater. I was glad Nick was smart enough to appreciate that.

I mouthed "thank you" to Gavin, who smirked at me, patting himself on the back. He earned it, he did good finding Nick for Lynds.

Shawn and Jeremiah showed up ten minutes late, but at least they looked good. Shawn must've spent longer than usual getting his hair to look perfectly messy. Seeing his honey blonde hair reminded me of another blonde I was missing, though. I couldn't help thinking how if Auntie Jen had been right and Shannon had been the Parker I was going with that she wouldn't have kept us waiting.

Shawn and Jeremiah hopped out of Shawn's topless doorless Jeep and I grimaced at Ava. Maybe we could get them to take my car, but I doubted it. Thankfully, Ava's braids were mostly immovable, and I had enough hairspray in that the wind probably wouldn't do too much damage on the short ride to the school, but it was still inconsiderate of them.

Shawn came over and said hi to everyone. I waited to see if he would seem the slightest bit sheepish or embarrassed that he'd kissed every girl here except for my aunt, but if he felt any sort of way about it, he didn't show it.

It hardened my resolve against him even more, but at least now I didn't have to keep my distance from Roxy at school anymore. Shawn closed the distance between us and kissed me on the cheek. Of course, he knew to avoid my lips to not ruin my makeup. He'd done this before. He was a pro. I smiled at him, trying to channel my newly acquired acting skills to make him think I was happy he was here. I was lucky he wasn't too observant, since I didn't seem to be fooling my aunt.

She frowned a little but kept her thoughts to herself, whatever they were.

We took a lot of photos. Some with just the girls and then with everyone, and then photos of each of us with our dates. By the time we finished, we were going to make it just in time.

"Don't stay out too late, and have so much fun," Auntie Jen cried out to us as we left. Me and Ava took the back of the Jeep while our dates rode in the front. Roxy took the others in her car.

# CHAPTER FORTY FIVE

It took Ava a few minutes to re-fix my hair for me when we got to the school. Shawn hopped out to talk to some friends in the parking lot, but Jeremiah stayed with us. He was glaring at Shawn's back and apologized to us both, saying he should've thought ahead and drove us. We both assured him it was okay, no harm done, and we didn't blame him. All of that was true. It wasn't his fault that Shawn only ever thought about himself.

The school had gone all out with the enchanted garden theme. There were fairy lights and flower garlands strung all over the place. It felt like a midnight stroll through a moonlight garden.

We claimed a table and took some pictures and in that ten minutes, Shawn managed to lose us. I wasn't sure whether I was thrilled or annoyed that I had barely seen my date. Everyone else were still in their couples, and when a Savannah Hollywood song we loved came on, we all ran out to the dance floor.

After a few more songs, I heard the voice of honey blonde yelling, "Bri!"

I turned and grinned, yelling, "Shan!" and pulled her into a hug. "You look beautiful!" I told her as I hugged her.

She was grinning as she pulled away to get a better look at my dress and said, "Auntie Jen outdid herself. It's stunning! You're stunning!" She spun me around and, for the first time that night, I felt truly beautiful. Of course, she outshone everyone here, myself included. She was wearing a light purple poofy skirted dress that was covered in a floral pattern and had a matching floral crown. Beautiful was an understatement and she fit the theme perfectly. I hoped whoever she was here with knew how lucky they were.

When the song ended, a slow song came on. Shannon looked around asking, "Where's your date?"

I shrugged. "He's your brother, you know how easily distracted he is. Where's yours?"

She looked around, frowning. I wasn't sure if she was looking for her date or mine, but I hoped she didn't find them. I wasn't worried about Shawn. I had the better Parker with me. I took her hand and her attention shot back to me. "Dance with me?"

She considered a moment before asking, "Really?"

"Yes," I said, and pulled her closer. I moved my hands to her hips, and she put hers on my shoulders as we swayed to the music.

"Having a good time?" she asked.

"Better now," I said honestly, before realizing that was probably a little too honest and adding, "No offense, but your brother doesn't make the best date."

She sighed. "I tried to warn you."

"I know you did. I should've listened. Thanks for coming to my rescue."

When the song was just ending, Shawn found us and clapped Shannon on the back, saying, "Thanks for taking care of my date, sis." He grinned and grabbed my hand from her waist, pulling me to him.

He steered me away from her and toward his friends. I mouthed, "I'm sorry," over my shoulder to her. She waved me off, and I was happy to see some of her drama club friends pulled her into a dance. I let Shawn pull me the rest of the way, wishing I could ditch him and go back to her, or to my friends, but knowing I was where I was supposed to be.

I was grateful when Ava and Jeremiah found their way to us and danced with us. We all danced to a few songs, after which I started looking around, trying to find an excuse to ditch Shawn. He was being handsy in a way I didn't like or invite, and I was a few more minutes away from ruining everything by telling him off.

Thankfully the DJ intervened, announcing it was time to crown the Homecoming King and Queen. Shawn's friends were already clapping him on the back, congratulating him. His win was a foregone conclusion, and I wished more than anything that anyone else's name would be called out.

The DJ announced Homecoming King first, stealing my sliver of hope of Shawn being overlooked. He pressed a kiss to my cheek before leaving me to go up on stage. When he got up there, he was given a microphone and thanked everyone. I was impressed he managed to sound believably humble while doing it. I was sure it was better acting than most of the people in the drama club would've been able to manage.

Mercifully, the DJ took the microphone from him shortly after, cutting what was sure to be a long speech short. I waited with some interest to see who Shawn would be sharing a dance with. I didn't know the seniors well, but there were some seniors on the cheer squad with Ava who were likely candidates.

The DJ looked at his script and announced, "This year's Queen is breaking tradition. With over half the votes of the entire student body, this year's Homecoming Queen is... drumroll please." I grinned at Ava as we followed everyone's lead. I was just happy that the Queen was getting more fanfare than Shawn did.

"Please welcome to the stage, your Queen, coming to us from the junior class..." The crowd audibly gasped at that. Shawn had won Homecoming King every year, but usually the others had told me that his Homecoming Queen was always a senior. The DJ paused, and I looked at Ava, who was already looking at me with expectant excitement, like it was going to me. *Yeah, right,* I thought, shooting her back an incredulous look. I was looking at the most likely girl in the room to be called up. "Ava Johnson!" the DJ called out, proving me right, and changing the look of delight on Ava's face to shock.

The crowd cheered, and I nudged her toward the stage yelling, "So proud of you!" after her.

When she got up there, her joy was palpable. I started tearing up a little when she did as she thanked everyone. When she finished, the DJ prompted Shawn to take Ava's hand and lead her off the stage and to the middle of the dance floor.

When the song started, I felt an elbow in my side and looked over to see Roxy grinning at me. "She looks beautiful, doesn't she?"

"Incredible," I agreed.

"Up for a little mischief?" she asked.

"Depends."

"Trust me?"

"Yes," I said, hoping I wouldn't regret it.

"Follow my lead."

She pulled me out on the dance floor and before I could pull away and tell her this was a terrible idea, she spun me around, pushing us toward Ava and Shawn. Ava shot us a look of confusion as the crowd began to murmur. Shawn hadn't seen us yet, and everyone, me included, gasped when Roxy stepped up to him and tapped him on the shoulder.

Everyone else had to be thinking we were about to see a confrontation for the ages, since Shawn was dancing with one of his exes in front of another one of his exes and his current date. Ava and I shared another look of confusion and mild panic while Shawn turned around. If he was worried about seeing us there, he didn't let it show.

He grinned and said, "Roxy, there's plenty of me to go around if you wait your turn."

She rolled her eyes and said, "Wow you've got yourself a charmer there, Bridgette." She turned back to Shawn and Ava, offering Ava her hand. Ava hesitated half a moment while they shared a glance, and then Ava took it. "I'm cutting in," Roxy clarified to a confused Shawn. "I would ask if you mind, but I don't actually care. I want to dance with my girlfriend."

Shock rippled through the crowd as Roxy spun Ava away from Shawn. He moved toward them, and I stepped in between them, offering him my hand. I didn't care if he danced with me or not, but he wasn't interrupting their moment.

He looked around and his eyes caught on someone in the crowd. I wanted to look to see who it was, but I was worried if I looked away from him, he'd push past me and ruin Ava and Roxy's big moment, so I continued to watch him, waiting. He surprised me by turning and heading into the crowd, leaving me standing there, alone. I froze. I knew this was bad for the plan and that I should probably go after him, but

I couldn't make myself move. I couldn't believe he had actually ditched me in the middle of all these people. My eyes dropped to the floor as the crowd's murmuring got louder. Suddenly, there was a familiar pair of purple pants in front of me. I looked up and saw Gavin grinning at me.

He dipped in a bow, offering me his hand, "May I have this dance, my lady?"

I laughed at that with a quick answering curtsy. "Of course, my lord."

He spun me around to a rhythm all his own, making me laugh. By the time the song ended, I was sufficiently cheered up. Even more so when Ava rushed up and pulled me into a hug saying, "She did it!"

"She did!"

"Did you know?" she asked.

"Not before you," and I still couldn't really believe she had done it.

Roxy grinned at us and Lynds was there a moment later with Nick, squealing and hugging Ava. Nick clapped Roxy on the back, making her grin.

A moment later, we were engulfed by the entire cheer squad. I held my breath, waiting to see how they would act, but it turned out I didn't need to be worried. They all congratulated Ava wholeheartedly and Roxy somewhat less so, but they still congratulated her and told her how lucky she was. I was surprised and relieved she was getting such a warm reception, but then again, this was Ava. She was one of the nicest people I knew. She deserved happiness, and I was glad to see her friends were true ones who were still willing to embrace the truest side of her.

Shawn reappeared, but stuck with his friends and left me alone for the rest of the dance. I knew I should have probably gone to him, but I couldn't bring myself to care what was going on with him. There wasn't any good reason for him to be upset, and I didn't want him anywhere near Ava tonight. I didn't want him ruining what was looking like a perfect night.

Ava and I squeezed into Roxy's car after Jeremiah apologized for the hundredth time that Shawn was still nowhere to be seen. It was for the best anyway; Shawn wasn't welcome at our afterparty. Of course, he was throwing the actual afterparty per usual, but we were going to our diner, and he wasn't invited. Ava had invited Jeremiah, but he had to go to Shawn's party and was able to get a ride with someone else from the team. I had grown to like Jeremiah, but I was still glad he wasn't coming. The diner was our place.

In our dresses, we were the fanciest people in the diner, but it was a perfect end to a perfect night sharing milkshakes and fries, celebrating the monumental step Roxy and Ava had taken in their relationship. From how Ava couldn't stop smiling, it was clear she couldn't believe this was real, and I was so happy for her. I was happy for all of us. Lynds hadn't stopped smiling since Nick had shown up at the house. He held her hand every second they weren't eating and looked at her with just as much devotion as she looked at him. Gavin made several jokes about how he and I were the extra wheels, but we both knew we couldn't be happier for our friends.

# CHAPTER FORTY SIX

Tiger Shark Tea's post on Sunday for the first time in a while wasn't about me. It wasn't surprising it was about Roxy and Ava, but I was surprised that, whoever Tiger Shark Tea was, was kind about it.

The comments, however, weren't.

There were a lot of comments about how they must have been toying with Shawn. There were even more comments from boys begging to watch. The ones about Roxy were the worst, though. People were calling her every version of a hoe they could without getting their comments flagged and removed. People were saying she was clearly a sex addict since she couldn't keep her hands to herself first with Shawn and now with Ava. It was horrifying. I texted the group, but Ava texted back they were taking a social media break for a bit, but that they were both doing okay and were happy they didn't have to hide.

It was somewhat reassuring that for every negative comment, though there were two positive ones. I also noticed that, whoever Tiger Shark Tea was, seemed to be monitoring and attempting to remove the worst comments since they kept disappearing.

It was interesting for sure, because I hadn't noticed them do that in the past, but to be fair, the past comments hadn't been anywhere near as bad as these were.

The whispers at school Monday were bad, but the cheer squad took it on themselves to look out for Ava and, by extension, Roxy. I was glad they were doing that since I didn't have any classes with Ava or Roxy and couldn't help protect them. I planned to sit with Ava at lunch, but she texted me that her and Roxy went home early. I was proud of them for sticking out the half of the day they did. If it were me, I wasn't sure I could've done it.

The moment I sat down at the table with Shannon, she looked up at me and asked, "So what are we gonna do?"

"About what?" I asked. If there was something going on today that didn't involve Roxy and Ava, I had missed it.

"About Roxy and Ava, I know you're close with them and we've all been seeing the comments." Everyone around the table nodded and Shannon repeated, "So what are we gonna do?"

I sighed. "I'm really not sure. Do you think Shawn would say something for them?"

I didn't really expect him to be willing to help, but it was worth a shot.

"Maybe if you asked him?" she said, but her tone didn't convey confidence.

"Him and I haven't talked since he was crowned," I told her.

"He's such an ass," she said. "So, he's out. Anyone have any ideas?"

"What if we made a statement?" I said slowly, the idea starting to form.

"No one's going to listen to us," Shannon said, sounding defeated.

"No, not us talking. I mean, what if we made a state-ment?"

She looked up at me and asked, "What do you mean?"

"Okay, so it's a little crazy, but hear me out..."

# Chapter Forty Seven

"You want to change the play?" Mr. Hayes asked, more calmly than I expected. "Not only do you want to change Shakespeare's classic, but you want to do it three and a half weeks before opening?"

"Okay, yes," Shannon said, taking over for me, "I know it sounds bad, but we want to change the play three and a half weeks before opening, but before our first rehearsal. It's not just that we want to change it, though, it's that we have this opportunity to make a statement, and we want to take it. We think some of our classmates need reminding that love is love and can come in all forms."

"You're really set on this?" Mr. Hayes asked, looking around at the cast. My heart soared, seeing everyone nod in solidarity. Not a single person objected.

"What do you think?" I asked. I couldn't believe how quickly everyone had jumped on board with what I had thought was a crazy idea.

"I think you all are going to give me more grey hairs than I already have," he sighed and added, "but I'll make a good-looking silver fox."

"Is that a yes?" Shannon squealed.

"Before I say yes, I need you all to understand what we're doing here," he said, looking around meeting each of our eyes. "There's a reason something like this hasn't been done before and there might be pushback from the school board, from the parents, from your classmates. I'm not sure what we're walking in to, and I need you all to be committed, not just to me and to the play, to the art, but to each other. If we do this, you have each other's backs. And if we do this, you're going to rehearse your butts off."

There was a loud chorus of agreement before he sighed and said, "You're not wrong; the play has an even stronger message this way."

Before he could change his mind, we all cheered, chanting his name.

He held up his hands, saying, "Okay, okay, now we get to the hard work." He started handing out tasks and assignments, and I couldn't believe we were actually doing this. I wanted to take the attention off of Roxy and Ava, but it was easy to see how this had quickly become more than that. The message was important, and it was one worth standing up for.

When the meeting was ending, Mr. Hayes came up to me and put his hand on my shoulder and said, "I'm proud of you, kiddo. I know suggesting that couldn't have been easy and that our school is apparently not always the most accepting place, but we've made so much progress."

"You think?" I asked.

He nodded. "When I went here, I never would've dreamed of putting on a gay play. I just wanted to say this is going to mean so much to people. You were right, this is what theatre's truly about. Real art takes risks. Real art makes you feel," he said, wiping away a tear from his eye. "And I'll be damned if this isn't already real art. You've got me getting all mushy."

I laughed at that and said, "Thank you so much. This means so much to me."

"And I'm so proud of you. Now get out of here, kiddo, so I can cry in peace."

I laughed at that, grabbed my purse, and ran out to meet Shannon where she was waiting outside to talk about our next steps.

# CHAPTER FORTY EIGHT

Tiger Shark Tea

*Tiger Shark Tea's message to the haters:*

*This page started as a way to call out the liars and dirty dirty cheats of Harris High and pass along the gossip. It was meant to be fun, but your comments are really showing why we can't have nice things.*

*It should have gone without saying that Tiger Shark Tea doesn't condone bullying, harassment, or homophobia. In light of y'all not being able to keep your opinions to yourselves, Tiger Shark Tea might be taking a hiatus.*

*This could be the last you hear from Tiger Shark Tea. If it is, I'll leave you on a high note.*

*I thought what I was doing was something that mattered, but you know who's doing the real work? New girl, Bridgette Tanner.*

*She took one look at the hatred y'all were spewing and decided to do something about it. Sources say she's the reason behind the new fall play.*

*If you haven't heard yet, what was going to be Romeo and Juliet is now Ramona and Juliet.*

*Bridgette reached out to us and gave the following statement, "This switch was inspired by the clear need our school has to be reminded that love is love. Love, in any form, isn't something to be gawked at, ridiculed, or hated. Romeo and Juliet is the original story of two star-crossed lovers separated by family and expectation. In this day and age, it's clear that no one knows and understands that struggle better than the queer community. Shannon and I hope we'll do the community justice and hope to see you all there. Part of the ticket proceeds will be donated to the Trevor Project, and if that's not enough to encourage you to attend, we haven't cut any of the kissing scenes."*

*I almost cut out the last part in light of how disappointed I am in y'all, but it was her statement, so I didn't want to change it.*

*I, for one, will be there showing my support for the people doing something that really matters and I hope I won't be the only one.*

Can you believe it?? Tiger Shark Tea actually did it.

I can't believe they didn't do something like that sooner, to be honest - it's ridiculous they let people bully Lynds, Roxy, and Ava in the first place.

I'm sure they did what they could.



I'm not so sure.

Well, at least they're stepping up now. With any luck, we'll get a lot of donations.



Especially since you made sure to remind people how much we kiss.

I sent a couple of laughing emojis.

What can I say? I know our audience - it's a big selling point.

The drama club was all hands on deck after the change. For the next couple of weeks, I was Ramona more than I was Bridgette or even Bri.

I had been anxious about actually implementing the change, since I felt a lot of responsibility for making sure everything went right since it had been my idea. It turns out I didn't need to be worried. As Romeo and Juliet, Shannon and I were good, but as Ramona and Juliet, we were incredible. I was dedicated to representing my community in the best way I could, and it seemed Shannon was just as dedicated to bringing to life the new changes.

No one in drama club was complaining about having to perform Romeo and Juliet anymore. Everyone was abuzz with energy, reinvigorated by the change.

Mr. Hayes mentioned some small issues with complaints, but so far had been handling them and kept telling us to go full steam ahead. Mr. Hayes managed to convince the principal and school board that it would be good for the school and got them to agree to give us the creative freedom this time. It was implied that if this didn't go well, we would be forced to be more traditional in the future, though. I was ecstatic Mr. Hayes stood behind us and believed in us enough to take that risk.

I was grateful that after the Tiger Shark Tea announcement, people were talking more about the play and Tiger Shark Tea than they were about Roxy and Ava. Of course, Roxy was acting like it never bothered her, but I was glad I managed to help. Even the loudest haters got distracted after a couple of "leaked" photos of me and Shannon kissing at practice ended up on Tiger Shark Tea.

I hadn't been sure it would work since Tiger Shark Tea was planning a hiatus, but the post appeared the day after Shan and I sent in the photos. Apparently, they felt like they owed us, and I wasn't going to take that for granted.

We kept the pedal to the floor right up until a few days before Halloween. Halloween was big for the drama club and apparently for the rest of the school as well. Shawn was having another one of his blowout parties, and I was told that everyone would be at this one. Apparently, that, for once, actually meant everyone, including the entire drama club and, to my shock, Lyndsey.

Nick asked her to go with him, and she was a little anxious about it, but was ecstatic he asked her, so she was going.

It was a huge amount of progress for her to agree to go to Shawn's house, and I was incredibly proud of her. If I hadn't already decided I was going, that would've done it. Of course, I wasn't going to let Lynds brave that mad house without being there for emotional support.

I wasn't sure Shawn would welcome me there, but when I told Shannon that, she waved off my concerns, reminding me it's her house too and that we're her guests.

# Chapter Forty Nine

I was apparently worried for nothing though since a couple of days before the party, Shawn came to find me at lunch. The team hadn't won a game since Homecoming and I knew rumors were flying that the team thought I was some sort of curse and good luck charm rolled into one, but I hadn't believed he believed it until he approached me.

"Can we talk privately?" He asked, looking meaningfully at Shannon.

I considered for a moment denying him, adding to his humiliation, but I was curious what he had to say and I wasn't sure he would stick around to say it if I denied him.

Shannon's smirk disappeared when I said, "Sure."

He led me toward the parking lot.

"Are we going somewhere?" I asked.

"No, just wanted a bit of privacy," he said, running his hand through his hair. He looked nervous, and I almost felt bad, almost.

"What's up, Parker?" I asked, hoping he'd just spit out whatever it was so my thoughts would stop racing.

"Look, I was a jerk at Homecoming. I'm sorry. I probably should've said that sooner." That was the last thing I expected him to say.

"You probably should have," I agreed.

He gave me a sad smile. "I acted like a jerk, and I know I don't deserve it, but I'm still hoping there's a chance you'll forgive me."

I couldn't tell if this was an act or not, but it felt more real than any other interaction I'd ever had with him, so my response was kinder than I planned.

"Forgiveness has to be earned."

He nodded solemnly. "I know. I'm willing to do what I can to make it up to you."

"Luckily, I know where you can start."

He perked up a little at that.

"I want you to put out something on your socials in support of Roxy and Ava."

"Why does that matter to you?" he asked.

"They're my friends and they don't deserve what people have been saying. A lot of those people think they're defending you."

"It's not my fault they-" he started, but I cut him off.

"I'm not saying it's your fault, but you saying nothing is making it worse. You throwing a fit and storming out of homecoming made it worse."

"That's what people are saying?" he asked with surprise so genuine I didn't think it was fake.

"Yeah, they're saying the girls hurt your feelings."

"That's ridiculous," he said quickly. "My pride maybe a little, but I didn't storm out and I don't care that they're together."

I wanted to ask what he thought he was doing if it wasn't storming out, but settling my curiosity was less important than taking advantage of the opening he'd given me. "So tell people that, tell them you don't care they're together and you're happy without them."

He looked at me incredulously. "And that would be enough for you to forgive me?"

I rolled my eyes. "I mean, you should do it anyway, but that would be progress."

"Okay, I'll do it. Can I ask you for a favor, though?"

My eyes narrowed, and he threw his hands up in defense. "It's a tiny tiny favor. I know you don't owe me shit, but I'm hoping you'll do it anyway."

"What do you want?" I asked.

"You know how I was joking about you being my good luck charm?"

I nodded, unsure where he was going with that.

"Well, you might've noticed we haven't won a game since Homecoming and the guys on the team have it in their heads that I was right, since the only two games we've won, you've been there."

"You can't be serious."

He laughed a little. "I mean, I don't really believe it, but the team's big on superstition and I think everyone would be less anxious and play better if you were there."

"You can't be serious," I repeated.

"It'd be good for school morale if we won. I'll post tonight but if you come, I'll do you one better. When we win, I'll tell everyone that Roxy and Ava's bravery inspired us to the win."

That might be worth it, but I wasn't sure I could trust him.

"Why would you do that?"

He sighed. "You might not believe it, but I really didn't mean to make things harder on them. I want to help, and I want you to forgive me. What do you say?"

"Okay, I'll do it."

"I have another idea if you're game?"

Again, my eyes narrowed. "What kind of idea?"

"It'll really help the school," he said slowly, and I knew whatever it was was going to be ridiculous.

That's how I ended up cheering from the sidelines with Ava and the cheer squad instead of anonymously up in the bleachers like I had every other time.

Shawn wasn't wrong, though. I watched as the team spilled out onto the field and their eyes widened when they saw me. Their energy was infectious. I was hardly a cheerleader, but they had an extra uniform and pompoms and Ava had simplified a lot of the cheers, promising to make sure I didn't look stupid.

I stayed on the sidelines during their halftime show, though. There was no way I was going to be able to fake my way through that.

We were one touchdown behind the Orcas. It was going to be a close one.

I wouldn't say I was the reason they won, but plenty of people said it to me that night and when the game ended, like promising Shawn made a quick heartfelt speech about how Roxy and Ava's bravery had inspired the team to victory. He finished it off by saying that he was extra excited to have his girl back cheering for him.

With that, him and a few of his buddies ran over and hoisted me onto their shoulders, parading me around the field. I couldn't help laughing and waving like a pageant queen. The whole thing was so ridiculous I couldn't not laugh.

If someone had told me last year as I jumped from school to school that this year I would be settled permanently in a school with a bunch of close friends and would be being celebrated by the school's quarterback, I wouldn't have believed them. I never stood out at my old schools. I wasn't there long enough to, and I had to admit, the attention wasn't the worst.

Especially when Shawn put me down and Ava and the rest of the squad ran over and pulled me into a group hug.

For once, Shawn wasn't throwing an after-game party, since tomorrow was his annual Halloween party. No one wanted to stay out too late since tomorrow was going to be crazy, but the team was going to get pizza after. Shawn invited me, thanking me for coming and hoping to see me tomorrow.

I told him I couldn't wait to come to Shannon's party and his laugh seemed genuine.

Ava invited me out with them, too, but I declined. She tracked my gaze to Gavin, who was easily visible because of his painted green face. She laughed, saying, "Every time I swear he won't be able to outdo himself and he always proves me wrong."

"You can't get away, can you?" I asked, nodding to Roxy.

Ava sighed. "Not this time, but I'll be with you guys all day tomorrow."

# Chapter Fifty

Auntie Jen's magic closet came in clutch again. I had no idea why she had enough costume pieces to outfit a small army on less than a day's notice, but she did.

When Lynds said her mom never threw away anything that could be potentially useful, she clearly wasn't kidding.

The majority of mine and Lynds's costumes came from her closet.

Ava, Roxy, and Gavin all came over to get ready and I invited Shannon, too.



The Better Parker



I took a quick survey of everyone's state of disarray and Gavin redoing his makeup a third time and told her,

No worries! Excited to see you! What's your costume anyway?

Don't judge, but my aunt had the crown already so I'm going as a princess - thought about adding some blood but the dress for a Carrie look, but it's too cute for that.



Pink?

I sent a few laughing emojis.

Princesses do come in other colors.



They do, but you're in pink.

Fineeee, yes I'm in pink. What are you wearing?



You'll have to wait and see.

No fair!

Shannon sent a string of laughing emojis and I put my phone away.

At least she wasn't making fun of my costume. I was really second guessing doing my own thing. Ava and Roxy were a light and dark fairy, reusing their Homecoming dresses with added wings. Ava's makeup was light and sparkly, while Roxy's was dark and otherworldly. They made the perfect pair.

They offered to let me join and turn the couple's costume into a group costume, but I didn't want to crash their thing.

Gavin, Lynds, and Nick, who was meeting us later, were dressed up as a rock band. Gavin was the lead vocalist and guitar, Nick was the backup guitar, and Lynds was on drums. The guys had neon colored inflatable guitars and Lynds had two thick glow sticks that she was calling drumsticks.

They invited me to join their band, but I wasn't feeling it. Maybe it was the amount of time I was spending as Ramona, but I wanted something a little more romantic, a little more whimsical, so I went with a princess. It wasn't the most original but in the pink poofy dress and tall silver crown, I felt and looked good.

I split off from the others when we got there and went looking for Shannon in the backyard.

She wasn't there, but Shawn was. My jaw dropped when I saw him. It was hard to miss him since he was dressed in an actual honest to goodness suit of armor. He was holding the helmet instead of wearing it though, so I could see his perfectly coifed golden hair. I felt my cheeks start to burn.

Before he could notice me, I turned around and whipped out my phone, texting Shannon.

> I just got here and we're SO not friends.

The Better Parker

> Upstairs if you're looking for me. Why're you breaking up with me though?

I quickly snuck a picture of Shawn and texted it to her with a selfie of me frowning dramatically.

The Better Parker

> Hurry your ass upstairs before he sees you!

I felt a tap on my shoulder and turned around, already knowing who was going to be there, but hoping I was wrong. I was right; it was Shawn. I wasn't sure how he'd managed to move quietly enough to sneak up on me, but as he reached out for me, I realized the suit wasn't actually made of metal, it just looked like it.

"You're here!" he said, picking me up at the waist and spinning me around as he yelled out to the crowd. "My princess has arrived!"

I wasn't sure whether I should be amused or cursing Shannon for not warning me. By the time he put me down, I still hadn't decided.

"I'm so glad you're here," he said with an easy smile and a kiss on my cheek. I was finding, much to my own annoyance, that I didn't mind this version of him as much as his usual self. I wasn't sure which version was closer to the truth, though.

"Can we talk?" he asked. I noticed with appreciation that he didn't seem to be drunk yet, and he waited for my agreement before pulling me off to the side for some privacy. When I noticed he had pulled me behind the trees I recognized from his make-out session with Roxy, I glared at him.

He looked around, noticed where we were, and held his hands up in protest. "Not like that, I just wanted to thank you."

"You can start by keeping your lips to yourself," I said, crossing my arms.

His eyes widened before he said quickly, "Oh, no-that's not what I meant. Geez, I'm bad at this. I meant I wanted to thank you, with words."

I waited, and he chuckled to himself, running his fingers through his hair. I wondered if he was actually nervous since there was no one around to be putting on a show for.

"Thank you so much," he continued. "We needed a win, badly. There were scouts there tonight."

My eyes narrowed at that. Of course, that's why it mattered to him. He'd used me to make the team play better.

"Wait- wait," he said, sensing he was losing me. "It wasn't for me. I'm already locked in with USC. This was for Jeremiah."

"Jeremiah?" I asked.

"Yeah," he said, looking around before saying, "his parents can't afford to send him to Stanford without more of a scholarship. He's got academic scholarships, but without the added football scholarship, he'll probably get stuck local."

I had no idea Jeremiah was that smart. Stanford was a huge deal. Apparently, Shawn was a better friend than I thought, too. I didn't know he cared that much about Jeremiah.

"We haven't been playing our best lately," he continued. "I know he's good enough. They'd be lucky to have him, but I didn't think they'd be too impressed if we couldn't pull out a win and the guys were convinced we would lose again if you weren't there. The guys are like my family, so thank you."

It was about the last thing I expected Shawn to say. I wasn't sure I liked how he was slowly becoming human.

"And it didn't hurt that we crushed the Orcas."

I laughed. "Of course it didn't."

"Can we keep this between us, though? Jeremiah's been keeping his parents' financial situation a secret and I don't want it getting out."

"Yeah, I'll keep it to myself."

"Thank you," he said, grinning. "You're the best. I've never really met anyone like you before."

He looked sincere enough, but that sounded like a line if I had ever heard one. Even if it wasn't, he didn't really know me. The times he'd spent with and talked to me, he wasn't getting to know the real me. I didn't know what I wanted to do about him now, though. I had given up on the revenge plan working after he ghosted me at Homecoming. Now it sounded like maybe he was starting to be real with me, and I didn't know what to think or do about it.

"I've definitely never met anyone like you before, either." It was true. He was turning out to be more complex than I expected.

He smiled at that and said, "Well I hope I can continue to surprise and impress you."

I crossed my arms, fighting back a smile. "Did I say you impressed me?"

He laughed. "Not yet, I suppose, but it'll happen. After all, I am your knight in *shawn*-ing armor."

The laugh that burst out of me surprised me.

He ruffled my hair teasingly. I laughed and playfully batted him away. Instead of moving away, he linked his arm through mine and led me back to the party. The crowd whooped when we reappeared and even though he waved them off, I noticed he was smirking.

I got away from him as soon as I could and escaped to Shannon's room.

I opened her door and quickly closed it behind me. Shannon and the rest of our drama club friends were still laughing.

"Why didn't you warn me?" I asked glaring at her. If I had known Shawn was going to dress as a knight, I never would have come as a princess.

"I didn't know, I swear," she said quickly.

"Did he know?" I asked.

"I might've mentioned it to him," she said, grimacing. "I'm sorry. I'm so sorry, but it's a little funny, isn't it?" she asked, fighting back a grin. Priya started laughing, and the others joined in. I did too, I couldn't help myself. Especially when Shannon zoomed in on the pic I had taken of Shawn and I noticed he was flexing his muscles, showing off to the crowd.

"He called himself my knight in *shawn*-ing armor," I said, and the room broke into hysterics again. "This is so your fault," I told Shannon.

"I told you to hurry up and get up here," she protested.

"Too little too late. He caught me."

She grimaced. "Sorry. Next time we'll stand guard at the door waiting for you, your highness."

I laughed against my will and said, "As you should, obviously."

I looked around, taking in their costumes, and saw that I was facing a bunch of witches and superheroes. I only recognized some of them, the others were a mystery to me.

Shannon's outfit in particular, I did recognize. She was dressed as a witch, but her makeup was all green tinged in a way that looked spooky and had to be on purpose. "The Wicked Witch of the West?" I asked.

She grinned. "We accidentally match since you're clearly Glinda the Good Witch and not a princess."

I couldn't help laughing at that. "So the green," I said, gesturing to her face.

"Was added after your text, yup. What can I say? Apparently the Parkers are shameless."

I laughed at that and asked, "So are we staying up here or going to put hexes on the others?" I asked of the witches.

The gang shrugged. Priya spoke up. "I'm not sure they're ready for us, but Halloween only comes once a year. Let's go party!"

"To the pub?" I asked Shan.

"Definitely!" she said, pulling out a small key from her desk drawer.

"You were gonna keep it locked up tonight?" I asked.

She laughed. "Maybe. They're animals."

"Let's go!" one of the guys said, and we all got up and started the trek downstairs. We were assaulted by the music and there wasn't an inch of unpacked space on the ground floor. We had to dance our way through the crowd, and it felt like hours by the time we all made it to the backyard.

It was less crazy out there thankfully and a lot quieter once the door was shut behind us. Shannon led the way to her pool house pub and cheers went up when she flipped open the shutters opening for business, so to speak. The Parker Pub didn't get to be the most popular pub in town by charging people.

Lynds, Nick, and Gavin found their way to us and Gavin started to put on a show for the crowd. Nick joined in and Lynds found a cooler to sit on to do air drums.

Roxy and Ava showed up shortly after to see what the crowd was looking at and Roxy transformed from a goth fairy into a punk rock singer, taking the imaginary mic from Gavin, who welcomed her onto his makeshift stage.

I sidled into the pool house to offer to help Shannon, but everyone was paying more attention to the air band now than they were to her, so she made me her Shannon Special, grabbed our drinks and shuttered the pool house. We went out and joined the others, sliding in between Ava and our drama club friends who were cheering and calling out requests to the band.

Roxy pulled Ava onto their stage, spinning her around and serenading her with a Savannah Hollywood love song. It was sickeningly sweet in the best way. I wasn't sure how long they'd been together, but it was clear it was serious for both of them. Ava looked at Roxy like she hung the stars in the sky and Roxy looked at Ava like she was the only person she could see, the only one who mattered. I wondered how they'd managed to keep their secret for so long. They really weren't discreet. I was so happy they didn't have to be anymore, though.

# Chapter Fifty One

The rest of the night passed in a blur of dancing and laughter. At one point Shawn found me and hoisted me up on his shoulders again saying I was his good luck charm and he wanted to keep me with him. He was drunker than he had been, but it was harmless enough.

When we finally called it a night, I dropped Gavin off at his house and then drove Lynds, Roxy, and Ava to our house to spend the night.

I should've known things had been too good to be true though since we woke up to a link texted by Gavin to the group chat.

It was Tiger Shark Tea again, of course, so much for their hiatus.

Tiger Shark Tea

*Shawn Parker Scores Twice in One Weekend:*
*Parker led the Harris High Tiger Sharks to victory Friday night, but he might say Saturday night was his bigger score. He and Bridgette were seen sneaking off together to the golden boy's make-out spot. When they*

> *rejoined the party, she hadn't bothered to fix her messed up hair, and he was grinning wider than when he won the game. I wonder if anyone told her how many other girls have seen that spot...no? Well cats out of the bag now.*

I swiped and saw a photo of me and Shawn walking arm and arm back to the party. There was nothing remotely scandalous about the photo by itself, but after the picture she painted, I could see how it looked a little less innocent now.

Especially when I kept swiping and saw other girls in the same area with him in similar photos. Tiger Shark Tea also reused the picture of Shawn kissing Roxy against the tree to really drive the point home.

I groaned and Roxy rolled over from the air mattress she and Ava were sharing on the ground and asked, "What?"

When she saw it, she sighed. "Welcome to the club. You got Parker-ed."

"I didn't even do anything, though," I groaned.

"I know you didn't," Roxy assured me.

"But that won't really matter, will it?" I asked.

She winced and shook her head.

By the time Ava and Lynds woke up and offered their sympathy, I had spent too much time looking at the post and reading the mean comments. Those didn't bug me nearly as much as Shawn's comment, though.

It read, "Tiger Shark Tea, come on, way to put me on blast. I don't kiss and tell."

That was the only comment Tiger Shark Tea responded to. They said, "Good thing no one thinks you just kissed."

He hadn't responded, but he didn't need to. The implication was clear, and he wasn't denying it. I was fuming. We hadn't even kissed, and he knew it. He could've said that. He could've denied it. I had half a mind to get his number from Shannon and tell him exactly what I thought of that, but I knew it wouldn't make a difference. I knew the song and dance from when the others went through it. He would try gaslighting me into thinking he had tried to deny it and that he was discouraging the rumors. It was a joke. We were all apparently a joke to him. Well, I wasn't laughing, and I wasn't going to sit around feeling sorry for myself and let him continue getting away with this.

"He's stupider than I thought," I said out loud.

The others immediately agreed, but Lynds was watching me more carefully and asked, "Why?"

"Because you guys had basically convinced me to let it go. You wanna know what happened with him last night?"

"Do we?" Ava asked confused.

"Him and I basically called a truce. He thanked me for helping the team and he actually seemed *human* and oh my gosh, I can't believe I fell for it."

"We've all been there," Ava said quickly.

"Don't beat yourself up over it," Roxy added.

"You know he's good," Lynds said.

"I know. I just thought I'd be safe, though. I wasn't going to fall for him, and I didn't fall for him that way, but I still fell for his tricks. He probably only took me out there for the photos."

"So are we doing something about it?" Roxy asked, raising an eyebrow at me.

"I was going to leave him alone," and I might still have done that if it wasn't for his comment. He was encouraging the rumors at my expense. He didn't care about me or about anyone else, just himself. "But he doesn't deserve mercy, and I have something he wants."

"You do?" Roxy asked.

Ava elbowed her, and she immediately added, "You're great, and obviously he'd have to be crazy not to want you."

I laughed at that. "Thanks guys but that's not what I meant. I meant the team thinks I'm good luck. He basically told me last night that he can't win a game without me there. It's definitely all in their heads, but that doesn't mean we can't use it."

"I knew I liked you," Roxy said, grinning.

"What's the plan?" Lynds asked.

"We're taking things a step further. We're going to destroy him. Ava, what are the odds they win the next couple of games?"

"With or without you?" she asked.

"If you isolated me, pretend for a second I never came to Harris High. What are their odds?"

"Well, next weekend's against the Stingrays. We won against them before but only at the home game. This one's away and we haven't won a single away game this season, so odds are low."

"And the week after?"

"Is against the Orcas. They give us a run for our money on our best day, so it's highly unlikely we'd win."

"And if the team is convinced they're cursed?"

Roxy grinned at me while Ava thought for a moment and said, "That would almost guarantee we lose both."

"Perfect, and if they lose both of those, they'll need to win the next two to get to the championship?" I was only eighty percent confident that I understood the stakes correctly, but Ava's answering grin told me I was right.

"So if a certain someone were to stay away from those two games," Lynds said slowly.

"Which I would've had to do anyway cause the play runs those two weekends," I added.

"Then Shawn would be desperate enough to do whatever you wanted," Ava continued.

"You'd have him eating out of the palm of your hand," Roxy said, grinning.

"Exactly," I said, grinning at them.

"You really did it," Ava said in awe.

"You played the player," Roxy said, her expression exuding respect. "So what are you doing with all that power?" she asked.

"By the second loss, he'll be offering me anything I want, begging. I bet he'll make me his girlfriend before Thanksgiving. Then I'll dump and humiliate him at his New Year's Eve blowout party."

"I don't know whether to be proud or a little afraid," Roxy joked.

"You think you can act like his girlfriend for that long?" Ava asked.

"You guys haven't really seen her act yet, but trust me, she's got this," Lynds said.

I laughed at that. "It'll be quite the show, that's for sure."

# Chapter Fifty Two

I'd been ignoring the nerves for weeks, and knew I was as ready as I could be, but standing in the wings waiting for my cue, I was nervous. Dressed in Ramona's flowy white shirt and tights, I looked the part, but I was freaking out.

I felt a hand on my shoulder and turned around, expecting to see Shannon had snuck out of hair and makeup to see me, but it wasn't her, or any of our other theatre friends. It was Mr. Hayes.

"You're shaking like a leaf," he said. "Don't worry, kiddo, you've got this."

"I can't believe I'm doing this," I said. "I'm excited, but so nervous."

"The moment you step out there, Ramona will take over. You've got this. You know the part like you lived it. I knew you were right for the part, and I know you'll do me and the bard proud."

That had been niggling at the back of my mind since he had announced the final casting. I wasn't complaining, of course. I was so excited to be playing the role I was, but I didn't understand why I was picked over Stephanie. She was a senior with acting experience and I was just me. It had felt disrespectful to ask, but it felt like this was an opening. "Thank you, but I have to ask, why me?"

"Why you?" he asked.

"Yeah, why am I Ramona instead of Stephanie?"

"You both have so much talent, but you were right for the part. A good director can tell when a part needs to be played by someone, and the part needed you almost as much as you needed it."

"I'm not sure I know what you mean," I said.

"Look at what you've already made of the show. In true Romeo fashion, you were passionate and brave enough to inspire change. This show wouldn't be what it is now without you, and as Mercutio, that wouldn't have happened. Besides, you and Shannon have a chemistry that can't be easily manufactured."

I was still wondering at that when I stepped on the stage. By the time Benvolio bid Ramona, "Good morrow cousin," Bri was gone, and Ramona was in her place, forlorn and lovesick over Rosaline, who wasn't willing to shame her family by admitting her feelings for a woman, for me.

By the time Shannon joined me on stage, I was feeling like I really belonged there.

When I saw her in her regal purple gown, I forgot myself again. When I kissed her, I did it as Ramona, like I wasn't worthy of her or her lips. It was the gentle kiss of a first love. The second kiss was a little less gentle, but quicker. Ramona, who twenty minutes ago had been despairing that her heart would never beat again for someone else, was enthralled by Juliet. She was determined to steal every kiss from Juliet that she could.

When the show came to an end, I was emotionally drained. The others had warned me about the adrenaline crash, but I hadn't expected it to hit as hard as it did.

In the dressing room, Shannon scooped me into a giant hug. "You did it! You killed it! You were so good!"

"So were you!" I told her immediately. "You were born to play Juliet."

"And you killed Ramona!"

"Literally," I joked, "with poison."

She grinned, squeezing me tighter. "We were so good!"

When she let me go, I checked my phone and saw that everyone was waiting for us. I rushed through getting changed. While I was getting ready to leave, I asked Shannon, "How's the rest of your night looking?"

I wasn't sure if Shawn was throwing another party or not. We had two shows tomorrow and one more on Sunday, and then three more shows next weekend. It was going to be hell for her if she was up all night because of Shawn being inconsiderate.

She checked her phone. "They lost the game, so Shawn's sulking. Apparently, it was bad enough he doesn't feel like partying, sent everyone home a little while ago."

In all the excitement from the play, I had temporarily forgotten about my plan, but I was glad that I was one lost game closer to having a boyfriend.

"Good, I'm glad. I was gonna insist you stayed over if there was a party there tonight."

She laughed. "Dang, just my luck; should've told you there was a party."

I chuckled but said quickly, "You're welcome if you want. We might stop for ice cream on the way home, but it'll be an early night for sure."

She paused for a moment, considering before waving off the offer. "That's okay. Don't worry about me. I'm exhausted. I can't wait to go home and get into PJs and go to bed."

"Alright, but the offer's always there," I told her. She thanked me, pulling me into one more hug before I ran out the door.

I exited the dressing room into the hallway and saw everyone was there waiting for me. Roxy, Gavin, and Lynds with Auntie Jen and Uncle Cam had been in the front row, but I had been shocked to see Ava there, too. I hadn't expected her until tomorrow since she was supposed to be cheering at the game tonight.

Auntie Jen wrapped me in a hug first and then Uncle Cam gave me pink roses, which had me in tears. "Thank you guys so much," I told them. "It means so much to me that you're here, that you let me be here."

I had never dared to dream that there was a world where I could have a family that took care of and supported me instead of me having to take care of and support them like I used to have to do with my mother.

"Are you kidding?" Auntie Jen said, grinning. "We're thrilled to be here." She pointed at Uncle Cam and added, "He's been telling everyone that we ran lines with the star of the show."

I laughed at that, turning to him. He shrugged. "We're both so proud of you."

The tears were fully flowing at that point.

Lynds stepped in to hug me next, but Gavin beat her to it, pulling us into a group hug that Ava and Roxy joined.

"I'm so happy you're all here!" I told them.

"Of course we are," Gavin said.

"Wouldn't have missed it," Ava added.

I tried to stick out the plan to get ice cream, but I was too tired. Roxy, Ava, and Gavin said their goodbyes, and I went home. The entire car ride home Auntie Jen, Uncle Cam, and Lynds were raving about my performance and it almost brought me to tears again. I was incredibly grateful to feel as loved as I did. They not only made sure to make me feel included, but celebrated, and if I thanked them every day for the rest of my life, I was sure it would never be enough to express the depth of my gratitude.

They came to every show even though I told them they didn't have to. The shows were all going to be the same and there were three more showings that weekend, but they all came to all of them. I was over-whelmed by their love in the best way.

# Chapter Fifty Three

I was surprised that even Tiger Shark Tea was talking about the play. Monday morning they posted a pic of me kissing Shannon to let people know there were three more shows this weekend. While the comments were a little gross, I was glad to see some supportive comments, too.

Shannon and I got catcalled by some people at lunch, but besides that, not much changed. I was glad that Shannon didn't feel like things were weird with us kissing as much as we did in the show and in the rehearsals.

I knew people would kill to be in my shoes and I couldn't help feeling a little smug about the fact that I was the one that got to kiss her. Of course, it was just for the show, but still, it made me feel special.

When half the week came and went without Shawn approaching me, I started to wonder if maybe I was wrong. Maybe Shawn didn't care enough about the team to try to talk to me.

I decided to give him until Friday morning. If he didn't approach me, I would talk to him about it and see what I could do about planting the idea in his head.

Thursday afternoon, he found me when I was on my way to rehearsal. He was clearly on his way to practice, since he was in his football jersey. "Hey Bridgette, can I talk to you for a sec?" he asked.

"I mean, you are already," I said, smirking a little.

He chuckled. "Fair enough. I don't really know how to ask this, though," he said, hesitating.

"I'd recommend going for it. Looks like you have somewhere to be," I said, looking pointedly at his jersey. "Besides I don't have long either."

"I need you," he said, pausing a taking a deep breath. "Not just me, the team does. We were trampled in our last game, and everyone's spirits are way down about tomorrow. They're all saying we can't win if you're not there and they know you have a show tomorrow."

I waited for him to say more, but when he didn't, I said, "I'm sorry things aren't going well, but I'm not sure what you want me to say?"

He looked sheepish but slowly said, "That's the hard part. I wasn't sure how to ask, but we need you there tomorrow."

I honestly couldn't believe his nerve. "That's a whole lot of audacity."

He had the sense to look embarrassed, but rushed on, "I know you have a show, but you have two more this weekend and you have an alternate, right?"

"They're called understudies."

"Yeah sure, whatever." He kept going, "You can have your understudy go on, but we need you at the game. The team needs you, hell, the school needs you. We don't play well when you're not there."

"Look, I'm sorry, but I'm not ditching my show for your game."

"Come on, at least think about it. Is there anything I can do to make you change your mind?"

I shook my head. "I'm sorry, but no. This is important to me and I'm not giving it up to come be your cheerleader. I'm not your girl, just some girl you're acting like you scored. Why should I come cheer for you? That's a girlfriend's job and we're certainly not together."

"If I asked you out, would you come to the game?"

I raised an eyebrow at him. "Seriously? how romantic," I deadpanned. "That's just how every girl wants to be asked out. I can't believe you're still single."

"Come on, tell me what to do and I'll do it. I'm trying here. You've gotta give me something. We need this win."

"I already told you no. Good luck with your game, though."

"You know we're going to lose. Come on, say you'll come."

"For the last time, we're not together. Why would I bother? I just went to one of your games and you haven't been to a single one of my shows. Clearly, you're only interested when it's convenient for you, and I'm not interested in being at your beck and call."

"It's not like that."

"I'm sick of waiting, Parker. I'd say call me when you grow up, but you still never earned my number."

With that, I walked off. I didn't turn around, but I imagined his jaw was on the floor. I felt untouchable after that absolute power move and couldn't wait to see what he'd try next.

# CHAPTER FIFTY FOUR

After our show Friday when I got to check my phone, I found out that they lost again and I couldn't help grinning at the news.

I sent a celebratory text to the group chat. They had to win their last two games to make it to the championships, and I had already planted the seed to Shawn about what I wanted from him, now I just had to wait and watch it grow.

When I saw Shannon the next morning getting ready for our matinee performance, she looked like she hadn't slept much.

"I thought you said there wasn't a party again last night?" I asked her, feeling a little guilty for not trying hard enough to have convinced her to stay over the night before.

She groaned. "There wasn't, but you have my brother all worked up."

"Me?" I asked. "What did I do?"

She laughed. "Besides being vexing to him because you're a girl not falling all over him?"

"Well yeah, besides that," I said, laughing.

"He's convinced you skipped the game yesterday to make him lose on purpose. He's bitching about how you're trying to manipulate him."

"Seriously?" I asked, playing dumb. "I have no idea why he thought for a second I would skip one of our shows to go cheer him on."

"I know!" she yelled. "I couldn't believe he actually had the nerve to ask you! I mean, actually I totally can, but god," she groaned, "he's really the worst."

"I get the game's important to him, but the show's important, too."

"Even more important, our show has a killer message thanks to a certain someone," she said with a grin.

"I'm just glad people are loving it."

"I mean, people do love seeing girls kiss," Shannon quipped.

I laughed. "Fair enough. I'm sure that's why all the shows have been packed."

I was loving the show, but it had taken up almost every free moment and thought for the last two weeks so I wouldn't be lying to say I was a little relieved we only had these last two shows today and then it would be over.

"What are we gonna do with all our free time when the show wraps?" I asked.

"We?" she said. "You mean you won't be too cool for me the minute the show wraps?" she joked.

"Of course not! Besides, you're the cool one here, not me."

"Hardly," she said, laughing, and turned back to her mirror.

I knew she was joking, but she planted the worry in my head that I wouldn't see as much of her after the show was over. It nagged at and distracted me until the moment I was out on stage and then took up my thoughts immediately after.

Shannon, of course, noticed I was distracted between shows and asked, "Do you want to talk about what's bothering you?"

"I'm exhausted and a bit ready for this to be over, but I also don't ever want this to end."

She sighed. "I know what you mean. It's so draining, but so worth it."

That was part of what was bothering me, but it wasn't all of it. I had my other friends, of course, but I adored Shannon and had grown attached to the rest of the drama club, too. "I'm just worried things will change after the show?"

"Change how?" she asked.

"I'm worried we wouldn't have as much in common or that I won't really see you guys as much."

She turned away from the mirror and put down the lipstick she was touching up. "What makes you think that?"

I shrugged. There wasn't really a rational answer to that. It just felt like Shannon didn't know the real me, not in the same way my other friends did. I was worried our friendship was hanging by a thread as it was and that without the show holding us together, the cord would snap. If I was being honest with myself, I was worried my relationship with her would be just as temporary as the other friends I had made in the past. Most of them had promised to stay in touch when I moved only for me to find out that when I was out of their sight and no longer shared a school with them, they forgot about me.

I knew I wasn't going anywhere this time and tried to convince myself this time would be different, but it was hard to believe that when I felt like I was keeping secrets from Shannon. She had always been so open with me and here I was plotting to hurt her brother. I wasn't even sure I deserved her friendship, but for once in my life I was going to be selfish and, like Ramona did with Juliet, I was going to take whatever Shannon offered me.

"No reason, really. I guess I'm just used to things falling apart."

It was the truth, but that didn't make me feel any less guilty when she wrapped me in a comforting hug that I wasn't sure I deserved.

This time when I saw Shannon, as Juliet, dead on the stage, I felt like I was mourning not only Juliet, but my friendship with Shannon. I didn't know if we could survive my plans for her brother. As much as I loved her, though, this was too important to give up, even for her.

Tears poured down my cheeks as I kissed her lips for the last time and drank the poison. Hearing the heartbreak in her voice when she discovered me dead, it was almost impossibly difficult to not break character and wrap her in a hug. When she collapsed on top of me, I squeezed her arm, not able to move more than that, but needing to touch her to reassure her and myself that I was right there with her.

When the show ended, the feeling of grief clung to me. Shannon seemed to be feeling it, too. The others were in more of a celebratory mood and we both tried to rally for the sake of the others, but I was failing.

I rushed through changing. The others were going out to celebrate since it was the last show. Shannon tried to convince me, saying it was tradition, but I wasn't in the mood and didn't want to bring them down.

I exited the dressing room looking for my family, who had come to every single show, but I was surprised when my eyes landed first on Shawn.

"Hey you," he said, grinning. "How's the star of the show doing?"

I pushed away my exhaustion and conflicting emotions enough to manufacture a smile for him. "Depends on what you're doing here?" I asked.

He was holding a bouquet of red roses that he held out to me, saying, "You didn't really think I'd miss your last show did you?"

I shook my head slowly like I was confused by this turn of events. "I guess not," I said slowly. "I don't know what to say."

"How about you say you're happy to see me?" he said, pulling me into a hug. "You were really hot out there," he said in my ear. I was glad he was hugging me and couldn't see me roll my eyes at that.

"Thanks," I said, pulling away. "I'm happy you're here and the flowers are beautiful," I said, taking them from him.

"Beautiful flowers for a beautiful girl."

"I bet you say that to all the girls," I joked.

He grinned. "If you'll have me, I'd like to only say it to you."

The shock on my face wasn't forced. I assumed it was coming, but I really thought he would've held out longer if I was being honest. "What are you saying?" I asked.

"I'm asking you to be my girlfriend. I can't get you out of my head. I've been going crazy thinking about you. I can't eat, I can't sleep, I can't play football well." I fought to not laugh that he couldn't even keep football out of his fake love declaration. "I can't stop thinking about you. I just want to be with you. What do you say?"

I noticed out of the corner of my eye that Lynds was recording. I gave the camera an 'ohmygosh can you believe how lucky I am' look before squealing and saying, "Yes!"

He pulled me to him and kissed me. It was a little more enthusiastic than our last kisses, but it still lacked any real passion from him. He pulled away and picked me up, spinning me around, yelling out, "She said yes!"

The people around us who had clearly been watching, even though they had pretended not to, were cheering for us now.

"She said yes! Bridgette's my girlfriend!"

When he put me down, my eyes landed on a different blonde who was frozen in the dressing room door. When she saw me see her, she smiled at me, but that didn't erase the hurt and confusion I had seen on her face a moment earlier. The worst part was that I couldn't even blame her for being upset.

I couldn't explain myself, couldn't be real with her, and even if I could have, she might still have been just as upset with me for trying to hurt her brother.

I had known this would hurt her, and I had chosen my revenge over her and her feelings. I deserved her scorn, so when she turned and left without a word, I didn't chase her down like I wanted to. Instead, I let her go, and later that night, when I laid awake wanting to talk to her, I didn't text her.

# Chapter Fifty Five

The video Lynds took ended up everywhere. Everyone was telling us how cute of a couple we were. Acting happy about it was turning out to be much more draining than my role as Ramona had been. Having to act like I was in love with Shannon was incredibly easy. She was so kind, caring, and beautiful. She was easy to love.

Her brother couldn't be more different. He was charismatic, but once you saw past the superficial charm, he was calculating. While it wasn't likely every piece of vulnerability he showed me was fake, I couldn't tell what was real and what was fake, so all of it felt targeted to manipulate me and everyone else around him.

I went to their next games, and they won. Shawn and the others made a big deal about me being there, but it didn't feel nearly as special as it did the first time. Regardless of how I was feeling, I performed the role of his girlfriend as well as anyone could want. I wore the colors, painted his number 49 on my cheek with face paint, and screamed for him with everyone else.

At school, he performed the role of my boyfriend well enough that no one had any doubts we were enamored with each other. Things had stayed weird with Shannon since closing night of the play, though. Despite her assurances things wouldn't change with her and the drama club, things felt off. I had tried sitting with them a couple of times, but it hurt how distant Shannon was acting, so I started sitting with Ava again.

It was better for the plan anyway since Shawn refused to sit with his sister's friends, but was more than willing to sit with me at Ava's table.

His company was a terrible consolation prize for the absence of Shannon's.

I couldn't help thinking that maybe I had made a mistake, because after this was all over, what would I have? I would have Lynds, and Ava, and Roxy, and Gavin, of course, but I had them anyway. I would get fleeting joy from exacting vengeance on Shawn, but I would lose Shannon, and I was severely doubting now whether the prize was worth the sacrifice, but there was no turning back down. I had chosen my path, and I had to see it through.

I threw myself into paying attention to Shawn. Thankfully, football practice kept him exhausted and busy, so I only had to contend with his attention at school. He was acting as taken with me as I was him.

I would have felt guilty if I wasn't sure that his feelings were as fake as my own. I wondered how soon after the championship game he would find someone new. I knew I had to beat him to that punch, though, so I gave him the ultimate ultimatum.

When he was talking to me about the championship game, I asked him, "Are you even serious about us or am I just a good luck charm to you?"

His smile dropped into a frown, and he rushed to reassure me, "Of course you're more than a good luck charm. I adore you. I'm crazy about you."

"I don't know why I'm even going to the championship game. You're just using me."

He paled and said quickly, "That's not true. I would never. You're my girlfriend."

"Until you decide you're sick of me," I said, injecting concern I didn't feel into my voice, before adding, "I mean if you really liked me, you'd have asked me to be your date to your New Year's Party."

He looked surprised by that and chuckled. "New Year's? It's the beginning of December and you're already thinking about the end of the month?"

I put on a pout and said, "It's all anyone's been talking about besides the championship game. It's 'Parker's big New Year's blowout' this and 'Parker's New Year's Rave' that, and you haven't even invited me."

He laughed again and said, "I don't invite anyone really, people just show up."

I frowned a little dramatically at him and said, "But I'm your girlfriend. Don't you want me to be your date to your party?"

He gave me an easy grin, saying, "Of course. You're so much more than a good luck charm to me. Please spend New Year's with me?"

"As your date," I prompted.

"As my date," he agreed.

Perfect. I had plans for him and something told me he wasn't going to love the bang his New Year was going to start with.

# Chapter Fifty Six

They won the championship, and I was said to be the luckiest girl in school to be dating Shawn Parker. I felt lucky at just how little time I actually had to spend with him.

I refused to go over to his house when he wasn't throwing parties. It was awkward enough seeing Shannon in English class when she would only talk to me when politeness wouldn't let her stay silent, but spending time at her house with her brother would've been too much.

For my own sanity, and Lyndsey's, I didn't invite him to our house, either. He seemed perfectly happy with our arrangement though, and continually joked I was keeping him a dirty little secret from my family.

After the championship game, studying for finals took over. I was surprised that Shawn seemed to take them as seriously as I was. We didn't see much of each other leading up to and during finals. Of course, with the championship game behind us, it made sense he wasn't paying me much mind anymore. I was grateful that he had already invited me to the New Year's party, otherwise I would be worried he was going to pull back entirely and ruin my plans, but I felt as secure as I could that he would stick to his word in this at least.

After finals, we headed to winter break, and I was relieved when Shawn relayed the "sad" news that him and his family would be spending the holidays until New Year's Eve at their lake house.

I was thrilled and kissed him a little more eagerly than I normally would have while saying goodbye. I laid it on thick about how much I was going to miss him and how sad I was that we wouldn't be able to spend Christmas together.

It took everything in me to wait until I was safely in my car with Lynds and driving away from the school to start celebrating my good luck.

A couple of days before the New Year's party, we had a group chat meet up at Lynds's and my house.

Once everyone else was settled in our room, I stood up, walked over to the door, and turned around dramatically to face them. "I bet you're all wondering why I've gathered you here today."

I couldn't hold my straight face when they all started laughing and Lynds threw a pillow in my direction.

"But for real," I said, grabbing the pillow from the floor and sinking down next to Lynds, bumping shoulders with her.

"You guys have been to his New Year's parties before. What do we think the move is?"

"Well," Ava said, considering, "we want maximum visibility."

"And maximum humiliation," Roxy added.

"I did have an idea," Lynds offered. "But I'm not sure how we could pull it off."

We turned to her expectantly, and I asked, "What are you thinking?"

She turned to Roxy and said, "You know how Shawn did the video wrap up last year?" They nodded, and she asked, "Does he do that every year?"

"He did the year before, too," Ava said.

"Well, I think we could make an addition to it," Lynds said.

"What are you thinking?" I asked.

"A video compilation of his various conquests taken from Tiger Shark Tea's page, over the years there's way more than enough, and then we have a video of you, or maybe you make a speech, I'm not sure, but you would let everyone in our your little secret that you set out to play the player and never even liked him but got him so under your thumb that you're the only official girlfriend he's ever had, and then you dump his ass."

"I love it!" Roxy said.

"Obsessed," Gavin agreed.

Ava turned to me and asked, "What do you think?"

"I think it's perfect. I just don't know how we would get access to add to the video."

"Are you still close with Shannon?" Gavin asked.

I considered before shaking my head. Aside from a "Merry Christmas! Hope you're having the best time," text I had sent her that was left on read, we hadn't talked since school was out. I hadn't talked to Shawn either, though. I was sure Shannon would've given him my number now if he asked, but he hadn't contacted me either. I was glad that I was on the same page with at least one of the Parkers.

"Haven't talked to either of them since school let out," I said, trying to sound more casual than I felt.

"No worries," Ava said, waving it off and quickly moving on. I appreciated so much that she understood without my saying it that I didn't want to talk about Shannon right now. "Forget the video," she said, shooting Lynds an apologetic look. "It really was a great idea, but there are always New Year's toasts and resolutions. What if you tell Shawn you want to make a toast as his girlfriend..."

Ava trailed off and Roxy finished, "And then you make your speech and dump his ass."

I thought about it for a moment, pictured everyone staring at me while I held a glass of champagne and toasted the player of the year. I found myself picturing tossing the champagne in his face. It was exhilarating. I had been building to this moment since those photos came out. We all had.

"Let's do it," I said, grinning.

We spent the rest of the day joking about what I should say and imagining everyone's reactions. I had never questioned whether Shawn deserved it, he did, but I had questioned whether it was worth it for me, but now I was all in. I had nothing to lose, and I was going to make sure he felt some of the pain he had inflicted.

# CHAPTER FIFTY SEVEN

Walking up to the Parker Palace for the first time in a few weeks was an odd feeling. I hadn't heard from or seen either of the Parkers since school ended, and I wasn't sure how I was going to be received.

In a perfect world, Shannon would wrap me in a big hug and spend all night with me, and Shawn would be politely indifferent to me, but none of that was realistic. Polite indifference was the best I could hope for from Shannon because, after humiliating Shawn tonight, I'd be lucky if she didn't hate me.

"Alright guys," Roxy said, looking at her phone, "it's nine now, which means we have three hours to enjoy ourselves before meeting in the backyard for the countdown."

"Sounds good to me," I said. She was about to say more but Nick found us and came over. He kissed Lynds, slapped Gavin on the back, and said hi to the rest of us. That stopped whatever she was planning to say. We all liked him, but weren't sure he would understand and go along with the plan, so it was easier to keep him in the dark.

"So what are you gonna do to kill time?" Ava asked.

I shrugged before saying sheepishly, "I thought maybe I'd see if I could find Shannon." I knew I should be spending time being seen with Shawn, making him show everyone at the party how much he likes me, but our plan didn't change the fact that the only Parker I really wanted to spend time with was Shannon.

She nodded. "Makes sense. Good luck," she said as she and Roxy headed off to find some of Ava's friends.

Against my better judgment, I went around to the backyard, skipping the house altogether, to look for Shannon. I figured Shawn was probably in the middle of the crowd inside and knew that once he found me, it would be hard to get away.

I was excited to see the pool house was unlocked and open, but as I got closer, I couldn't see her. I looked around, surveying the yard. There were plenty of people here, plenty of other blonde girls, but I didn't see Shannon. I sighed and took a seat on one of the barstools.

I almost jumped out of my own skin when I heard her voice ask, "Vodka for your thoughts?"

I looked around, and a moment later, she popped up with a bottle. On seeing me, her face ran through surprise, joy, and sadness quickly before turning to politeness and saying, "Hey, good to see you. How was your holiday?"

"It was good," I said slowly. "How was yours?"

She waved off the question, pouring a shot. "It was fine, but I'm sure my brother told you all about our exploits at the lake."

"I actually haven't seen him yet," I told her.

She looked at me with surprise. "Needed a drink first?" she asked, gesturing to the bar behind her. "Fair enough. He can be quite vexing. What can I get you?"

I swallowed hard. I hadn't expected to find her friendly, but this aloofness hurt more than I thought it would.

"You know I don't drink," I said, "but if you're offering, I'll take a Shannon Special."

"I thought I knew a lot about you," she said, shrugging. "But the girl I knew wasn't my brother's girlfriend. I figured other things might've changed."

"I haven't changed," I said carefully.

"You could have fooled me." She gestured again at the shot glass. "You sure?"

I again declined.

"Suit yourself," she said before raising it mock toast to me before swallowing the vodka. She grimaced, but poured herself another.

"I didn't know you drank," I said.

"Apparently you hardly know me either."

It wasn't true, though, and it hurt to hear her say something like that.

"I'm really sorry, Shan. I didn't mean to hurt you." I said, telling her the only truth I could offer. I knew it wasn't good enough, though, and her face remained unchanged.

She gave me a placid smile and said, "Don't worry, your favorite Parker has been singing your praises since school ended." I almost slipped and told her the truth, that my favorite Parker was standing in front of me, but I bit my tongue. The truth wouldn't make things easier and even if it would, I was too committed now to ruin things by telling the truth now. She frowned when I didn't say anything, and I realized that by not speaking at all, I had managed to make things worse again. "Why don't you go find him?" she said.

"I wanted to see you first," I admitted.

"Ah, for the drink." She turned around and started gathering ingredients. "You know, I'm the only one that makes a liquid sunset."

I chuckled at that, saying, "I'm not sure if you're the only one, but you're certainly the best."

She scoffed. "I'm sure if my brother made you one, you'd swear it tasted better."

I was a little surprised by her harshness and went with the truth. "If I did, I'd be lying."

She gave a sad smile at that, offering me the drink and said, "My dear Ramona, always the flatterer."

I smiled a little at that. At least she was smiling, even if it was tinged with sadness. "I missed you," I said, taking the drink from her hand.

She stiffened a little at that and said, "I know what you're doing, but you don't need to anymore."

I felt I had already lost the plot of the conversation. "If you know what I'm doing, I'd love to know, because I feel like I'm stumbling and tripping through this conversation."

All traces of happiness were gone when she said, "Shawn told me what you said. I was just giving you your space."

"What did he tell you?" I asked quickly, grasping to understand.

"Don't play games with me anymore," she said, and before I could say anything else, she closed the bar shutters in my face.

I blinked in shock at them, waiting for them to re-open, for her to greet me with a joke and a smile, but the only thing that happened was the door following suit with a slam. I knocked on the shutters, asking her to open up softly at first, then louder, but she didn't relent.

I had no idea what was happening, but I knew who might. I grabbed my drink and headed to the house in search of Shawn.

# CHAPTER FIFTY EIGHT

Before I could find him, Gavin stumbled into me. He was halfway through a joke when he noticed my face and his smile dropped. He looked around before pulling me to the edge of the yard, away from prying eyes, and asked, "What happened?"

"I don't know," I said, all hurt and frustration. "Shannon's been icing me out since I started dating Shawn, and I know I shouldn't care because I know she's going to hate me after tonight anyway, but I wanted to talk to her. I miss her, and I know she'll hate me in a couple of hours, but I have no idea what I did to hurt her now. I know it must've been awkward for her that the girl she had to kiss during the plays is now kissing her brother, but I thought we were friends."

Gavin just stared at me. "You're joking right?"

I stared back and he continued to watch me before saying, "You're not. It would be funny if it wasn't so sad."

"What are you talking about?"

"The Parkers have been fighting over you, and Shannon thinks she lost."

That sort of made sense. I supposed I hadn't really thought about the consequences of my actions, but I had come between them whether I intended to or not.

"I guess I can see what you mean. She feels like I chose my relationship with him over my friendship with her."

Gavin shook his head saying, "No. She feels like you chose him over her."

"That's what I just said."

"No, you said friendship. Shannon's not upset as a friend because you're dating her brother. She's upset because she's in love with you and you chose her brother."

"What? You're crazy. She's not in love with me," I insisted.

"Fine, maybe love is a bit dramatic, but she likes you as more than a friend."

"You can't be serious?" I asked. I hadn't seen any-thing about her friendship with me that was much different from her friendships with the others in the drama club or my own friendships with Ava and Roxy, but as the thought came, I had to recognize that it wasn't quite true.

She always seemed a little happier to see me than she had almost anyone else. Her smile seemed a little brighter and softer towards me than it was with other people. When I used to sit with them at lunch, she would accidentally brush up against me several times while we were eating and when she asked something of the table or said something particularly funny, she usually looked at me first. Sometimes in English, I used to look up and catch her watching me. She'd smile at me, and I'd return the smile, but I couldn't think of any time I had caught her looking like that at someone else. Surely that just meant that she liked me best of all her friends, though.

"You're serious?" I asked again.

He nodded. "I would've said something earlier, but I thought you knew how she felt."

"Are you sure she feels like that?" I asked. I wasn't well versed in relationships and crushes, but her liking me didn't make much sense to me.

"I'm positive and, to be honest, I have no idea how you missed what's obvious to pretty much everyone else."

"Is that why Tiger Shark Tea kept posting about me and her?"

"Without knowing who Tiger Shark Tea is, it's hard to know for sure, but probably."

"So she's upset that I chose him?"

"No, she's upset you chose him over her."

I threw my hands up in the air at that. "That's not fair, though! I didn't know she was a choice, and I didn't really choose him."

Gavin looked at me appraisingly and asked, "If we ignore the Parker problem, how do you feel about Shannon?"

"How do I feel?"

"Do you like her?"

I started to respond that I adored her, before I stopped myself. He wasn't asking about my friendship with her; he was asking if I had deeper feelings for her, and to be honest, I wasn't sure. I didn't have much experience and while I had gone on an occasional date, I wasn't sure I had experienced attraction to anyone I had dated.

"How do you know if you like someone?" I asked Gavin.

He looked at me incredulously, looked like he was about to make a joke, and then seemed to realize I was being sincere and vulnerable and instead he said, "I used to be really confused myself. I thought liking someone was a more elated form of friendship where you're close enough with someone that you can tolerate kissing them and having them touch you. That was all I felt for the girls I dated, but then I dated a guy and realized I'd just been looking in the wrong place."

"Who was he?" I asked.

Gavin waved me off. "Ancient history, just a guy I met at summer camp, but it wasn't until then that things clicked into place for me. I found myself being pulled toward him, wanting to be around him more than anyone else. Whenever something was funny or made me happy, he was the first person I wanted to tell. When I was sad, I wanted him to be the one to comfort me and tell me everything would be alright.

I was right about it being an elevated friendship, but with him I never had to tolerate being kissed."

"He didn't kiss you?" I asked, confused.

He laughed loudly at that. "I didn't say that. He kissed me, but I didn't just tolerate it. With him, kissing wasn't a chore. It wasn't something to be tolerated, it was something I enjoyed. Tell me, did you enjoy kissing Shannon?"

"That doesn't count, though. We were acting."

"Did you enjoy kissing Shawn?" Gavin countered.

"No," I answered immediately, and he raised an eyebrow at me. "That's different, though. With Shannon, we were different people, and I was having to act like I loved her."

"Which is super different from what you were doing with Shawn as Bridgette because...?"

When he put it like that, I didn't know what to say.

"It's hardly the same thing, though. Shawn's the worst and she's her. Of course, kissing him would be worse."

"Do you think she's beautiful?" Gavin asked.

"Of course I do," I said quickly. "I might be demi but I'm not blind."

"And I might not be into girls, but I think someone here is... into a particular girl anyway."

"I-I don't really know," I said. "I've never been anywhere long enough to have deep enough connections with people to form feelings. Do I like her like that?"

"I know it's confusing. Trust me, I get that better than most, but only you can decide that. From the outside looking in, though, it looks like you do."

I thanked him and headed toward the music again. I wandered toward the house, feeling unmoored. It felt like my entire life I had believed the sky was blue, only to now be told it was green. Now when I looked at the sky, I was struggling to see the blue I had thought was there before.

I knew I loved Shannon's friendship and objectively I knew she was beautiful and that I loved spending time with her. I hadn't realized that I thought she was beautiful in more than an artistic way, though. Now I was wondering if I did want more from her, if I was attracted to her and wanted to be with her.

My phone chimed, and I looked down to see it was somehow already half past ten. I only had an hour and a half left. After that, regardless of how I felt about her, she would know what I did to her brother, that I didn't choose him over her, but that I chose revenge over her, and I wasn't sure if that would be better or worse.

I needed to hurry. I needed to find Shawn and find out what he told Shannon. Maybe that would help me make sense of the thoughts and feelings buzzing around in me. I knew it was the wrong time and place for this, but I couldn't shake the feeling that it was now or never. I felt in my heart that if Shannon went into midnight, into the new year still mad over this hurt, there wouldn't be room for our friendship to heal from the hurt that was coming.

I found him on the dance floor, and he pulled me to him, kissing me like he had missed me. I stiffened in his arms but let him. When he pulled away, I leaned to his ear to be heard over the music and yelled, "Can we talk?"

He smiled, nodding, pointed to the ceiling and mouthed, "Upstairs?"

I nodded quickly. It was quieter up there and we'd be alone, which was better than the back or front yard where people might be able to see or overhear us.

He clapped a few of his friends on their backs and took my hand. I heard him yelling to them, "My girl missed me!" I rolled my eyes at that, but let him keep hold of my hand. I only had to play the girlfriend for another hour and a half. I could do that.

He led the way through the crowd, pulled me up the stairs, and opened the door to what I assumed was his room. I went in and he quickly followed, shutting the door behind us.

"Missed me?" he asked, stepping toward me to kiss me. I took a step back and found myself in front of his bed. I paused a moment. I could play into this and lead him on a bit more, but I was tired and confused and couldn't stop thinking about Shannon.

"Course I did," I said quickly. "Shannon said you guys had a great time."

He frowned a little at that. "You're still friends with her?"

I wasn't really sure how to answer that, so instead I said, "She's been really weird actually and I was hoping you might know why."

He raised an eyebrow at that. "Why would I know what's got my sister worked up?"

"She said you told her what I said, which didn't make any sense to me, so I figured I'd ask you. What did you tell her?"

He came forward and pulled me into a hug. "You sound upset. I'm sorry she upset you. This is what I was trying to protect you from."

"What do you mean?" I asked, getting more suspicious by the moment.

"She was being weird about you for ages before we got together. I don't think you two should be friends."

I pulled away from him and crossed my arms. "That's not really up to you." I told him. "What did you say to her?"

He shrugged. "I just told her the truth."

"Which is?"

"That you were using her to get close to me."

I gawked at him. "You didn't."

He shrugged. "I don't see what the big deal is. It was true, and it was the only way she was going to get over her little crush that you clearly weren't reciprocating."

"What? Why would you say that?" I demanded.

"Because it was true. It wasn't the first time someone's been her friend to try to get with me," he said.

"That wasn't what I was doing!"

"You can drop the act," he said, grinning. "It worked so you don't have to lie to me."

"You actually believe that, don't you?" When he didn't say anything, I said, "You're delusional. I wasn't using her. No wonder she hates me now. I have to go find her."

I moved around him to the door and grabbed the handle. Before I opened it, Shawn stepped toward me, reaching out to me, saying, "Bridgette, wait."

I turned around long enough to glare at him and say, "I know you've got everyone else fooled into thinking you're some perfect golden boy and that you're the big man on campus, but let me tell you something, Shannon's twice the person you'll ever be."

With that, I turned back around and whipped open the door to see a stunned-looking Shannon staring back at me.

"Shan! I was just coming to look for you. Can we talk?"

She looked over my shoulder at Shawn and whatever she saw there had her grabbing my arm and saying, "Yeah let's go to my room."

Before Shawn could say anything, she had us in her room with the door shut. She stood in front of the door, waiting. When, after a minute, he didn't follow, I breathed a sigh of relief.

She turned around and asked, "Are you okay?"

"Yeah, I'm fine. How much did you hear?"

"Enough to know that maybe I shouldn't have listened to Shawn."

"He told me he told you I was using you to get to him and that's so not true," I said quickly, needing her to hear it and hoping she would believe me.

"Yeah," she said slowly. "I ran into Roxy and Ava earlier, who both basically told me you'd been really upset I wasn't talking to you."

I grimaced. "I'm sorry. I promise I didn't tell either of them to bother you about it."

"You were really upset, though?" she asked, assessing me.

"Of course I was. I adore you and you started icing me out after the play ended."

"Well yeah, I thought we were building something, and you spat in my face becoming my brother's girlfriend. It made no sense to me and then my brother tells me that you want me to leave you alone. After you said yes to him, I felt like I didn't even know you, so when he said that, I listened. I didn't want to get more hurt." She started to tear up, and I wanted to pull her into a hug, but I wasn't sure if she would welcome that, so I reached out and squeezed her arm instead. "I thought distance would help, but that hurt, too."

"I'm so sorry," I said. "I never ever meant to hurt you, I promise. It's just- it's hard to explain."

She looked up at me sadly and said, "You don't owe me an explanation. You're allowed to like who you like. Bad taste isn't something you should have to apologize for." She cracked a small smile at that and my heart shattered all over again seeing the lies and half-truths continue to hurt this girl that I cared about so much. In less than an hour, the truth would be out anyway, so I figured there was no reason to keep holding back.

"I have to tell you something. Well, a lot of things actually, and I don't really know how to start. It's a long story and you might hate me afterward, but I have to get it out there. You deserve to know."

She looked at me warily and asked, "How bad is it?"

"Bad enough that I want you to promise to hear me out until the end, and then if you want me to leave you alone after that, I'll understand and will listen."

After a moment of silence, she nodded. "Okay, hit me with it."

"So you know Lynds is my cousin." She looked like she was going to interrupt which made me smile, so I said, "I know, but hear me out. A month after I moved in with Lynds, Tiger Shark Tea leaked that Shawn was triple timing Lynds, Roxy, and Ava. I watched Lynds be devastated by that and hated Shawn for it. Long story short, I reached out to Roxy, and then Ava ended up joining, too, and we all decided that we were going to do something about it. We decided that a boy like that-" I paused, saying quickly, "I know he's your brother and my boyfriend, but let's be honest, he sucks." She looked confused but didn't interrupt so I continued, "We decided that a boy like that shouldn't get to treat girls however he wanted without repercussions. We decided to give him a dose of his own medicine and play the player."

"Wait what?"

"I'm getting to it-" I started to say but she didn't let me finish.

"You set out to play him and managed to catch feelings for him?" she asked in disbelief.

Now it was my turn to look confused. "Feelings? I didn't catch feelings for him."

"But you're dating him," she said slowly, before her eyes widened. "You're dating him," she repeated to herself.

"Until the midnight toasts, yeah," I said.

"What's happening at the toasts?"

"A bit of a roast," I hesitantly admitted.

"You dated my brother for the last six weeks just to dump and roast him at his blow out party of the year?"

"I did warn you it was kind of bad." She put her head in her hands, and I rushed to say, "I know he's your brother, but he really hurt my cousin, and he doesn't seem to care who he hurts. Maybe I should feel guilty for lying to him and plotting to hurt him, but I know he doesn't care about me either. All he cares about is his reputation, which is why it was so important for me to hit him where it hurts."

I watched as her shoulders started shaking. I was frozen, not knowing what was okay to do. I reached out again and squeezed her arm. When her head popped up a moment later, I saw, to my relief and confusion, that she was laughing.

"I can't believe you were a good enough actress that you fooled me, too," she said.

"You're not mad at me?" I asked, feeling a small amount of hope.

"No? Why would I be?" she asked. "Shawn's my brother, but he runs through girls way too quickly. That's why I warned you off of him from the jump. I was worried about you, and I'm so glad you didn't actually fall for him."

"Does that mean we're friends again?" I asked cautiously.

She looked at me and said, "Maybe, but I have a question for you first."

I swallowed hard, instantly worried again.

"What is it?"

"Okay, a statement and a question really," she clarified. "I've spent the last six weeks trying to avoid thinking about you being with my brother, only to find out I was jealous for no reason, so I'm cutting to the chase. I like you a lot... as more than a friend."

She looked at me expectantly, but I was waiting for her to continue.

"Well?" she asked.

"Well," I said slowly, "you said you had a question, too. I was waiting for the question."

She chuckled and asked, "What do you think about me?"

"I'm not really sure how to answer that," I said truthfully. I saw her deflate a little and quickly added, "No. I'm being serious, I don't know what I think, really."

She scoffed and said, "Come on, we're friends. If you don't like me like that you don't have to save my feelings, I can handle it."

"I- so um... I'm demisexual."

Her eyes met mine, and I watched a few emotions pass over her face too quickly to read before she asked, "I know that means a lot of different things to different people, so what does that mean for you?"

I started to tear up a little at that. She hadn't thought that made me weird. She had accepted me and asked about my boundaries. It was a level of acceptance I'd never experienced in a romantic context before and it was making me emotional. I swallowed back the lump in my throat and tried to explain. "Well, to me it means I've never really had strong feelings for someone, so I don't really know what it feels like. You know I used to move around a ton, so I was never somewhere long enough to form a connection deep enough to catch feelings for anyone. I imagine if I did catch feelings for someone, though, that it would sneak up on me."

"What do you mean?" she asked, and I searched for a better way to explain.

The best I could come up with was a Pride and Prejudice explanation and I was happy to know she would get the reference. "I mean like how Darcy tells Elizabeth in Pride and Prejudice that he was in the middle of falling in love before he knew he had begun. I think if I were to fall for someone, that I would be caught off guard by it. I know I love spending time with you. You get me and make me feel seen, but I don't know if what I feel is deeper than friendship. I know you're objectively a beautiful girl, but how do I know if I'm attracted to you?"

After a moment she said, "If you want me to answer that for you, I might have an idea."

"Please, if you know a way to make me feel less confused, I'm willing to try anything."

She scooted a little closer to me on the bed and said, "We're going to play a game of chicken. Mirror what I do and stop if you get uncomfortable, okay?"

Sounded easy enough, but I was nervous. I really liked her and wanted her to be happy. The stakes were high, but I knew I had to be true to myself. If I wasn't comfortable with her or attracted to her, leading her on wouldn't do her any favors.

She reached out and touched me on the arm. With my other hand, I reached out and did the same. Someone making me nervous like this was a new sensation that I didn't dislike. She trailed her hand up my arm and as I copied her, I felt my heart start to race as she got to my shoulder and worked her way up my neck. It wasn't like I hadn't touched her before, but this intentional touching, this intentional exploration felt more sensual. Her hand got to my chin, and she cupped my cheek, running her thumb over first my top and then bottom lip. I shivered a little at the touch as I did the same to her.

"Feeling okay?" she whispered.

"Yes," I said, feeling a little breathless, but I was okay.

"Then let's try something," she said, pulling my face slowly to hers, giving me ample time to pull away as she slowly brought my lips toward hers. I didn't though.

Her soft lips met mine as she kissed me gently. It wasn't like any of the other kisses I had shared with her. This one was slower and more cautious. She was asking a question of me with her lips. She was trying to taste and explore my boundaries, first with her lips and then with her tongue. When her tongue stroked mine, my brain stopped working. The thoughts stopped whirring, and it was just me and her existing together, sharing a passionate kiss. We were the only two people in the world, and she was the only one that mattered.

After what could have been a few minutes or a few hours, she pulled away breathless and asked, "So...?"

"Damn," I breathed out.

She bit her lip, and I found myself mesmerized by the action for a moment. She cleared her throat softly, and I looked up, meeting her hazel eyes. The question was written in them, but she asked it anyway, "Do you think you're attracted to me?"

I laughed at that, grinning at her. "I think that's the only time I've ever kissed someone where my brain shut off."

"Is that good or bad?" she asked.

I struggled to think of how to explain before saying, "Usually when I kiss someone, my brain is running through a checklist of how to do it right. Usually, my thoughts are racing with how much pressure to apply, how much tongue to use, how long to kiss them before pulling away, how much to lean into them, whether they're enjoying it, and how long I have to keep kissing them before I can pull away and still have it feel normal. With you, I was in the moment. I enjoyed it."

"So," she said, a grin spreading across your face, "if I'm understanding right, you love me as a friend, think I'm beautiful, and enjoy kissing me. I think that's a pretty solid basis for something, but what do you think?"

"I think we should test the theory a little more," I said, pulling her to me and kissing her just because I wanted to. She melted into me, and I lost myself in her again.

When we eventually pulled apart, she asked again, "So what do you think?"

"I think the school's going to be in an uproar that I upgraded from a Parker boyfriend to a Parker girlfriend," I said, grinning before it hit me and her at the same time. "Shit, I have to dump Shawn." I jumped up, pulling my phone out of my jean pocket. My heart dropped when I saw it was already past twelve and the group chat had been blowing up.

"You missed midnight," Shannon said, checking her own phone.

I clicked into the group chat and saw a string of 'where are you's' and then a few 'abort missions' and more 'where are you's'. I glanced at Shannon quickly and saw whatever she was seeing on her phone was upsetting her, too.

I quickly fired off a text to the group.

### Shawn Parker Must Die

I'm so sorry. In Shannon's room. I screwed up the plan big time, didn't I?

Roxy

YOU'RE STILL IN THE HOUSE?!

Gavin

We've got to get you out.

What's going on??

Ava

Explanations later. Now we need you to haul ass out of there quickly and quietly.

Roxy

Front door, not back, car'll be waiting out front.

I looked over at Shannon and said, "No clue what's going on but the group chat's a mess."

Another text came through.

Lynds

Bring Shannon if she wants to sleepover/get away.

"Do you want to sleepover my house tonight?" I asked. "Whatever's going on is apparently big enough that I'm supposed to make a quick escape."

She looked up, startled, before taking a breath, grabbing a bag from her closet, and shoving some clothes into it with impressive speed. A minute later, she looked at me expectantly and said, "Alright let's go."

I took her hand, and we raced down the stairs and out the front door together. Adrenaline pumped through my veins at everything that had happened. I was a little anxious about what had everyone so freaked out, but I knew whatever it was we would be able to face it together, especially now with Shannon by my side.

The minute the car door was shut, the others all started at once. They all asked some form of 'where were you'.

"I'm so so sorry," I said quickly. "I promise I have a good reason, but I really screwed up and I'm sorry."

"How good a reason?" Gavin asked.

"I'd say pretty good," I said, grinning at Shannon and squeezing her hand. "Have you guys met my girlfriend, Shannon?"

The car exploded into cheers and hoots and hollers and I felt some of the anxiety dissolve that despite whatever was going on, it didn't stop them from being thrilled for us.

"How'd that happen?" Roxy asked.

"No," I said. "First, what's going on?"

"Well," Ava said, "when you didn't show up toward midnight, Shawn started to get more and more agitated. At first, we thought that was part of your plan to keep him on his toes and really get him worked up, but when the countdown started and you weren't there, he grabbed Grace instead and kissed her at midnight."

"Really? Grace?" I asked.

"Probably cause she was convenient," Gavin said. "She's always following him around like a lost puppy."

"He kissed her in front of everyone and then made a speech about how he was on to bigger and better things in the new year and leaving the trash in the past."

"He called me trash?"

"I had to restrain Roxy," Ava said.

"I wish you hadn't," she grumbled.

"That's not all," Gavin said. "He told everyone that you slept with him and then he found out you'd been cheating on him."

"Seriously? He's trying to make me the bad guy?"

Gavin nodded. "Seems like it."

Lynds squeezed my shoulder and said, "I'm really sorry. He's the worst."

"I'm sorry, too, guys," Shannon said. "None of you deserve what he did to you. He's unfortunately my brother, but he's the worst."

"What are we gonna do?" I asked. "Has Tiger Shark Tea posted anything?"

"Not yet," Ava said. "They probably won't until tomorrow, though. I'm hoping they wait until the afternoon to give us time to plan how to spin things."

"I can't believe I messed this up. I'm so sorry, guys."

"No need to apologize," Ava said. "You didn't have to do anything for us."

"Seriously, you were badass and stepped up. Not your fault he's managing to continue to mess with us," Roxy said.

"Besides," Lynds said, "this seemed to work out a little too good for him. It felt like he had the exit strategy planned. There's no guarantee that even if our plan had gone smoothly, that he would have come out of it looking like the bad guy."

I was grateful they weren't mad at me and that I finally didn't have any secrets from Shannon. We dropped Gavin off and he told us he'd be over for breakfast and made us all promise not to make any plans or do anything exciting without him.

By the time we got to our house and settled everyone into bed, we were exhausted. Like our last sleepover, Shannon was tucked into my arms, but unlike last time, having her this close to me had me feeling energized and wanting to explore my newfound attraction to her.

Unfortunately, it was late, there were a lot of other people in the room, and we were all exhausted. Besides, it sounded like we'd have a lot to do tomorrow, so I just hugged her tightly to me and tried to ignore my racing thoughts about how close our bodies were and how little clothing she was wearing. They were thoughts I wasn't used to having, and they surprised and delighted me.

I thought she had fallen asleep until she made my heart swell by turning and giving me a goodnight kiss. As I drifted off to sleep with her in my arms, I knew I could very easily get used to this.

# CHAPTER FIFTY NINE

When we all went down to breakfast and Auntie Jen saw Shannon and I were holding hands, she exchanged a knowing look with Lynds before grinning at me and saying, "About time."

"We were up late," I joked, knowing she wasn't actually telling us we were late for breakfast.

Uncle Cam looked at everyone before his attention turned back to his wife and asked, "What'd I miss?"

She just laughed. I sat in between Lynds and Shannon. Roxy and Ava sat together on the other side of the table. Auntie Jen was about to ask something when the doorbell rang.

"That'll be Gavin," Roxy said with a chuckle, holding up her phone.

"I'll go let him in," Lynds said.

Auntie Jen laughed again, saying, "That boy can't stand the idea of girl's time, huh?"

"Or any tea time that doesn't involve me," Gavin said as he pulled out a chair next to Roxy.

"Are we talking good, bad, or ugly?" my aunt asked me.

"A mix," I said.

"I figured since you left with a Parker boyfriend and came back with a Parker girlfriend?"

The table's cheering and mine and Shannon's smiles confirmed it for her.

"So what happened?"

There was no reason to keep her in the dark anymore, so we all took turns explaining our plan and how things had turned out.

"So basically," I summed up, "I was supposed to dump him last night, but instead I secretly made out with his sister who's now my girlfriend and he made out with Grace in front of everyone and we have no idea what the narrative is gonna be about it, but I guarantee I'll come out of this looking like the villain."

"Has anyone checked Tiger Shark Tea lately?" Gavin asked.

"They haven't posted anything," Ava said.

"Yet," Roxy added.

Shannon had been quiet, so I was surprised when she cleared her throat and said, "Actually, there's a little bit more you guys don't know."

I racked my brain for something that happened between me and Shannon that I'd left out, but I couldn't think of anything. Then I noticed she was looking at me. Everyone else was watching her, so I turned my attention back to her.

"I know who Tiger Shark Tea is," she said slowly.

I stared at her in shock, running through the past posts, and it started to click for me. "It's Shawn, isn't it?" I asked. With how idolized he was because of those posts, even if they looked like they were targeting him, it would make sense.

"What? No. Where'd you get that from?" she asked.

"The posts. They're so focused on him and airing out his tea, yet somehow, he always comes out of it fine."

She threw her hands up in the air, frustration all over her face. "It's ridiculous! It's like he can't do anything wrong! Every time I post, I keep telling myself that this'll be the thing that's too much for everyone. This'll expose how he actually is, but no one holds him accountable."

She stopped her rant when she saw we were all staring at her.

"You're Tiger Shark Tea?" I asked.

She nodded, saying quickly, "But I swear everything I posted was to help you guys," she said. "When I found out Shawn was running around with all of you, I wasn't sure any of you would believe me if I came to you solo, and that would've given him time to get his story straight. When I posted those, I thought I was exposing him and that he would catch all the heat for it. I never thought for a second you guys would. I thought everyone would be sympathetic to how you guys were hurt. I'm so sorry."

"Clearly I wasn't too into him," Roxy said, smiling at Ava, who said, "Ditto."

I turned to Lynds. My thoughts and feelings were racing, but most of the turmoil was coming from worrying about how Lynds would respond.

Relief coursed through me when she smiled at Shannon. "You did me a huge favor. Before you did that, the best people in my life were Shawn and Grace. Now I have a boyfriend who cares about and shows me off and the best friends a girl could ask for. We're good."

"Really?" Shannon asked with tears brimming in her eyes.

Lynds nodded, saying, "On one condition."

"Anything," Shannon said quickly.

"Keep making Bri happy and we're good."

I laughed at that, and Shannon jumped out of her seat and hugged Lynds and then Roxy and Ava.

"What about me?" Gavin pouted, who then got a hug, too.

Auntie Jen pulled her into a hug before Shannon could sit back down. "You're a brave girl and I'm glad we'll be seeing you around more."

At that, Shannon actually started crying. My aunt hugged her tighter, and I went over and joined them. When Shannon regained her composure a few moments later and sniffled her thanks, it felt like no matter what happened back at school, I'd be able to handle it knowing this family I'd built had my back.

Uncle Cam excused himself and my aunt, saying that they should leave us to our talking and planning.

Auntie Jen looked like she might protest, but he whispered something to her, and she smiled and left with him.

"So," Roxy said, pulling us back to the moment, "we have Tiger Shark Tea on our side now."

"Which means we can control the narrative," I said slowly.

"Sort of," Shannon said. "I mean yes, I hear things and see them first, but usually if I don't post them, the person who submitted them will."

"So you can't bury things," Gavin said, "but you can get out in front of them."

"Exactly," she said.

"Like with everything you posted about me, you, and Shawn?" I asked.

She blushed a little. "I'm not gonna lie, a lot of that was for me. I was worried he was going to hurt you because I cared about you, but I was jealous and wanted you to consider how maybe there was a better Parker out there for you."

I laughed at that. "That makes so much more sense. I could never figure out why Tiger Shark Tea was so obsessed with me."

We all laughed at that.

"So if you weren't here," Gavin asked, "what would you be posting this morning?"

She got serious again and said, "I got a lot of submissions this morning, and they're not great," she said, hesitating when she looked at me.

"Rip the bandaid off," I told her.

"Okay, so there's a lot of Shawn and Grace kissing that I'm obviously using, but people caught pics of you and Gavin sneaking off to Shawn's make-out spot and are implying Shawn's right that you cheated first."

"What?!" Gavin and I asked at the same time.

Ava and Lynds were staring at us, shocked, but Roxy started laughing.

I looked at her, and she held her hands up saying, "In my defense, that's kind of hilarious."

When she said it and I tried to picture it, I couldn't help laughing, too.

"This is the point where I say, but wait, it gets worse," Shannon said, killing the laughter. "Gavin, they caught you sneaking off with someone else before Shannon."

That didn't seem like a big deal, but when I looked up at Gavin, he was pale. "Who?" he asked her.

"Are you sure you want me to say?" she asked.

He paled further. "We were so careful. I can't believe this, Jer's gonna be devastated. It'll destroy him if this gets out."

I looked around and saw my shock was mirrored by Lynds, but Roxy and Ava didn't seem all that surprised. It made sense. Ava seemed close with Jeremiah and Roxy was obviously close with Gavin. I wondered if they knew or just weren't surprised, but either way, it didn't matter right now. What mattered was fixing this.

"So what do we do?" I asked, turning back to Shannon.

"To bury that, we have to give a better story. I know I can post about Shawn and Grace, but that's not enough," she said apologetically. "If I don't give them anything about you two, they'll do their own digging, which is dangerous."

"Could we release something about me and you?" I asked.

She considered for a moment before saying, "I don't know if that would help."

"Shannon's beating around the bush," Roxy said, "so I'll lay it out straight. The best way to protect Gavin's reputation is to sacrifice yours."

"What do you mean?" I asked.

"Well, I wouldn't have put it quite like that," Shannon said.

"But I'm not wrong," Roxy replied.

"No, you're not. The best way to protect Gavin would be to show proof you were cheating with him."

Gavin looked like he was going through all the stages of grief at once, but managed to pull himself together enough at that to say, "Bri, you don't have to fall on your sword for me."

"It doesn't have to be forever, though," I reasoned, "just until things die down a bit, then I can do the whole coming out song and dance and announce that I'm with Shannon."

"You're doing a song and dance? Way to upstage my coming out dance," Roxy joked.

I laughed. "What can I say? I'm a drama kid. We're dramatic."

"I know you were kidding about the song and dance," Ava said, "butttt if you wanted to make a grand gesture, the Valentine's assembly would be the perfect place to do it."

"Are we really doing this again?" Gavin asked.

I looked at him and said, "You guys are family. I've spent this long being Bridgette, I can go another six weeks to help you out."

"Wait," Shannon said, "what do you mean, being Bridgette? That isn't your name?"

I grimaced, saying, "It's Bridget, not Bridgette, and everyone here calls me Bri."

"Why would you change it to Bridgette for school?" she asked.

I looked at Roxy, who looked at Gavin, who shrugged. I turned back to Shannon and started laughing. "Some people here thought your brother would be more intrigued if my name sounded exotic and French."

We all burst into laughter at that and when she regained her composure Shannon said, "The sad part is how true that is. He kept going on about how exotic and mysterious you were."

We spent the next couple of hours crafting a new plan. They all continued to check in with me about whether I really wanted to do this, but I knew I could handle it. Pretending to be the school's slut was going to be so much easier than pretending to be Shawn's girlfriend.

# CHAPTER SIXTY

Tiger Shark Tea

*Shawn and Bridgette call it quits.*

*It seems like Bridgette and Shawn both took the motto 'new year, new me' a little too seriously. During the big New Year's Party at Parker Palace, Bridgette was seen again at Shawn's make-out spot, but this time she was with Gavin and there aren't pictures, but multiple sources say they heard things they wished they didn't.*

*What I do have for you is this picture of them leaving the secluded spot to go off to who knows where. What we do know is that Bridgette didn't go see Shawn. Just before midnight, Shawn was still alone and, to everyone's surprise, grabbed and kissed Grace to ring in the New Year.*

*Good for Grace finally getting pulled off the sidelines. Looks like Bridgette moved on, and apparently our golden boy didn't waste any time moving on either.*

School was intense, to say the least. I was glad my friends had my back, but I was called every name under the sun, both to my face and behind my back. Shannon had to turn Tiger Shark Tea's comments off, something she'd never done in the past, but she wasn't okay with seeing the comments that were being made about me.

Maybe I should've been more upset, but honestly, I was happy. I had really good friends and was in a real relationship for the first time in my life and I didn't have to pretend to tolerate Shawn anymore.

He tried to talk to me that first day, but I shut him down real quick, telling him, "Honey, if you had my number you'd be blocked but you didn't even make it to 'saved in my phone' stage."

Maybe I should've been nicer, or acted like I was more hurt, or heard him out, but I was sick of him. I knew rationally it wasn't his fault people were attacking me, but he wasn't doing anything to stop it.

After that, though, he went public with Grace, who instantly made things worse.

She started telling everyone that would listen about how he was born again and had seen the light and that she had saved him. *Please.* There was nothing holy about that boy.

Her and her friends started bumping into me and shoulder checking me in the hallway. Then they would loud freak out about whore being contagious and tell me they were going to pray for me.

If I didn't get to spend English and lunch with Shannon, I would've been losing my mind. I wasn't sure if Mr. Hayes was up on the school gossip, but the fact that we were studying the Scarlett Letter right now seemed pointed and ironic.

To make things worse, when Shannon turned the Tiger Shark Tea's comments back on, people were doubting that Gavin and I were together, wondering who I had really been with and saying he was probably gay.

We could've called it quits then, and maybe we should have, but I wasn't a quitter and we'd already come this far.

After school, we all went to the diner. It was refreshing to be able to hold Shannon's hand there and not have to act like we were just friends. Holding her hand made what I was about to suggest even weirder, but I didn't think there was any way around it.

"I think Gavin and I have to have steamy make-out photos leaked," I said once our food had been dropped off.

Everyone's eyes shot to me immediately. Gavin was the first to break the silence, saying, "If you wanted to make out with me you could've just asked."

I laughed at that before saying, "I'm saying it doesn't seem like everyone's buying the *you* part of the equation and I think we have to give them a bit more."

"I thought you were getting all the heat you are because people believe it," Lynds asked.

"I mean, they believe the worst in me and that I hurt Shawn, but they don't seem to believe that Gavin's straight."

Gavin rolled his eyes. "We have the stupidest peers of probably any high school in the country, but it's just my luck they're perceptive about this."

"Well, do you want to be a ladies' man a little longer?" Once I came out as being with Shannon, he'd need to find another way to keep the charade going if he wanted to, but I was happy to help him for now.

After a moment he said, "Sure, why not."

"How romantic," I quipped, and the table erupted in laughter.

## Tiger Shark Tea

*Since some of you have to see it to believe it, here's some spicy pics I didn't share earlier of Gavin and Bri getting hot and heavy under the bleachers.*

*Someone call the janitor because they're really getting down and dirty.*

The pictures gained more attention than I expected and as I walked down the hall with Gavin, it was hard to miss how differently we were being treated.

Gavin was getting nods of respect from the guys and checked out by some of the girls. I was being glared at by the girls and leered at by the guys.

When I spotted Shawn and Grace coming our way, I almost turned around, but I knew that wouldn't actually help anything.

"Bridge," he said, nodding to me. That had been a new development that I felt sure was Grace's doing. Apparently they were calling me "Bridge" because I let anyone on top of me. It wasn't the most clever insult I'd heard, but it still stung.

I didn't have the energy to bother with him, so with a look to signal that to Gavin, we kept going.

It ate at me that day and the next day, though. I was still thinking about it when I went to English. We were still talking about the Scarlet Letter, and I had been ignoring a lot of the lesson to pass notes with Shannon, but Mr. Hayes caught my eye and tapped the board meaningfully.

It drew my attention to the word rebellion. I tuned back in and realized he had been talking about how Hester's rebellion was in embracing her punishment and forcing people to not be able to ignore it. The idea that there could be power in embracing a bad reputation sparked an idea for me.

Mr. Hayes asked me to stay after for a minute. Shannon told me she'd wait outside.

I was worried I was going to get lectured or punished for being distracted, but instead he said, "I won't pretend to be blind or deaf. I know high school can suck and I know kids can be cruel. I know you're having a rough time, and I hope you were really listening to my lesson."

I thanked him, relieved to not be in trouble, and asked, "Am I okay to leave?""

He nodded, but called back out to me right before I made it to the door. I stopped, and he added, "If you need someone to talk to, my door's always open."

"Thank you," I told him, meaning it, but his lesson was sinking in, and I was inspired. I had a feeling I was going to be just fine.

After school, Lynds, Shannon, Gavin, and I went on a shopping spree. The thrift store turned up some really cute corset tops, which were just what I needed. For the finishing touch, we stopped at a craft store so I could get thread and red fabric.

Once I finished surgery on one of the corsets, I texted a picture to the group chat and was met with fire emojis, clapping, praising hands, and heart eyes. No one tried to talk me out of it or second guessed it, so I guessed I was actually doing it.

The next day, I wore the corset top with a newly sewn on scarlet letter 'A' with matching red lipstick. I was taking a page from Hester's book. They were trying to shame me and put me down, and it would only work if I let them. *Let them talk; I'd give them something to talk about.*

When Gavin and I encountered Shawn and Grace in the hallway, I didn't wait for him to talk or give him a chance to notice me. I stepped directly in his path and was rewarded with seeing his face jump from surprise, to confusion, to appreciation as he took in my new look. I wondered if he even noticed he had dropped Grace's hand. She was torn between being angry with him and glaring at me. Apparently, I won out, since she looped her arm through his and glared at me.

"Parker," I said, closing the distance until I was standing toe to toe with him. Grace gasped, but I didn't give her a chance to say whatever she was planning to. I gave Shawn my attention and said, "Surprised you still can't stay away from me."

That brought him a little to his senses, and he backed up a step.

I took a step closer, following him, "How's your little girlfriend feel about you worshipping me?"

"The only thing he worships is our Lord and Savior," Grace piped up, taking his hand in hers again and squeezing it.

"I don't know. He seemed pretty intent on worshipping me with his tongue last month."

His look of shocked surprise played into the lie, and I could see she was squeezing his hand hard enough it might fall off. "Better tell your girlfriend to stop squeezing your lover so hard."

She gasped and pulled her hand away, crossing her arms. She leveled a glare at me and said, "Shawn's a new man now. He would never sin like that, unlike you."

"Whatever you need to think to sleep at night," I told her. Nodding to Gavin, we moved around them, and almost in an afterthought, I called back, "because we both know Shawn'll be thinking about me at night."

The rumors and name calling were going to get worse after that, but I still felt like it was worth it. The power I felt from putting him down like that stirred up something in me.

I felt back in control. It reminded me of how Roxy had handled things when the photos came out, and that gave me another idea.

"Are you sure this isn't too far?" I asked Shannon, showing her what I was about to post on Facegram. The photo was of me in my 'A' corset, blowing a kiss and winking at the camera. I'd felt ridiculous taking it, but I wanted something over the top, and this was definitely over the top. It was the caption I wasn't sure about, and Shannon was laughing too hard to respond.

When she managed to calm down, she said, "No it's perfect, and I'm writing about it on Tiger Shark Tea the second you post it."

---

**Tiger Shark Tea**

*The New Girl versus the New Shawn*

*No matter how much Grace tries to rebrand Shawn as being reborn, I'm not buying it. What do you guys think? Are you buying that he changed overnight? That the only love he's chasing is God's?*

*According to the New Girl's latest post, I'm not the only one doubting it.*

*'For everyone wondering if Parker's new persona is real, I can tell you there's nothing virginal about that boy. Shawn, just a heads up, it still counts even if you only last ten seconds.'*

---

After that, things spiraled more. The others started hearing about me having slept with Jeremiah. Then the rumors started flying about pretty much everyone on the football team. At first it was entertaining. I played into it, wearing different custom 'A' corsets for a full week, but after a while I started to worry about what would happen when I told everyone the truth. The truth was on my side, but with how out of hand things had gotten, I was starting to worry if that would be enough.

# Chapter Sixty One

I was a bundle of nervous energy as I headed to meet up with the others outside of the Valentine's Day assembly. It was really just a Valentine's Day themed pep rally where the school crowded a cutest couple. We knew it was going to be Shawn and Grace. Grace had been telling everyone since the moment voting started to vote for them. On her own, she wouldn't stand a chance, but Shawn had yet to be beaten in a popularity contest. Lucky for me, I wasn't trying to beat him, just steal his spotlight.

I couldn't wait for this charade to be over.

I found the others waiting for me outside the gym. Shannon was there, too. At this point, she'd become one of us even if she hadn't started out that way.

"Are you ready?" she asked, squeezing my hand.

"She's definitely ready," Ava answered for me. I was glad she had confidence in me.

"You got this," Lynds reassured me.

"Of course she does," Roxy said and then, turning to me, said, "You're gonna kill it."

"You're a natural actress and this is just another stage," Shannon said, pulling me in for a quick hug and whispering to me. "Just remember, it's your last performance, so pull out all the stops and break a leg."

I was still grinning at her when Ava pulled me away toward the locker rooms to finish getting ready.

"Are you sure about this?" I asked Ava as she and a few others unrolled the giant heart banner they'd be holding.

"Absolutely!" she said with enough confidence for the both of us.

# Chapter Sixty Two

I listened for my cue from the locker rooms and heard Shawn and Grace announced as this year's cutest couple. When their intro music played, I opened the door to the locker room. Ava and some of the other cheerleaders on the squad were standing a few feet in front of me with the giant heart banner pulled taut. Shawn and Grace were supposed to stand in front of it, using it as a backdrop for their thank you speech and couple photo, but first Shawn stopped at the microphone and said, "Thank you all so much for-"

That was all he managed to say before his microphone cut out and over the loudspeakers came a recording of my voice saying, "Let me be the first to congratulate the happy couple, Grace and Shawn, or should I just say Grace since we all know she's the only one happy with their new arrangement."

Gasps rang through the gym, but my voice kept going, "Since we all knew Shawn would get voted cutest couple no matter who he's with, I think it's time for a new superlative, your favorite heartbreaker, let's get a drumroll please."

The sound played over the recording just in case, but it turns out our classmates were more than ready to play along since the noise of them stomping their feet echoed through the gym.

"Turn your attention to the front and let's see who your favorite heartbreaker is."

I couldn't see from behind the poster, but I imagined people were looking around in confusion for me, waiting to see me step forward, or if they didn't know my voice, to see who stepped forward.

The music changed, and I looked over and saw Ava give me a thumbs up. I took a couple of steps back before running at the banner.

It had been slightly ripped in the middle and the cheer squad girls holding it pulled hard when I ran at it, the moment I made contact with the banner it broke and I emerged on the other side, the giant heart ripping down the middle, revealing me. Our classmates were in chaos on the bleachers. There were cheers, boos, and gasps. Before any of the teachers could do anything, Ava dropped the banner, grabbed the mic from the stand in front of Shawn, and tossed it to me.

"Well, Harris High, say hello to your resident heartbreaker. Who wants to bet I can have Shawn and Grace broken up in five minutes or less?"

The room was in chaos. I looked over at Shawn who wasn't even hiding his staring at me and Grace, who looked livid. "It looks like Shawn is really hoping I'll try, but that's not why I'm up here. Tonight, I'll be live on Facegram spilling all the tea. I know you're all wondering how Shawny was as a boyfriend, how he was in bed, how the rest of the team was in bed-" I had to pause there as the school gasped, cheered, and booed. "I'm spilling all the tea tonight with some special guests and you won't want to miss it."

I saw the principal coming my way and tossed the microphone to him. Even through his surprise, he managed to react quick enough to catch it. I bowed to my audience with a wink before turning and high-tailing it back to the locker room.

School was letting out for the weekend after the assembly anyway, so I grabbed my stuff and waited by my car.

Lynds and Shannon were the first there. Shannon pulled me into a hug and Lynds gave me a thumbs up and a giant grin.

Gavin showed up next, with Roxy and Ava bringing up the rear. "So we're really doing this?" Lynds asked, looking around at everyone.

"We're really doing this." I paused, taking a deep breath before continuing. "At least I am. It's a little too late for me to back out now." I pulled out my phone and swiped down a bit, showing them the influx of Facegram followers I was getting. I was going to have a lot of eyes on me tonight. "It's not too late for any of you to back out, though," I said, looking at Roxy and Ava for a moment before turning my attention back to

Lynds. I knew Roxy and Ava well enough to know they weren't backing out, but if Lynds didn't want to be involved, I wouldn't blame her. "You know you don't have to do this for me to know you have my back."

"It's not about that," Lynds said, before quickly adding, "Of course I have your back and I love you like a sister, but that's not why I'm doing this. I'm doing this to hold Shawn accountable and make sure no one else gets blinded by his lies. I'm doing this for me. I didn't get to tell my story before, but now you made sure people are going to listen." We were both tearing up as she said, "Thank you for that. You coming here was the best thing to happen to me in a long time."

"The best thing to happen to us all," Ava added.

Shannon's hand found my shoulder and squeezed. "Best thing to happen to me, too, even if my sorry excuse for a brother wouldn't agree."

"You definitely made this year more interesting," Gavin said, grinning.

"I'm glad you found your way to us," Roxy added.

"Alright, alright," I said sniffling, "let's get going and get ready before you saps make me cry off my make-up."

Shannon and Lynds hopped in with me after arguing about who was sitting in the back. Shannon thought she should since Lynds was family and Lynds thought she should since Shannon's my girlfriend and girlfriends don't ride in the back.

They were both being ridiculous, but Shannon caved and sat in front, and everyone seemed happy with the resolution, especially when Shannon immediately put on one of our favorite Savannah Holly-wood songs.

# CHAPTER SIXTY THREE

Roxy's car with her, Ava, and Gavin in it pulled in right behind mine. If Auntie Jen was surprised at the intrusion of teenagers, she didn't show it, just asked what we were up to tonight.

I guiltily looked over at Lynds, who looked back at me, looking just as caught.

"We're having a tea party," I joked.

"Oooh," Auntie Jen said with a little chuckle. "About time you guys said something. Shawn's the guest of honor, right?"

I shouldn't have been surprised she'd understood what I meant. "Something like that," I said, laughing.

"Well, if you guys need any help or anything, just holler."

"Will do, thank you," I said.

"Thanks Mom," Lynds said, smiling at her.

"Thanks, Mrs. Matthews," the others chorused as we went up to our room.

We had an hour left until showtime and I was starting to get nervous. The others had been trying to make a game plan and distract me from the nerves, but it wasn't working.

I was telling everyone I was fine for the hundredth time when Lynds interrupted and said, "You don't have to lie to us. I know how nervous you are. It's a big deal. I think it might be time for some professional advice."

Everyone looked at her, confused. It took me a moment to understand her meaning. "Ollie?"

"Well, preferably Gwen, but I'm sure Olls would have advice, too. Not sure how good it would be, though."

I laughed at that as she pulled out her phone. "I'll video call him."

The others were still looking confused. I didn't realize they didn't know who Lynds's brother was or who he was friends with. This was going to be entertaining.

"Who's her brother?" Gavin whispered while the phone rang.

"Just wait," I said.

A moment later, the phone stopped ringing and Lynds grinned. "Olls!"

"Lynds," he said. I could hear him grinning. "What's going on?"

"Have you been following Bri?"

"I thought so. Not closely enough apparently, though. Why? What's going on?"

"Hang on, let me fix you." She propped her phone up on the tripod and we all squeezed in.

Ollie grinned when he saw me. "Bri, how's it going? Who's everyone here?"

"Is that Lynds?" we heard Gwen ask from the background.

"What's going on?" another voice I recognized asked.

"Hang on," Ollie said, laughing. "You're calling into family night. Headphones or speaker?"

"Definitely speaker," Lynds told him.

"Sounds good. Let me get you guys set up."

The phone wiggled and moved, before settling and focusing on a group of people that had everyone except me and Lynds gasping.

On Ollie's end was him, his boyfriend Eli, and the people who had the others gasping, Gwen, her girlfriend Mor, and their best friend Arty.

Ava started squealing before rounding on Lynds. "You guys know Gwen Pendragon?!"

"And Mor," Shannon added, waving. "Talk about sapphic royalty."

"And Arty," Gavin added. "You guys are legends!"

"I can't believe you guys were holding out on us," Roxy said.

The others were laughing and Eli piped up saying, "Hey I'm pretty cool, too."

Ollie grinned, squeezing Eli's shoulder. "Of course you are. You're important to me, babe,"

"Hi Eli," Lynds said, waving.

"Hey Lil' Lynds," he said, grinning back. "Bri cheese," he said, waving to me. He and Ollie were adorable together and had the same ridiculous sense of humor.

"Good to see you guys!" I said.

"Should we do intros or skip to the elephant in the room?" Ollie asked.

"What elephant?" I asked.

"The fabulous outfit," Gwen said, nodding to me. "That corset is putting in work."

"And the 'A' on there," Arty said, moving closer. "Scarlet Letter?"

I nodded.

"I'm so glad you guys called!" Gwen squealed. "This is the end of the revenge arc, isn't it?"

"I feel like I'm missing several things," Arty said.

"Okay, pivoting back to intros first," Ollie said.

"Wait wait wait," Gwen said, running off screen. We heard the door open and a couple more people came into the frame.

"Good call," Ollie said to Gwen.

"For real," Gwen said, laughing. "If Sam missed the tea, there would've been hell to pay."

The other two slid in and waved. I recognized them enough to know that the one waving enthusiastically must have been Sam, which made their other friend Ben.

"You guys know my little sister, Lynds." They all nodded. "Well, the girl in the corset is our cousin Bri." He paused, and Gwen took over.

"Bri called a while ago about Lynds's boy being a cheater and was looking for advice, and I think after that she reached out to the other girls."

"That's us," Ava said, raising her hand that was holding Roxy's. "I'm Ava and this is my now girlfriend, Roxy."

"That's a whole story I'm gonna need later," Ollie said.

"I'm Gavin," Gavin introduced himself, "Roxy's best friend and the token testosterone of the group."

We laughed at that before everyone, both on and off screen, turned to me and Shannon. I took the cue and said, "And this is my girlfriend Shannon,"

"Girlfriend?!" Ollie yelled out while Gwen squealed behind him.

I squeezed Shannon's hand, waiting for them to chill a bit.

"Why are you guys freaking out so much?" Mor asked.

They looked at each other and back at me, not sure what to say. Ollie and Gwen knew I was demi, but they obviously didn't want to share anything I wasn't comfortable with, but I trusted them and their judgment in friends.

"I'm demi and she's my first ever partner," I told them, and everyone in their room "awwed" and squealed, leaning closer to the screen.

"That's adorable!" Eli called. "So happy for you guys!"

"Welcome to the fam, Shan," Ollie said, grinning.

I looked at her quickly, a little embarrassed at how Ollie was acting. He was always over the top, but she and I were new, and I didn't want to scare her off. Luckily, she was beaming at him.

Apparently, I had nothing to worry about.

"I'm just glad it's me you're saying that to, not my brother," she joked.

The other room was full of confused looks, so Shannon said, "The lousy guy who cheated on the others is my brother."

"Tough break," Mor said.

"We'll need that story, too," Gwen said.

"Seriously, like pronto," Ollie said.

"But first," Gwen elbowed him, "manners."

"What?" he asked her.

"Introductions," she said, chuckling. "I think you all know Lynds's brother Ollie," she said gesturing at him, "and this is his boyfriend, Eli."

Eli waved and grinned at the others.

"They'll have dumb nicknames for you in no time," I told the others.

"I heard that, Brie cheese," Ollie joked.

"You were meant to, Oxen-free," I quipped back.

Gwen continued, saying, "This is Ben."

"Hi guys," he said with a head nod.

"And I'm the not man, the not woman, the not myth, but definitely the legend, Sam."

The others laughed, and Gwen said, "They/them pronouns and fabulous."

"Obviously," Sam said, grinning.

"And I'm Gwen, Ollie's best friend," she continued.

"They definitely know you, Gwen," Ollie said, rolling his eyes. He wasn't wrong. She was by far the most famous person I knew, and I was pretty sure everyone in the room followed her socials.

"And this is my girlfriend, Mor, and our best friend, Arty."

Again, they were people that didn't need an introduction. Gwen and Mor's love story had been all over the internet when Gwen came out as a lesbian in the middle of a packed book convention cosplay contest to the crowd and to everyone who tuned in to watch her live. It's why we were calling her now. If anyone knew a thing or two about stressful internet situations, it was Gwen.

Mor hadn't been as big as Gwen prior to that, but after hers and Gwen's public declarations of love, Mor's following skyrocketed. Anyone who knew Gwen usually also knew Mor, and anyone who knew either of them knew Arty.

Not only was Arty well on his way to becoming an influential politician that would bring some much-needed change, but he was also about to be reality show royalty. After his public breakup with Gwen, and Gwen and Mor's public getting together, he had been reached out to by 'Finding the One' to be one of their next contestants. From what Ollie's said, it took Gwen and Mor a lot of convincing to get him to agree, but he finally did.

The show brought 16 singles that the show runners had found perfect matches for. The object of the show was for each person to find their perfect match. Unlike a lot of other dating shows out there, on this show, the contestants worked as a team. The house either won or lost together.

The promos had just started airing and Lynds and I couldn't wait to watch it. We loved the show and couldn't wait to watch him on there. It was so cool we actually knew someone on the show.

Besides, if anyone deserved to find love, it was Arty. I'd never heard or seen a single bad thing about him, and I knew from Ollie how good Arty had been to Gwen. Anyone would be lucky to be with him.

"So," Gwen said, turning back to us, "now that that's out of the way, what's going on?"

"I'm going live in," I paused to glance at the time, "twenty minutes and I'm telling everyone what actually happened with Shawn and I'm freaking out."

"You think people will be upset with you?" Ollie asked.

"Worried about backlash at school?" Gwen asked.

"They can't act worse than they have been, so no, I'm just nervous."

"People are bullying you?" Ollie asked, narrowing his eyes.

"Not really," I said quickly, but Lynds said, "Kind of," and Roxy said, "Our school sucks."

"Can we do anything?" Gwen asked. "I could come on at the end and say something about how bravery like that should be applauded."

"You would do that for me?" I asked.

"Of course. In a heartbeat. You're family."

We talked over the plan for a few more minutes before we had to go finish getting ready.

"I'll text Ollie when we get close to the end," Lynds said.

"Remember, deep breaths and be yourselves," Gwen said.

"Easy for you to say," I said to her.

She chuckled before saying, "Believe me, it wasn't always easy and sometimes it's still scary, but it used to be much scarier. It gets easier every time, and living my truth is enough of a reward for the scary parts."

"You got this!" Ollie said.

"See you guys soon!" Gwen called before Ollie hung up.

"Did that really just happen?" Ava asked, looking around.

Gavin leaned over and pinched her. "Ouch! What was that for?"

He laughed. "Just helping you make sure."

"I can't believe you guys never mentioned your family friends with the Rainbow Round Table," Shannon said.

"Seriously though," Ava chimed in, "next you're gonna be saying you're besties with Savannah Hollywood."

Lynds and I laughed at that. "If we were you would've heard of that," I promised.

"Alright, alright," Gavin said, "we're running out of time. We've gotta get this set up right."

I spent our last few minutes touching up my make-up while the others set up and tested my phone camera. They set it up facing my desk. I sat in the swivel chair and they pulled another chair over, setting it up like a talk show. The bed was behind us in the frame, which would be good for when Roxy, Ava, and Lynds all joined.

They set up the tripod and started a countdown on the live, I swiveled around in my chair, facing away from the camera. I didn't want to miss my moment to be over the top.

When they cued me that the live had started, I waited thirty seconds before turning slowly and saying, "Well well well, I bet you're all wondering why I've gathered you here today." My friends suppressed giggles which felt like a win. I turned my full attention to the camera, ignoring my nerves and avoiding the box at the top that would tell me how many people were watching.

"Hi everyone, thanks for coming. I promised you all the tea about Shawn, and boy am I ready to spill it, but before we dive into that, we have to take it back a little bit, since I might be the end of this story, but it didn't start with me. It starts with our special guest, Lyndsey Matthews, also known as my cousin."

Lynds plopped into the other chair and waved to the camera.

"My story with Shawn starts with Lynds and Shawn's story."

I nodded at Lynds who took a deep breath and said, "I know most of you saw how Shawn and I ended, but you guys didn't see the beginning. You didn't see how he sweet-talked me, how he swooped in, as a junior, as the quarterback of the football team, as Harris High's golden boy, and sweet-talked little band geek freshman me. I didn't get why he paid attention to me in the first place and still don't, but I was smitten. I was half in love with him, and I foolishly thought he cared about me. Maybe he did in his own way, but he kept me a secret and you all saw the photos that told me why."

"That brings us to special guest number two."

Ava hopped onto the bed behind me before I could finish introducing her.

"Hey everyone!" she said, waving to the camera. "I know you guys have been wondering what happened with me and Shawn and now me and Roxy, and honestly, I'm sick of the rumors, so let's get into it. Shawn and I had been friends since I was a freshman on the cheer squad, and he had just made varsity as a sophomore. You guys know the cheer squad and team hang out all the time and people started trying to nudge us together. Eventually toward the end of my sophomore year and his junior year, he started really trying to pursue me. We were never official or anything, but we went on dates. I didn't really feel a connection with him in that way, though. I don't know if he did. I was never mad at him for not being into me since, if that was the case, it was mutual, but I was mad at him for making me part of him hurting other girls."

"I never blamed you," Lynds said, reaching out for her.

Ava took her hand and squeezed it. "I know you didn't, but him making me a villain and pitting us against each other is something I won't quickly forgive and forget, especially since he never apologized."

She paused a moment and said, "When the photos came out, I was a little relieved since I felt like I was leading him on by letting him take me on dates when I wasn't into him like that, but with the team and squad being so close and us being friends I didn't really know how to turn him down. But I will say the picture of him and Roxy upset me."

Roxy joined in the frame on the bed next to Ava and kissed Ava on the cheek. "You never had anything to worry about," she said.

"Shawn and I weren't a thing before or after that party, but I'll be honest, I make rash decisions sometimes and he's not the worst kisser."

We laughed at that before she said, "Backtracking a little, though. We'd all been hearing rumors about him and Ava dating for weeks and I was sick of hearing about him and little miss perfect over here. Everyone was talking about how lucky she was and how perfect they were together and, frankly, it annoyed me. When Shawny boy pulled me aside at the party and came onto me, I was shocked, but I let him lead me to the clearing and I let him back me against that tree and stick his tongue down my throat, but the whole time I was thinking of you," she said to Ava.

She turned back the camera and explained, "I was thinking about how little miss perfect wouldn't have her golden boy anymore and maybe then the school would stop talking about them. After I left the party, it hit me what I'd done, so I DMed her and we met up. I really thought you'd hate me," she said to Ava.

"And I couldn't believe my luck, especially when you realized you were jealous of him not me."

"That was the first time we kissed."

"Wait a second!" I burst out. "You two were together since before school started?"

They both shrugged, looking guilty. I looked over the camera at Gavin, who mouthed 'later' and pointed at the camera. Fair enough. Not the time or place.

"We thought that's where things would end," Ava explained.

"Neither of us had any idea he was seeing you, too." Roxy said to Lynds.

Lynds nodded quickly. "I don't blame either of you, I promise."

"When we saw the pictures, though," Roxy said, "and found out that after making out with me, he'd then made a move on Lynds, we were pissed off."

"A boy like that didn't deserve any of us," Ava said.

"He deserved to be as upset as we were," Lynds said.

"He deserved revenge," I finished for them, "which is where I came in. When the photos came out shortly after I moved here, I reached out to Roxy, and we all agreed to team up."

"We quickly decided that Bri..." Ava said, pausing a moment to explain, "Bridgette actually goes by Bri and I'm sure you'll all be excited to get to know the real her."

I smiled at her and mouthed 'thank you'.

She returned the grin before turning her attention back to our audience and saying, "We decided that Bri had what it took to play the player."

"And we set out to destroy a boy and his reputation," Roxy said.

"I stopped being Bri or even Bridget, and became Bridgette. Bridgette was curated to get and keep Parker's attention. The plan worked a little too perfectly, though, since I caught not only Shawn's attention, but Shannon's attention, too. We hadn't planned for the other Parker. I'd planned to get Shawn to lock me down and then dump his ass at the New Year's party and embarrass him publicly with how I never liked him and was stringing him along like he did to my cousin, but I never got the chance since I was too busy upstairs ringing in the New Year with his sister. I ended last year dating one Parker just to start the new year dating the other Parker. Shannon's my not so secret anymore girlfriend."

I paused, letting that sink in before continuing, "I know you're wondering why I didn't let things go then. I kissed Shannon that night and Shawn kissed Grace. Clearly, we were over, and we both were happy, but I couldn't let it go. I couldn't stand seeing him happy and letting him feel like he had won, especially when he was now dating Lynds's ex-best friend. I can't honestly believe that was a coincidence.

"Shawn, if you're watching, it was a bad call, calculated or not. If it had been anyone else, I might've let it go, but it being Grace made things worse. When he kissed her in front of everyone, beating me to the punch, she and him were both too smug about it and it pissed me off. I hadn't put all this time and energy into that boy for things to end like that. He couldn't win, so I kept going.

"For the record, Shawn and I never did anything more than kiss, but since no one believed that, I used that to my advantage. Shawn, if you had made people believe the truth, they wouldn't have believed all the rumors we started about you being terrible in bed. I would apologize, but that's your own fault. When you didn't deny the rumors and let people slut shame me, you gave me power over you. I won't apologize for using it.

"Gavin and I were never actually a thing, though. I just needed someone by my side to rub in Shawn's face, but you all took it and ran with it. By now, I've heard all sorts of crazy things about me with pretty much everyone on the football team. Not that it's any of anyone's business, but I've never been with anyone like that, not Shawn, and certainly not the whole football team. You all believed what you wanted to, but none of that had anything to do with me. I'm not the villain in anyone's story except maybe Shawn's, but he was the villain in ours first and his story needed one.

"So now you all know. This was all I, all we, ever wanted...for you to listen to the truth. The fact that it took half a year and a whole lot of public spectacles for you all to listen to the truth is a big part of what's wrong with the world. We don't want to have to listen to uncomfortable truths, but here's the truth: Shawn

Parker is a player. He's a damn good player on and off the field. It took all four of us working together to unmask him for what he is, and I know even still some of you will choose not to listen, but we've done everything we could, so to the girls of Harris High, you've been warned. Shawn Parker is a player. Proceed with caution if you enter the game."

"I wish I'd had someone to warn me when he started paying attention to me," Lynds said, "and we're trying to do that for you. If you take one more thing away from this, it's that Bri's the best friend you could have."

I grinned at her. "I'm ride or die for my family and friends." I turned back to the camera and said, "From now on, I'm living my truth. My real name is Bridget Tanner, but I go by Bri and I'm falling in love with a girl named Shannon Parker."

The gasp coming from behind the camera warmed my heart, and I wanted to go to her, but I had a live to finish. "Living your truth takes courage, and I hope some of you can take inspiration from this and start being honest with yourselves."

"No one knows more about that than our final surprise guest," Lynds said, adding in Gwen.

I glanced real quick and saw the viewer numbers jump up as Gwen popped up on the screen and waved to everyone.

"Hey guys. I heard you've been less than kind to two very special girls I call family and to each other. I wanted to hop in here to remind you all that the scariest thing you can do in this world is to be yourself and live your truth. Each one of the girls sitting here before you is loudly, proudly, living their truth. Can you say the same? I know it's scary coming to terms with who you are and what you want. Hell, I struggled with it for years. Each of these girls had the guts I didn't, to live authentically and true to themselves at their age. It took me about a decade after high school to start living authentically, and I'm so, so proud of all of you," she told us, and we grinned back at her. Ava and Roxy were holding hands and Lynds and I were squeezing each other's hands.

"And to everyone else, I hope you'll make me proud by congratulating and celebrating their bravery instead of putting them down for it. High school can be a mean, lonely place, and I'm counting on each and every one of you to prove that Harris High is above that." With a final wave and a wink, she signed off.

"Well, that's all we had for tonight. If you'll all excuse me, I have a hot date with the other Parker. See you all Monday." With that I stood up and clicked off the live. Shannon launched herself into my arms. We were jumping up and down screaming as the others piled in, making it a group hug.

I couldn't believe that just like that, it was over. I was free to be myself again, and I couldn't be happier about it. I didn't care how people treated Shawn after this, whether they believed me or not, I was just glad that we all had spoken our truths. If people chose not to listen, at least the truth was out there.

We hopped in our cars and moved the celebration to our diner. It felt right. It was family tradition now and I couldn't be happier that Shannon fit so easily into the picture right next to me.

I might not have loved all the bumps in the road it took to get here, but looking around at Roxy with her arm around Ava's shoulder, Lynds laughing with Gavin, and Shannon holding my hand while talking to Ava, I knew none of us would have changed a thing about how we got here.

# CHAPTER SIXTY FOUR

"Can we talk?"

I turned around and saw my ears weren't deceiving me. It was the last person I expected to want to talk to me.

Shawn Parker.

The universe really had turned upside down over the weekend. My reception at school had been night and day from Friday to today. Friday, everyone was whispering about me, and the worse people were yelling things at me in the halls. Today, people were going out of their way to say hi to me and to compliment me on my bravery and say they liked my hair or my outfit.

I had gotten used to the negative attention and having to play a role, so getting to be myself and getting positive attention for it was going to take some getting used to. Even Grace had only scowled at me, which was practically an olive branch from her. Things were looking bright, especially when I was able to hold Shannon's hand in the hallway and walk to English with her. We even snuck a few kisses between classes.

Now school was out for the day, and I was excited to go find Shannon. The last thing I wanted to do was stop and talk to Shawn, but thinking about Shannon made me curious what Shawn could want from me. He found out with the rest of the world a few days ago that his sister and I had been dating since he and I broke up. I wondered if he wanted to talk to me about that. I didn't really have anything to say to him and thought about turning him away, but curiosity got the better of me and I agreed to talk to him.

Besides, if I was going to make things work long term with Shannon, which I very much wanted to, it would be nice to be able to be civil with Shawn for her benefit.

He pulled me away from the parking lot to a picnic table out front that was out of earshot of his friends and everyone else around.

"So," he said, running his fingers through his hair, "I'm not really sure how to say this."

I waited. I didn't have the first clue what he was going to say and didn't have any desire to fill the silence until I found out.

"Well, first off, I saw your live."

I nodded. "I figured you might've."

He didn't say anything. I waited, but he stayed silent so I prompted, "And?"

"And I ended things with Grace."

I couldn't have heard him right.

"What? Why?"

"Because I saw your live, and it made me do some reflecting."

"My live made you break up with your girlfriend?"

"Your live made me rethink a lot of things."

I waited for him to say more, but he didn't, so I asked, "Like what?"

He sighed, "I think, well I think *and* was told that I owe you and your friends apologies, but Shannon insisted I start with you."

I was going to have to talk to her the minute he left. "She told you to talk to me?"

"Sort of. She and I had a long talk yesterday about a lot of things and I told her I thought I owed you an apology and an explanation. I asked her if she thought you'd want to hear it. I didn't want to bother you with an apology if it was going to make you feel worse. Once she heard me out, she agreed that hearing it from me wouldn't be good for just me and that it might do you some good, too. I promised her I'd talk to you today since she only promised to keep our conversation secret from you for a day."

I smiled at that, and he said, "She really must be down bad for you cause I asked her for a few days silence and she was only willing to give me one." He grinned before looking at me and saying, "Shannon's special. She might be my annoying little sister, but she's got such a big heart, and she thinks the world of you."

I couldn't decide whether to smile or roll my eyes. "Of course she's special, and you're literally the least qualified person to talk to me about treating a girl right."

He frowned a little at that, saying, "Fair enough. Yeah, sorry, I got a little off track. I saw your live, and it really forced me to face what I'd been doing and how I'd been treating people, specifically girls. I haven't been a stand-up guy and even though you were trying to manipulate me, I owe you an apology. I'm sorry I hurt Lyndsey and that my actions could've hurt Ava and Roxy, and I'm sorry I was such a douche at every single one of my parties and especially at New Year's. I'm sorry I let people talk about you the way they had been this past month. Shannon really laid into me about that and she's not wrong. I never would have let people say things like that if I'd known Shannon cared about you as much as she did. I knew you guys were friends but definitely never guessed it was more than that on your end or more than a little crush on her end, but even without knowing that, I should've stepped in. Shannon reminded me that our mother would be disappointed in how I've been acting, and it really made me take a long look at myself."

"Did you like what you saw?" I asked half joking. No matter the rest of his flaws, he was objectively handsome, and he knew it.

"I didn't," he answered with an honesty I didn't expect. "Shannon and I had our first honest talk since before our mother died. Your live and the things your friend Gwen said really stuck with me. I talked to Shannon about everything, and I want me and you to be cool, well as cool as we can be. I know I have a lot to make up for and I'm going to work my ass off trying. I know this won't fix things, but I want you to know I had a reason. I wasn't just being an ass to be one. I'm trusting you here, but Shannon promised I could, and I trust her-" He paused, taking a deep breath and said the last thing I expected, "I'm gay."

I inhaled sharply, waiting for the just kidding, but it didn't come.

"Really?"

He looked around, making sure we were still alone, and nodded. "My mom guessed and talked to me about it before she passed, but after she passed, no one else did. I didn't think our dad would understand, and I thought if I didn't tell Shannon or anyone else that maybe it would go away, and I could be normal."

"There's nothing wrong with being gay," I said quickly.

"I know that rationally," he said, dragging his fingers through his hair again with a sigh, "but you don't hear of many gay football players for a reason. I didn't want to put my future at risk, but when I got into my sophomore year without being seen with any girls, people started to talk. I thought Ava would solve that. She seemed happy enough with being seen with me and play the role of my girlfriend without an actual label, but after a while, that wasn't enough to stop people talking.

"I couldn't have people talking, so I branched out. I got caught making out with girls at my parties. It was never anything serious, and I tried to make it clear to them that it didn't mean anything to me, but I should've realized then that I had no right to protect myself by hurting other people. I messed with different girls, thinking if I kept rotating people, they wouldn't get hurt, but I got careless and I ended up hurting Lyndsey. I didn't mean to. I had no idea she had feelings for me. I should've been more careful, though. When the photos got released about me being with Ava, Roxy, and Lyndsey, I was relieved that it gave them all a reason to hate me. It meant they would stay away from me and gave me a reason to stay single for a while. After all, a player like that couldn't possibly be gay, but then you came along-"

"And played the player," I finished for him.

He grinned. "I should've known you were trouble."

"And I can't believe I never realized you weren't into me. I kept thinking how weird it was how respectful your kisses were," I said, laughing a little at that.

"That was weird?" he asked grinning.

"Out of character," I amended.

"Fair enough," he said with a chuckle.

"The others were right. You would've killed in drama."

He grinned a moment before saying, "I would've killed, but Shannon would've killed me. It's her thing. Besides football's kept me too busy. A body like this is made for the field not the stage."

I laughed openly at that, and he joined in. I couldn't believe that he and I were actually sharing a genuine laugh. When it died down, he said, "I really appreciate you hearing me out. I know it's no excuse, but I wanted you to know. I know how important you are to Shannon, and if we had met under any other circumstances, I'd like to think you'd think I was a cool guy."

I let him sweat a moment before saying, "These glimpses of the real guy behind the act are the cool guy. Unlike the rest of the school, I don't like Shawn Parker, the man, the myth, the legend, but I don't mind Shawn."

"Just Shawn, then," he said with a small smile.

"I'm sure the rest of the school could learn to like just Shawn," I said carefully.

He looked thoughtful but after a moment shook his head, "Maybe someday, but I'm not ready yet. Hearing Gwen talk about how being yourself is the bravest thing a person can do, though, and seeing you and my sister and Roxy and Ava all out and happy and living your best lives, it gives me hope that when I'm ready, maybe things won't be as bad as I think."

I took his hand and squeezed it reassuringly. "When you're ready, I know a kick ass group of queers who'll be at your side ready to kick the asses of anyone who has a problem with it."

He laughed at that, and I couldn't help joining in.

"You know," he said, "if anyone tried to tell me that this year my ex-girlfriend, who had been plotting my downfall, was now my sister's girlfriend, and was offering to inflict violence on others to protect me with a group of my other exes, I wouldn't have believed a single word of it."

I grinned back at him. "Because when you say it like that, no sane person would, but hey, you're not too bad, just Shawn."

"Neither are you, just Bri."

When I walked away from him, I couldn't help feeling like this was the start of something good. I hadn't fully forgiven him, that would take a while and more transparency and honesty from him, and Shannon and I would kick his ass if he even thought about treating another girl like he had been, but this was definitely a step in the right direction.

Tiger Shark Tea

*A Farewell from Bridgette Tanner and Friends:*

*I'm sure you've all seen the jaw dropping live that Bri, formerly known as Bridgette, the new girl, and her friends put on over the weekend shedding some light on the darkness lurking behind the mask of Harris High's golden boy Shawn Parker.*

*I reached out to Bri to see if she or her friends had anything else to say to the school and she said the following:*

*'This is the last time I'm talking about Bridgette before letting her truly lay to rest. I took up the mantle in order to play the player who was running through the school breaking hearts left and right without any consequences. The others tried to tell you the truth before, but you were all too wrapped up in worshipping Shawn Parker to listen. He was the school's golden god, and we were just mortals, but now we've taught him a lesson and made you all stop and listen, and we hope this is something you'll remember.*

*'We hope you all remember that the truth came out in the end. Shawn Parker, the star quarterback of Harris High, the golden boy, was bested by a group of nobodies.*

*Signed,*

*the band geek*

*the cheerleader*

*the racy rebel*

*and the new girl*

*(bonus mention to the guy you all called 'probably gay' and who would definitely kill us if he wasn't listed - he would like you all to know he was a very integral part of the plot)*

*Sincerely yours,*

*The Shawn Parker Must Die group chat*

*(for legal purposes and clarification's sake - we never set out to kill a boy, just his reputation, and as to whether or not we succeeded, we'll let you be the judge)*

So, what did you think of The Other Parker?

I would love to hear any and all of your thoughts! If you would be so kind as to leave any review it would be greatly appreciated. Any review, good or bad, short or long, is always welcome.

For updates on my next books, you can find me:

Visit my website:
Thelibraryofsarahzane.com

Or follow me on TikTok or Instagram:
@LibraryofSarahZane

Or my Facebook page: Author Sarah Zane

If you want to read more about Gwen, Ollie, and their friends, check out:

_Cosplay and Confrontation_
_A sapphic rivals-to-lovers cosplayers romcom that takes place at the same fantasy convention in Off Script._

# About the Author

Sarah Zane is an author of happy endings for traumatized queers.

As a bisexual, it should be shocking to no one that she has more than one genre she loves and writes. She writes across genres but guarantees that a Sarah Zane book will always be queer and always have a happy ending eventually. She has a particular fondness for writing sapphic pairings since they tend to be underrepresented in books.

She lives in New England with her 2 black cats named Gatsby and Mr. Darcy. When she isn't writing, she can be usually be found taking forest walks, visiting castles, planning exotic trips she can't afford, or cuddled up with one of her cats crying over fictional characters or yelling at them about how badly they need therapy.

For more from Sarah Zane, check out...

*The Beautiful Fools Duet*
*Beautiful Little Fool – Book One*
*An Illusion Shattered – Book Two*
*A sapphic, feminist retelling of the Great Gatsby from Daisy's POV.*


*Off Script: A Book Ball Fantasy Adventure*
*A fantasy adventure story about Sadie, a fantasy author whose first convention goes haywire when her characters literally jump off the page.*


*Under Lock and Key*
*A sapphic cozy fantasy retelling of Bluebeard about a blue-haired temptress innkeeper and the mysterious woman who wanders into her inn and falls for her charms.*


*Becoming A Bi-con*
*A sapphic spicy rivals-to-lovers fake dating popstar romance about Savannah Hollywood and her ex-best friend/old costar Maya Ryder.*


*The Santerran Sea Stories*
*A High Seas Heist – Prequel*
*The Siren's Song – Book 1*
*and more coming soon...*
*A story about ex-nuns turned pirates who team up with the sirens of the ocean to fight against the patriarchial religious society that is seeking to commit siren genocide, with some sapphic pirate x siren romance.*

# ACKNOWLEDGEMENTS

Sometimes I have to labor over books to get the story to come out just right, and sometimes the story has been sitting there in my head and flies onto the page, this story was one of those. This story needed to be told and is one I would have loved to have read back in high school. I hope it finds the people who need it as much as I did back then.

To every single young queer that's reached out to me through my DMs or told me at author events how much the sapphic stories and queer joy in my books meant to them – this one is for you. Your bravery astounds me and I'm so proud of you all.

To my family and friends, thank you as always for continuing to support me.

Last but not least, thank you to you, dear reader, for supporting me and my books.

From the bottom of you heart, I love you all.

www.ingramcontent.com/pod-product-compliance
Lightning Source LLC
Chambersburg PA
CBHW020324010826
48973CB00005B/1111